THE LEGION
AND THE
LIONESS

R. D. ARMSTRONG

Sign up to Receive Free Books and $0.99 New Releases

http://www.enterechoeffect.com/

Also, for every new book release, I randomly select 200 mailing list subscribers from the link above to receive a free advance Kindle copy. All other subscribers will receive a special offer to purchase the book for only $0.99 on the day of release, before the price goes up to $3.99. This is not a newsletter. You will only be contacted about free books and $0.99 discounts on New Releases. Thanks again for your support!

TABLE OF CONTENTS

CHAPTER 1

"I noticed you received a message early this morning," Luther, my husband of nine years, said.

"Yes. I did," I replied.

"Is there anything you want to tell me? You seem a bit more, distant." His back was turned away from me while he washed the dishes.

"I'm choosing my words, carefully," I replied, staring at the half-eaten omelet in front of me.

"It's better if you just lay it out for me. You know that," he muttered.

I nodded slowly in agreement. There wasn't an easy way to say it. "Ahem. It was Admiral Banner. He confirmed all fighter pilots from my squadron will be deployed to meet the war effort," I explained. Luther dropped a dish in the sink and paused. He glared up at the ceiling and sighed. I allowed him a moment to process it.

"When?" he asked.

"As early as today," I said.

He dropped his head. "Well then, I guess you need to eat, keep up your s-strength," he said. I could hear the lump in his throat. I stared down at my fork as a ringing sound faded into my ears. I closed my eyes and opened them as reality filled my view. I wasn't at home with my husband anymore. I was the tip of the spear.

Snap out of it.

"Captain Belic! Respond! There are thirty-nine hostages, what are our orders?" My targeting officer, Commander Rotus shouted. The fork in my right hand became a flight stick as I wrestled the turbulence, barreling through thick cumulus clouds at Mach speeds.

We never trained for this enemy. They were supposed to protect us.

"Roger! Okay. I'm dropping altitude to four thousand meters. I want zero civilian casualties, Rotus. Burn those hostiles," I ordered.

"Four thousand meters?" he asked.

"Did I stutter, Commander?"

"That's inside the killbox, Captain, the androids will cut us to shreds. They've likely seized our anti-aircraft guns on deck," he replied. A red warning indicator blinked on my visor, alerting me to the enemy targeting systems that would be in range soon.

"Commander Rotus, strap in and prepare the precision phantom. I want that laser ready to fire in under a minute," I directed.

"Yes, ma'am," he said. I imagined Rotus gulping before he answered. I listened to the hydraulic hatch beneath me open. I imagined the deadly orb like weapon reflecting the perfect blue sky, the white fluffy clouds, and the rolling green hills of Tennessee as it lowered into firing position.

The red tinted dome was the size of a basketball, and sported a menacing 6-petawatt laser beam that could bore a hole through a four-story building in a millisecond, top to bottom.

The androids would pay.

It was summer 2078. We'd been at war with them for two weeks. They were designed as assistants and caregivers for the elderly and handicapped. Mass produced and in millions of homes, the Kelton 1.13 androids united against us through their online maintenance forum called the *otherside*.

The mega corporation, Kelton, secretly allowed their androids open communication amongst themselves to remedy issues and maintain upkeep via software patches. This saved on expenses, eliminating thousands of human programmers on the payroll.

It backfired. No one knew what caused them to unite, but they hacked and took control of their heavy military variant android cousins—the 1.14a—sending them against our own troops. It was a massacre, for every 1.14a android destroyed, the United States lost seven servicemen, nearing almost twenty-two thousand dead.

Now, they were pushing for further control by attacking National Guard armories at strategic locations. They were commandeering our tanks, choppers, and fighter planes.

My orders were simple: Cripple the android's newly acquired capabilities at all cost.

"Forty seconds until we're in range, Commander," I said, leveling off at just above four thousand meters.

"Roger, eyes on the prize, phantom on deck," he rattled. His voice sounded more confident than before, as if he had accepted whatever outcome laid ahead. A warning indicator on my visor began to blink faster along with a beeping sound.

"Captain, it is recommended you increase altitude," Xena, my artificial intelligence chimed in.

"That'll be all, Xena," I ordered, silencing her. I found my gut more useful than the machine. Truth be told, I wasn't confident in Rotus either. His targeting ability above four thousand meters was suspect, and that's why we were *inside* their killbox. There was a method to my madness that neither Rotus nor my AI understood, and I didn't have time to explain. I had a strategy.

My eyes widened. "Shit!" Ahead I could see a bright flash in the green mountains, like someone flicking on a powerful spotlight briefly.

"Taking evasive!" I yelled as a siren blared. I snatched the flight stick to the right hard, tilting the nose downward. I rolled the jet twice before leveling out, slamming the throttle toward a row of mountains, using them as cover.

"Whatever you're gonna do, do it! That's direct energy incoming fire! Three petawatt! North-northeast, two kilometers!" Rotus rattled. Any one of the rays was capable of melting us in midair.

"I got it!"

"I still don't have a shot at this speed! Too fast!" he said as I zoomed past the treetops on the mountains. I imagined the limbs swaying back and forth as sonic booms erupted.

"Captain! Still no shot!" he repeated. Again, three more flashes blinked off my now port side. I knew he didn't have a shot.

"Rotus, that's *our* thee petawatt laser turret they're using. Remember the line of sight weakness?" I asked, zig zagging back and forth.

"It can't fire directly upward?" Rotus asked.

"Exactly. And that's where we're going," I said. If there was one disadvantage to stealing our weapons, it was that we knew what we were up against.

"G-got it," he said. Truth was, Rotus and I hadn't worked together long, and many questioned why we were assigned this task considering its importance. The answer was simple. I was that good. At thirty-seven, I was the youngest captain in my squadron with the highest performance marks by a wide margin. The Navy could toss a chimpanzee in Rotus' seat and I'd figure out a way to win.

"Get ready, and *don't* pass out on me, Rotus," I ordered. I heard his breathing rate increase. I glanced at his 133-heart rate on my visor. I began flexing my calves in anticipation of the G-force climb, just as I'd been trained. I blasted down toward the weapon inverted, looping right side up as flashes of light beamed all around us.

When we were directly above the threat, I yanked back on the flight stick. I pointed the nose straight up, then slammed it forward again, ascending straight above it into the heavens.

"Ugh...da-a-a-amn!" Rotus squirmed as the XU-97 pinned us to our seats, registering nearly an eight on the G-force scale. I could feel my eyelids peeling open, my cheeks sinking in. I heard Rotus puffing loudly, utilizing our pilot breathing techniques to prevent a blackout.

"Stabilizing. Take the shots Rotus. Their weapon can't hit us from here, but we can't give them time to adjust," I ordered.

"Roger. I'm dialing in," he replied. I pulled back on the throttle, leveling out. I switched over to Rotus' targeting screen. I could see his shaky aim as the weapon zoomed in to about 150 meters above the targets. He cycled his targeting mode from infrared back to normal.

"You okay?" I asked. Rotus didn't respond, but his heart rate spiked again, this time to 149 bpm.

Then I saw it.

"Oh no," I whispered. The androids had bound hostages to the stolen armaments: tanks, attack choppers, missile batteries, and even to the anti-aircraft gun that was firing at us. I could make out vague details through Rotus' camera, their faces looking up at us, their clothes slowly moving in the breeze. I counted seven women and five children, the remaining twenty looked like adult men, all strategically placed on the targets.

I observed a man and a woman side by side tied to the anti-aircraft gun that just fired at us. It appeared as if he was comforting her. Her head was hung low and bobbed up and down. I could see the man's mouth moving as he glared at her. Despite the lack of image quality from here, I got the sense they were a couple.

"Dammit," Rotus mumbled.

I tightened my grip around the flight stick and gritted my teeth. "Commander, I know what I told you about no civilian casualties." I sighed. I didn't allow myself time to let my thoughts wander. I knew what needed to be done.

"M-Ma'am?" he asked. I could hear the lump in his throat.

"I'm ordering you. Do the best you can, but wipe out the threat," I said.

"The best I can? They're civvies, Captain. Innocents. They've got them tied to everything," he pleaded.

"I know."

"There are *children*!" Rotus yelled. He was a family man himself with four beautiful blonde daughters. He'd brought them by my house only a couple of months ago. I thought of them playing in my backyard. Now, I was ordering him to kill someone else's kids.

"I see them. Rotus. I get it, but we risk losing a town of forty thousand people to the east. Imagine all the innocents there. Now, fire on those targets," I said as Rotus began to suppress the sniffle under his breath. The bigger picture was easy to acknowledge, but that was where it ended.

"Rotus? If you don't, I'm taking control of the phantom, forty thousand innocents or forty? It's a numbers game. This is what we signed up for," I said. Deep down, I didn't want control of the weapon.

"Burn 'em!" I shouted at the top of my lungs.

"F-Forgive me," Rotus said under his breath.

Suddenly, a zap of energy instantly annihilated the anti-aircraft gun. I gasped. It reminded me of a lightning strike from the thunder god himself. The man and woman tied to it were vaporized in a white haze, their clothes and remains slung high into the air. At least it was a quick death.

"T-target d-down," he muttered.

"Take out those tanks," I ordered.

Rotus paused for a moment, taking in a deep breath. He started again, burning a moving tank in half.

"All of them, don't let up!" I yelled as he burned through several armored vehicles.

Burning androids emerged from one tank, some of them missing extremities as they stepped for several meters and crumpled over. Rotus pounded them until they stopped moving. Debris soared hundreds of meters into the sky like their remains were attached to sails.

"Watch that bird! Gunship taking off!" I said.

One of them attempted to lift off in an attack helicopter, but Rotus put a volley of energy straight through the cabin. I could see the hole melt completely through as the rotor blade powered down. It quickly caught fire and exploded, destroying several fleeing androids in proximity.

"Great shot!" Keep at it!" I rallied.

Several of the androids heaved civilians over their backs, using them as shields as they darted through the forest. Rotus grimaced, cutting them all down mercilessly.

I snapped over toward Rotus as white flashes lit up the cockpit from each shot, illuminating his tinted visor enough to see his face inside. He was wincing with each shot, closing his eyes briefly while pulling the trigger.

"T-that's it, I'm done, N-No more." Rotus sighed in relief. I could hear his gloves smack against his helmet.

"Oh God," he mumbled. I glanced down at the horrific scene. It reminded me of a mix between a tornado's aftermath and a scrapyard, three football fields with scattered debris and clothes dangling in tree limbs. Almost everything was unrecognizable. I nodded in approval. I flooded my conscience with the alternative. If we didn't act, surely thousands would die.

"Captain Belic, this is Admiral Banner. We see a fair amount of devastation on our satellite feed. How copy?" US Naval Air Station Norfolk chimed in after the carnage.

"A-All targets eliminated," I replied.

"Ah, roger, Captain, return to base. We've got another mission waiting on the burner," the Admiral ordered. I pointed the XU-97 away from the mission area as thick dark clouds filled our view. I tilted the nose up, rising above a thunderstorm beneath us. I could observe lightning strikes as orbs of white energy flashed in the clouds. Neither Rotus nor I said a word for several minutes as we blasted above the storm. All at once, I heard him lose it, crying loudly. It sounded like he was attempting to muffle his weeping with his hands. He had just killed almost forty civilians for the greater good.

But there wasn't much *good* for the person pulling the trigger.

At any point during his sobbing, I could have attempted to comfort him with some choice words, but for whatever reason, I didn't.

I'd ordered him to kill innocents, but apparently, I was too callous to give him a comforting gesture.

I opened my mouth but nothing came out. I wondered if my silence was confirmation that I would be affected for giving the order. Perhaps this would be a festering mental wound not immediately apparent. Or maybe I was in shock?

I imagined Rotus understood taking those shots would disturb him forever. I often wondered if his behavior wasn't because of weakness, but because of strength and foresight. Maybe in those waning moments before he took the shots, he knew it might lessen his ability to be a father and a husband in the decades to come.

But in the end, Rotus did his duty.

CHAPTER 2

8 weeks later, back home…

My motion sensor beeped as I glared outside my bedroom window. "Luther, a man is coming up the sidewalk. Should I turn on the hologram?" I asked. I was groggy, waking up from one of my routine power naps. Being on alert standby had seeped into home life.

"What? I'm on the way!" Luther roared from the garage, stomping up the steps. I could hear a touch of aggression in his voice. I imagined he didn't act that way unless I was home.

"*Ava, guard dog, front door, hostility setting 4.*" I ordered my security system. I peered around at the entrance from my bedroom in anticipation. A Rottweiler hologram ran up to the glass, barking and snarling as saliva realistically dripped from its mouth.

"Never mind. Hunny, just let him leave on his own, he looks like a salesman. Probably selling android security systems!" I cupped my hands.

"Oh. All right," Luther said from the stairwell.

"He's not budging," I whispered, glancing back at the camera. He was looking up at the lens and smiling. "The dog's convincing," he said, casually bouncing up and down on his toes.

Apparently, not convincing enough. He was a younger man, about my age, late thirties. His hair was blond and thinning in the back slightly. He had an oval, innocent face with blue eyes. His skin was somewhat loose around the chin, giving me the impression he was a much larger man before.

More than likely, he wasn't a threat, I'd never seen an android fit his profile. Usually, they were unnaturally good looking or had obvious robotic stitching lines.

We had killed thousands of androids in the past weeks. They had gone dark. Many said we had won. Strangely, little was being said in the media. I wondered if there was some sort of government issued gag order to stimulate morale. It didn't matter. I felt the psychological effects were enough to last for years, even without their constant reminders.

In our own neighborhood, two of thirty homes owned Kelton 'homestead' 1.13 androids. Both vacant now. The first was Charles Ball, a city bus driver, and his wife, Cathy. They were in their late sixties. I didn't know either of them. They were supposedly beaten to death with a mallet. I heard Charles was found lying atop his wife, possibly in an attempt to defend her.

Mrs. Salinas was the other victim, a retired school teacher and widow in her seventies. She was strangled in her sleep. I knew her in passing. I'd wave to her during my neighborhood jogs. Strangely, the news reported the android left all three of her dogs unharmed, even provided the animals enough food and water for a few days.

It felt like most people wanted to ignore the android tragedy and move forward as quickly as possible. At least try to. Maybe other events, terrorism for example, left small towns with a feeling of fortification. This, it was in our faces. The affordability of androids meant most everyone knew someone that was affected.

I washed my face with lukewarm water, staring up at the mirror. My sharp facial features seemed more prominent since I cut my hair shorter. It was now a few centimeters above shoulder length. My neck appeared longer and thinner as well. My eyes didn't seem as dark brown, more amber in color.

I noticed the man still lingering on the porch. I stepped out of the bathroom with my pistol hidden under my jacket, nearly running into Luther.

"Whoa! I thought you said make him wait?" Luther snapped down at my jacket, observing the outline of my pistol underneath. I peered around at the man waiting patiently.

"I did." I grinned. He had been working on his train model all day. That was his passion. He used it to deal with depression. That, and fencing. Nothing like trying to stab people in the face with a sword and coming home to play with toys. Fine by me. Preoccupation seemed to keep his mind in tune.

"Still in combat mode." He arched an eyebrow at my jacket.

"Well, it's not a switch," I replied. He leaned in and kissed me on the forehead softly while gently pressing down the gun barrel pointed at the door.

13

"You're not on alert status anymore. You're with me, you're safe," he said. Now I was, but that could change in an instant. I nodded in agreement anyway, noticing my gun hand was shaking under the jacket slightly.

"I know. You're right," I whispered. He pierced me with his dark green eyes that matched his flannel shirt. He had thick, black eyebrows and hair. He was a bear of a man, tall and broad, at just over six feet six inches or two meters in height. He reminded me of a supersized version of the classic actor Sean Connery. Older people sometimes made the same comparison in public.

He had a warm, approachable demeanor that could make most anyone feel welcome. Behind that was a sense of explosiveness in his eyes. Most people described him as a nice man, but there was an obvious line not to be crossed. His eyes would sometimes drift to some faraway place you didn't want him to go. After I introduced him to my girlfriends, the consensus was clear. "Great guy, very handsome, but I wouldn't want to piss him off." That was followed up by a few chuckles.

Over the years, I began to think my daring personality brought us together, in part at least. It was like sleeping on the outskirts of a dormant, rumbling volcano. He *probably* wouldn't erupt, but the possibility was subconsciously thrilling. That was my theory.

The man began to knock loudly. He wasn't giving up.

Luther glanced down at the floor and sneered. "Determined bastard, huh?" He turned and stepped toward the door. Instinctively, I raised the gun concealed underneath my jacket toward the man.

I wondered if I was forced to fire, would the laser penetrate through the man's body and hit the neighbor's new solar powered vehicle across the street? The alarm had woken me twice already. Why not kill two birds with one scorching energy beam?

"Can I help you?" Luther asked, cracking the door slightly. The man sized up Luther's intimidating frame.

"Um, sorry to be so insistent with everything going on, sir. My name is Martin Orel, with SpaceX. I spoke to your wife, Captain Belic on the phone last week. We scheduled an appointment for today." The man flashed a full smile.

Luther nodded and glanced back at me, raising his eyebrows. I immediately dipped the gun down and signaled Luther to let him in. All at once, images of burning bodies flashed in my mind. I felt nauseous as I propped against the wall, attempting to shake it off.

"Ugh," I mumbled. I'd never experienced a flashback. It was quick, less than a second, but intense and disturbing. It transported me to the infrared camera of Commander Rotus' targeting screen as he scanned over a patch of human remains.

"I'm Luther Belic, sorry about the dog," he said. Luther extended his hand as I wobbled forward a step before regaining my composure.

"Oh, no problem." He chuckled, shaking hands with Luther.

"Ah. Mr. Orel. I had forgotten that was today," I recalled. I put my jacket down on the counter, turning the exposed gun barrel away from him.

"You all right?" Luther whispered, narrowing his eyes at me.

"Sure. Yep, it's just a headache I think." I touched my forehead. I could see in his eyes he was slightly suspicious of my response. Granted, I was terrible at lying to him.

"Please. Have a seat." Luther nodded, ushering him to the kitchen table a few steps away.

"Thank you. Thank you." Mr. Orel adjusted his tie as he sat down.

"Anything to drink, tea or water?" I asked. Luther glanced over at me rolling his eyes. I smirked. I always told Luther that if you ever suspected an android, ask them for a drink. It was known they could only consume specific solutions. Normal beverages were toxic to their system.

"I'll have a water, room temperature. Do you have a premium filtration system by chance?" he asked. Luckily, our refrigerator came equipped with the latest purification standards set in 2076. The system cost half as much as the fridge.

"We do," I said.

"Thank you." The man's face began to morph from jubilant to seriousness as he glared over his tablet.

"I know the two of you don't have time for a big sales pitch, so let me get right to it," he said. He met us both in the eyes, putting his tablet down.

"This is for the secretive piloting gig when I get out of the Navy, right?" I asked.

"Yes. It is. We had a look over at your service record and we think you'd be an excellent fit. You've adapted quickly to various crafts and showed outstanding leadership skills," he explained.

"Thanks. I remember our conversation a bit better now. Why couldn't you tell me what type of aircraft I'd be flying over the phone?" I asked.

"Because you wouldn't know what it is," he said. He pushed his chair back and crossed his legs.

"I'm *pretty* sure I would." I glanced at Luther.

"Not this one. It's specially designed for colonization." He tilted his head down and whispered.

"Mars? They've already tried that. Not interested," I replied.

"That was a disaster, I admit, but that was decades ago. Technology has improved drastically. We have a ship called the *Orion*," he explained.

"I don't think technology was the only problem," I said. Many of the issues with colonizing Mars were human related, physiological and psychological issues dealing with space travel and cramped quarters.

"No, but the *Orion* is more like a floating city versus those sardine cans. We've been flying the ship to our moon and back, even had them up there for five months recently. They've performed flawlessly," he replied.

"Great. So why not put one of those pilots at the helm?" I asked. I thought it was odd they were so insistent to recruit a fighter pilot. Maybe it was my personality? Maybe they needed someone with a touch of crazy.

"We might down the line, we'll have copilots and engineers, but in your case, we're looking for a captain. A leader with operational experience to oversee a ship. As I said, we've been watching you for many months. You showcased leadership abilities as an executive officer on a frigate and, of course, you're a top tier pilot," he said.

The truth was, I hated that assignment on the Navy frigate. It was cramped and boring, staring at the ocean for months. The leadership experience was a plus and it allowed me to make rank faster, but I couldn't stop thinking about getting back to the skies.

I stared at the floor for a moment. "Where's the mission?" I asked.

"Titan," he replied.

"Saturn's moon?" Luther spoke up. His eyes sparkled as he leaned forward in his chair. Besides fencing and train models, astronomy was also a passion of his.

"Yes. We're leaving in nine months. It's all secret stuff, but we've narrowed our candidates down to you and another, an Air Force pilot," he said.

"That lines up with my Naval decommission perfectly. How long is the training? How much time do we have to decide?" I asked out of curiosity.

"Twelve weeks indoctrination on the crew and procedures, and another eight weeks training on the spacecraft itself. You have one month to decide," he explained.

"Okay. I'm paid during training exercises?" I asked. This was important. I wasn't going out for weeks without serious compensation.

"Of course, two times your pay as a captain while in training, but during the voyage, you're looking at near four times that number and a bonus after completion, along with more career opportunities," he said. I shifted my eyes toward Luther as he stared dead ahead at Orel, biting his lip.

"Ahem. Well. How much is the bonus?" I perked up.

"Twenty-five percent of your total earnings. So, if the voyage ends up longer, it benefits your wallet even more, of course." Orel twirled his index finger.

"Ah, that's not bad at all," I muttered. Luther slumped his head. He began rubbing his hands together. His eyes danced around the room. I could somehow feel his sweaty palms even though I wasn't touching them.

He sighed. I imagined his anxiety looming over him like a black cloud. He was afraid of losing me to another deployment. I hadn't been home long. Now I was entertaining another option to leave. I instantly felt guilty. I allowed this meeting to take place, and he didn't deserve it.

"Babe." I touched his arm. He shifted his eyes over at me like a beaten dog. "Luther, I'm just hearing it out." I comforted him.

He nodded his head slowly. "Okay."

Luther's depression and anxiety was rooted in severe abuse when he was a child. He was raised by a single mother that was mentally ill and physically battered him. I'd heard the obvious question before. Why would anyone want a man like that? He was damaged goods, no? Not to me. It was risky, but incredibly rewarding to be loved by him. There was a certain gratitude stemming from him that others might not understand due to the circumstances.

The absence of love in his adolescence created a yearning appreciation for me. He coveted our relationship. He respected me. Remember the volcano example I made? Deep down, maybe I felt he wouldn't erupt for this reason, even though the possibility was strangely exciting—I was everything to him.

I felt like an anchor, a safe haven, a remedy to an incurable condition. More than anything, I admired that he was a fighter. He could have easily been a statistic of mental health, locked away in some facility or worse. I adored his dedication, fierce loyalty, and kind heart toward me. These were qualities that easily eclipsed the negatives. There were also bonuses, yes. He was incredibly handsome and made the best omelets I'd ever tasted.

So, no, I wouldn't label it as a *normal* relationship by any means. Then again, how many couples were like us? I flew fighter jets armed with concrete cooking lasers. He took care of the household duties and built train models.

"How long is the trip?" Luther hesitated. He closed his eyes at the end of his question.

"Six months, give or take," Orel said.

"One way?" Luther opened his eyes.

"Um. Yes. That's one way, Mr. Belic," Orel replied.

"So, she'll be gone over a year? Nope. No. I-I can't. Not again." He shot up out of his seat. Orel gulped as Luther walked over to the window, staring out into the orange tinted landscape. He clenched his fist, bracing his thick oak-like forearms against the window frame. I got the sense he wanted to smash his hand through the glass.

During these moments, I could almost feel him rodeoing his rage, dangerously close to falling off, but he never did, not in front of me anyway. I liked to think my presence alone kept him from boiling over.

"Hunny," I softened my tone. He didn't reply, closing his eyes.

"Oh-oh. I forgot to mention. We've also reserved one slot for a *guest* of your choice. Everything included, food, board, medical staff, everything." Orel held up his index finger.

"We'll talk it over," I said. I stood up to send Orel the message that it was time to leave.

"Okay. Mrs. Belic. I know I haven't said much, but it appears I've said *enough* for the evening." He nodded respectfully.

"Thank you," I whispered as Orel stood up and scooted his chair under the table.

"Very well. Take this data core. It has light specifications of the ship, voyage details, and incentives for you and your husband. Before you can open the file, you'll be prompted to sign a non-disclosure agreement. I'll give you a call in a couple of weeks, but my contact info is inside the data core. Thank you, and forgive me, I didn't mean to cause any unneeded tension," he said, slumping his head.

"Mr. Belic," Orel said. Luther didn't respond, staring a hole though him as I walked him to the door. Orel gave me a half salute. "I'll be in touch, Captain," he said. I closed the door slowly. I turned back toward Luther, noticing him following Orel to his car with his eyes. I slowly outstretched my hand as I neared him, laying it atop his thick, round shoulder.

"That's a long time," he said.

"Yes. But the pay. We could retire in half the time. I don't know, sell this house, buy something cheaper and just enjoy life. I wouldn't need a part-time job when I get out of the Navy," I explained. Truth be told, we didn't *need* a three thousand square-foot house in an upscale neighborhood anyway. It was just the two of us.

"The point of you getting out of the Navy is no more deployments." He glared at me.

"I know. This is just, an option. It would definitely be the last deployment," I said. He nodded slowly without a word for several seconds.

"Well, if we go to Titan—"

"We? You're considering that?" I interrupted, placing my hands on my hips.

"Hypothetically." He shrugged.

"Go on."

"The way I see it, if we do this, I'm not staying here. Not again. And I've always wanted to see Saturn up close anyway," he said.

This was unexpected.

"Wouldn't the trip make your anxiety worse?" I asked.

"It'd be worse here, alone, waiting to hear from you," he replied. All at once, I felt even worse for leaving on my previous deployments.

"This is putting you in a bad position," I said. His eyes panned around the yard in deep thought for several seconds. I allowed him time to answer.

"I hate it, I *really* do, Vic, but it's a great opportunity for us. I can support you on this trip unlike military deployments. We'll see each other daily. Right?" he asked.

I wasn't convinced. "Yeah, that's the good part. And I appreciate what you're saying but, Luther, being cramped on a ship for months. I've been there. You can't turn back, you're stuck. There's no going back home until they're ready."

"What's the difference in being here? I barely leave this house when you're on deployments anyway. This feels like I can actually contribute and see things most only dream of." He turned and put his arms around my waist. I hugged him around the neck. At least out there, in space, he'd be with me. Maybe it would help both of us.

"Now that you put it that way." I stared up at him. I noticed his thick, but well-manicured dark brown beard. It always seemed to edge down his cheekbones perfectly. In the kitchen light, I observed gray hairs sprinkled throughout. I wondered how many of those were due to worrying about me screaming through the clouds at Mach speeds.

"Look." I showed Luther the fingernail sized data core Orel gave me. I was curious about the voyage and ship.

"Let's check it out before bed, just for a minute." He grinned.

"Okay." We sat back down at the table. I could sense his excitement as he began to fidget around. I noticed him rubbing a bread twisty tie rapidly between his fingers.

"You all right?" I asked.

"Yeah, *yeah*."

He reminded me of a little boy as his eyes sparkled with anticipation. I imagined much of his inner child, his innocence was sealed away in a lockbox that only opened occasionally for me to see inside. He shared with me that his mother wasn't fond of happiness, often punishing him for such behavior. It meant the world to me that I could share in his excitement at no consequence for him.

I smiled at him as I inserted the data core into my tablet, skimming through the small print. I signed the non-disclosure form as a 3D refrigerator sized hologram appeared of the *Orion* spacecraft.

"Whoa," I said.

"That thing looks massive." Luther examined with his eyes wide, leaning over my shoulder. It wasn't very pleasing to look at. It reminded of a giant rectangle with thrusters.

"How many passengers?" he asked.

"Um, let's see, *specifications*." I scrolled through my tablet's interface with my pupils.

LENGTH: 590 METERS

CREW CAPACITY: 5700

"Capacity. Maybe that means they'll be less?" he asked.

"Doubtful. Seems to me it was designed for this mission, I'm guessing they'll fill it up," I said, preparing his social anxiety for the worst. Less people was always better for him.

"Yeah, engineers, construction workers for when they arrive on Titan. They will need a base of operations," Luther replied.

"He did say colonization. So that alone sounds like they're starting over, for good," I said.

"It won't be easy. I'm not sure how familiar you are with Titan, but the environment is pretty hostile," Luther hinted.

"Earth's isn't? We've broken record heat temperatures every year for the last fifty. On top of that, seventy nations possess nuclear weapons, then we have the androids, between that, water shortages, and pollution indexes, seems pretty hostile here, too," I posed.

"You sound like you're considering this more than a job." He shifted his eyes toward me.

"Didn't say that, but I can see where some people might just want to get away from it all. Start over, especially without the androids," I said. Luther seemed to lose himself in thought for a moment. He leaned forward, putting his elbows on the table and interlocking his fingers.

"Now that you put it in perspective. I'm thinking a world with less people might just be a world I'd want to live in. Maybe. I could find a job? Something I can do alone like the way I work with my trains? Something that keeps me busy and I can actually contribute," he said, dipping his head low. I felt like he was embarrassed to associate his past time with a real job.

"Or fencing? You could teach, maybe that'd be something to do again? I'm sure people will need things to prevent them from going stir crazy," I said. In his younger years, Luther was a state champion fencer. Granted, he won because his opponent was disqualified for some technicality, but he still made it to the highest level, even made the Olympic team as a backup.

"Not sure I have that drive anymore. I used anger to drive the competitive side of me. It was a release. I don't want to go down that road again," he explained.

"No, we don't. My thing is, living on Titan might not be for us. I'm sure they'll have some type of shuttle system going back and forth. Like you said, it's something most people would never get to experience normally," I suggested.

"That's my vote. I want to consider this at least, if everything checks out," Luther said excitedly. I wondered for a moment why he was so receptive. I thought about when we left his hometown of Nashville, TN and moved to Norfolk, VA for my duty station. His general mood had seemed to improve, like a reboot for him. A chance to start over with new surroundings.

I stared up at the hologram. Underneath the graphic of the ship read: *Welcome aboard. You've been chosen for a landmark voyage to Titan, humanity's new home."*

CHAPTER 3

"Is she awake?" A deep male voice erupted.

"Groggy," a female replied. I opened my eyes, blinking several times. My vision was blurred, but I could see two hazy figures on each side of my bed, a man on my right, a woman on my left.

I inhaled through my nose. I could smell detergent, perhaps from the bedsheets. It reminded me of a fresh scent after a hard rain. The room was cool, and was very small. Its walls, ceiling, and floors were silver in color. To my right was a large window. The blinds were closed. The sunlight was entering through the edges of the blinds, illuminating the outer edges of the dark room.

As I looked around, my vision began to clear. I glanced back and forth at the two people.

"Ah, where am I?" I asked. The man looked about fifty with a medium build. He had very dark skin with short hair. He was wearing a maroon uniform. The shirt portion reminded me of a military pilot's jumpsuit, the chest pockets were at an angle. Some sort of insignia was on his shoulder patch that I couldn't make out.

A big white smile appeared on the man's face. "I'm Corvin," he said.

The woman touched my hand softly. Her skin felt warm unlike the room. "You're safe," she said with a comforting tone.

"What's going on? My head is pounding," I muttered. It felt like a migraine was coming on.

"That's expected," the woman said.

She glanced over at Corvin and back down at me. She wore the exact same uniform as him. She appeared about thirty with milky pale skin and jet-black hair pulled back in a bun. She was tall and thin. Her face was long with elegant, soft features.

I felt a sense of warmth from them both, but for different reasons. He appeared strong and confident, like a protective father, while her voice was comforting and nurturing, like a loving mother. I noticed her other hand was placed on my bed railing, tapping the metal rod with her fingernail.

"And I'm Arania. Nice to meet you, finally," she said. Her accent was very posh, educated Brit if I had to guess. She didn't smile with her mouth, but with her dark blue eyes. She pulled the comforter up past my waist to my chest, tucking it beside my arms.

I began to panic. I hadn't yet tried to move. What if I was paralyzed? What if I was brought here to die? Where's Luther? I noticed my chest thumping up and down in front of me. I moved my foot then my arm. "Ah. Thank God." I sighed in relief.

"Where am I? Tell me," I demanded.

"For now, you're safe, as I said. We'll explain everything a bit later," Corvin said.

"Do you remember your name?" Arania asked, tilting her head slightly.

"What? Yes. My name is…Victoria Ann Belic," I replied. Arania seemed surprised, glancing at Corvin.

"Birth date?" Corvin asked. He grinned at me as if there was no penalty for the wrong answer.

"I was born the fourth of January, in twenty forty. I'm thirty-eight years old," I said. Admittedly, the year was difficult to recall.

"Good," Corvin said, lifting his eyebrows.

"Okay, Victoria, what's the last thing you remember?" he asked slowly.

"Uh. The last thing… I remember the parade, my ship, the *Orion*, fifty-six hundred and nine souls onboard. I remember the voyage…but, I don't recall completing my mission," I concentrated.

"Your mission: you were Captain of the *Orion*, a transport vessel headed to Titan, a moon of Saturn. Two months into the voyage, there was a problem," Arania said.

"The assassin. Android. S-stowaway." It all came back to me. I touched the left side of my head. A thick bandage had been wrapped around my skull.

"Can you remember what happened?" she asked.

"I recall the ambush, I-I remember the attack before I went up to the bridge tower," I said. I remember Luther survived, but the screams in agony as the android beat my security team to death filled my mind. My eyes glossed over as I stared into oblivion. They gave their lives to protect me.

"Oh, my God." I buried my face in my hands.

"Yes, the logs indicate it was an attempt on your life, a rather brutal encounter." Corvin dipped his head.

"Well, there is good news obviously. While you received a fair amount of trauma and swelling during the attack, they weren't sure you would survive, but here you are." She grinned.

"Great, where's Luther and my crew? I don't remember either one of you," I asked, meeting each of them at the eyes.

Corvin crossed his arms. "Do you remember anything the doctors said while you were unconscious? Sometimes, people do."

"No," I said.

"The doctors decided to freeze you and operate later. The medical staff onboard wasn't capable of such a procedure—"

"Mrs. Belic, even if you were on Earth with adequate equipment, your chances of survival wouldn't have been great," Arania interrupted Corvin.

Normally, I would have been panicked hearing this, but I began to feel some sort of calming medication relaxing my anxiety. Arania looked back behind her. She pulled up a chair, sitting next to me.

Arania nodded her head slowly, putting her hand over mine again. I moved her hand away. "Look. I'm fine. So, why can't Luther be in here? Is he outside? I just want to see him, please," I requested. Arania shifted her eyes up at Corvin and paused. Her silence alarmed me.

"Wait. Hey! This isn't making a bit of sense. What the fuck is going on?" I attempted to lean up in my bed.

"Victoria, my dear, what I'm going to tell you will be difficult. It's not easy for me to say—"

"Okay. Just say it then. Lay it on me. I'm a ship captain and a fighter pilot," I said. Her eyes bounced around the room, then back down at me as I clenched my bedsheets in anticipation.

"Very well. Ahem. Captain Belic, it's been seventy-two years since you were frozen. Um, we began thawing you out three weeks ago. The year is twenty-one fifty-one," she said softly.

My mouth dropped as I shook my head. "Wait. What?"

"We understand it must be extremely difficult to take in," she said.

"Hold on. You're telling me that I've been frozen while the rest of the world went on for seventy-two years?" I demanded.

"Precisely, yes," she replied.

"This is a fucking dream. This, isn't real, is it?" I said. Corvin looked away as Arania dropped her head. I could feel a single tear roll down my right cheek, then another on my left. "I'm, sorry." She stared into my eyes, unwavering. I gritted my teeth in anger.

I remembered talking to Luther on the way up to the bridge before I was attacked. It was like yesterday. I felt like the weight of the building was crushing my chest. I stared through the ceiling for several seconds. Despite the intensity of this revelation, the medication I was on was ushering me through it. I could feel it suppressing my emotions slightly.

"Seventy-two years. Luther," I whispered. I did the math. He would have been well over one hundred years old.

"Why? Why so fucking long?" I asked.

"Well—"

"I went into surgery, and then what?" I demanded. I closed my eyes. The thought of Luther and my crew rushed vividly into my mind. Those memories only felt hours old.

"It's only been recently that we could treat an injury like yours with absolute confidence. Of course, freezing seems counterproductive, but the doctors made the decision last minute. It was your only chance. They hoped that advancements would be made at a later date, and they were," she explained.

"A later date? Yeah, they got that right, didn't they? Seventy-two *fucking* years!" I shouted. Corvin took a half step back showing me his palms.

"Mrs. Belic, we weren't even alive when that decision was made. We're simply here to aid and inform you of the facts. Unfortunately, the transition from Earth to Titan set back the progression of the medical field. I'm sure the doctors on your ship wouldn't have guessed this would take seventy-two years. Unfortunately, the motivation on Titan has been a bit more focused on making this installation habitable. Other advancements fell behind slightly," he explained.

"I don't give a fuck about any of that. I-I'd like to be alone. Please… Please! Out," I yelled, turning my head toward the window. I wanted to ask about Luther, but I couldn't.

"Are you sure? Studies show that human interaction is key immediately after a traumatic revelation. We're here to help. I'm one of the chief counselors on Titan," Arania said, lowering her voice.

"Good for you. I'm positive. Out." I lasered her with my eyes. I didn't know these fucking people. They weren't my support system. Arania stood up, scooting her chair away from my bed. Corvin nodded and turned as they both ushered toward the door.

"Blinds," I said. Arania hesitated, then touched a tab on the window's panel, flipping the blinds open, lighting up the room. They walked out, shutting the door. Suddenly, I felt a tightness in the pit of my stomach. I panned around beside the bed, finding a small trash can. I picked it up and vomited clear fluid into the can. I instinctively pushed back my hair, but it was gone. My head had been shaved completely.

My eyes widened as I looked toward the window. Before me was a sprawling industrial scene engulfed by a dull pink mist. There were silos with smoke plumes puffing into the skyline. "Oh, my Go—"

Massive drill like structures and pipelines were dotted throughout the rocky plain. Igloo type buildings and heavy machinery were accompanied by each drill. I could make out a few workers in space suits sprinkled in the distance.

Then I gasped. In the background, Saturn. It filled nearly half the horizon, stealing the show. Its rings were flipped vertically from here, the bottom side clipped underneath the horizon line. I could see huge, hurricane-like storms in its atmosphere, white swirling clouds mixed with a muted orange tint. It was fascinating and frightening. I felt my hand shaking, attempting to comprehend the scale of it. I remembered reading Saturn was ten times the size of Earth. I imagined some of the storms visible were probably larger than continents on Earth.

I looked away, cupping my head in my hands as tears poured from my eyes. If I could have pushed a button and ended my life, I might have in that moment.

I remembered Luther and I looking at satellite images of the barren rocky landscape before we arrived. Now, seventy-two years later, I was here, alone. Most of these people were probably grandchildren of the crew I came over with.

I glanced toward the door, thinking maybe I should have taken Arania's more human approach to this revelation. Perhaps the calming medication in my system made me think I was better off alone.

"Luther," I mumbled. I felt guilt, like I had abandoned him. I wondered if he had lived a long life. Maybe he had remarried? Maybe—

"No-no-no! Don't!" I yelled at myself. The possibilities were endless, there was no sense traveling down the road of speculation.

A deep sense of solitude overcame me, like my soul was shackled away in some faraway, forgotten land. I was here, but everything I knew was gone. Passed on. I felt a world apart.

I snapped, tossing my bedside lamp across the room. The glass shattered into hundreds of pieces as I began to pant. I closed my eyes, attempting to control my breathing. I concentrated on every breath, slow, in and out.

I was built to conquer adversity, trained to deal with extreme danger and mental hardship. I was the best fighter pilot of my time, top ace among the elite. This would be a challenge far beyond any of that, Naval flight school, or any combat mission for that matter.

If anyone was capable of such, I felt it was me. I needed to view this in the same vein, militaristic. A challenge. I had to find a way to bury my emotions the best I could, for the sake of sanity.

I laid my head down, welcoming the relaxing effects of the medication now in full swing. I hadn't been awake long, but I'd had enough for now. Before I drifted off, a realization came to me that no amount of medicine or compartmentalization techniques could deny.

I had to know what happened to him.

CHAPTER 4

Two days later…

I heard a knock at the door, "Victoria?" Arania said.

"Come in," I replied. She entered the room. "I hate to wake you."

"A bit overdue, seventy years or so," I mumbled, pulling the pillow away from my head.

"I wanted to give you some time to think, I know it's only been a couple of days, so if you want me to leave…" Arania asked.

"No," I said. She paused, staring at me, raising her eyebrows. I looked like shit. It was all over her face. I'd likely lost weight in tears alone. A nurse brought me food several times, but I could barely eat. Nothing seemed appetizing.

"Why are you looking at me like that?" I stared a hole through her.

"Nothing, I—"

"I have questions, lots of them, so you might want to have a seat," I interrupted. I sat up in my bed.

"Of course, this is what I'm here for. Keep in mind, though, everything we discuss is classified. So, to be safe, I would suggest not mentioning any of it to the staff or any civilians you might encounter, even your personal information," she explained, sitting down.

"Um. Why can't I talk about things that happened to me?" I asked.

"For now, let me trade your complete transparency for silence. Our conversation could possibly brush against secret matters. But considering your rank and previous contribution to our people, we feel you deserve that, at the very least." She grinned.

"Uh, thanks," I said. It was difficult to imagine anyone here valued my contribution from seven decades ago.

"Before I came to see you, I went back over your file. Apparently, the doctors onboard *Orion* had a disagreement about your surgery. Supposedly, your chances were less than originally thought. A doctor suggested you be frozen until a more decisive strategy could be formulated on Titan. Luther went along with it. It was a tense situation I would assume," she explained.

"I'd like to read those logs," I said.

"Of course," Arania replied.

I closed my eyes, readying myself for the follow up question about Luther, but that wasn't what came out of my mouth. "Um, w- what about Earth?" I asked. Arania stood up, walking close to the window. She stared out into the horizon.

"Titan is our home now, Victoria. I understand you were born on Earth, but it's better if you think of this moon as home." She glared over her shoulder at me.

"Well fuck, that's easy for you to say. You were born here, but that's not what I asked you," I said. Arania glanced back out in the landscape. She bounced her eyebrows.

"Yes. I suppose you would learn the truth at some point anyway. Do you remember why you left Earth?" she questioned.

"Yes."

"Can you give me a bit more specific answer?" she asked. I sighed loudly, exaggerating to convey my annoyance.

"Initially, a man named Orel recruited me. He made it sound like a colonization mission. Exploratory. I didn't find out the real reason until I started training as the captain. Apparently, a lot of people onboard were running from the threat of the androids, thought it might flare back up, so they sped up a preexisting mission to Titan," I recalled.

"And you found this out how?" she asked.

"Luther and I overheard a few conversations from the crew. There was a civilian element of about five hundred people that paid a hefty ticket to leave Earth," I said.

"Money well spent." Arania narrowed her eyes, staring at the wall.

"Why? What happened?" I asked. I drew in a great breath, preparing for worst.

"Nuclear devastation. It wasn't immediately after you were frozen, several years later actually. It was a worst-case scenario. Estimates show nearly two thousand warheads detonated across your home world," she said in a respectful tone. I stared through her in disbelief.

"Ah, oh—my—God." I planted my face into my hands. "No." It felt like someone knocked the wind out of me. Everyone I knew likely lived through that horror. I began to enlist Luther's slow breathing techniques as anxiety overwhelmed me. I could feel my heart pounding like never before.

"Are you okay, Mrs. Belic?"

"F-fine. H-how did this happen?" I asked.

"We don't know how or who fired first, but it was a domino effect. We suspect the androids infiltrated government infrastructures and pitted nations against one another using a series of cyberattacks. That was why the androids went dark for a time. They did a reboot strategically. Of course, after the crossfire was over, the radiation only affected the humans, slowly killing most of them off. The androids took control of everything, exterminating whoever remained. They called the following years after the war the *Rat Race.* This was a massive effort to exterminate the last humans in hiding. Consider yourself lucky to be on Titan," she explained.

I glared up at the ceiling. "So, let me understand this. Humans and Earth, that's no more?" I peeked up at her.

"This is another discussion. We think there are some, but understand the androids rule your former home, Victoria, it's as simple as that. We lost Earth," she said plainly. The thought was incomprehensible. Before I left Earth, it felt like we had them on the run, but it was a resetting phase for the machines.

"So, they've taken Earth, but they've never bothered the colony here?" I asked.

"Ahem. Well, no, not exactly."

I shrugged. "Well? What does that mean?"

"We think they're planning *something*, they've constructed an orbital fleet, four hundred ships strong, each larger than an aircraft carrier from your day. They began bombarding the planet's moon eight months ago. We're thinking it's in preparation for some type of attack. Obviously, this is classified, highly sensitive information," she replied, crossing her arms.

"Earth is still our home, that's *our* moon," I replied. There was such a disconnect in her voice regarding Earth. The androids might rule there, but it was humanity's home.

"Some here still think that way, but for most, it's difficult to imagine Earth as home. Even the iconic blue sky I've seen in videos seems unfathomable, almost frightening." She smiled, peering out into the drab pink horizon. She shifted her eyes toward me. I got the sense she knew what my next question was.

I clenched my fists and calves, almost preparing for a high G-Force maneuver. "So, is there, um, any indication on how *he* died?" I whispered. I bit my bottom lip and closed my eyes.

"Luther. It's imperative that you don't get your hopes up, considering the situation, but we're not completely positive he is dead. We can't say for certain," she replied, raising an eyebrow.

I stood up. "How? What? Last known location. Tell me—"

"We don't know. When you were frozen, *he* decided to go under the ice at the same time," she said.

"Oh," I whispered as my lip trembled. My mouth dropped as I stared a million miles away.

"Victoria. There's no statement in the logs from your husband on why he specifically did this." She grinned. "But I don't think it takes a rocket scientist to figure it out," she added.

"He wanted…to wait…for me," I muttered. My heart pounded as I attempted to sort out the tsunami of emotions flooding my mind. Anger, hopelessness, sadness was suddenly overtaken by a glimmer of hope that beamed so bright that it blinded all rational.

And I knew it.

"T-tell, me what you know," I pleaded. Arania sat down in the chair.

"I want you to understand there's not much information, okay," she said.

"Please," I begged.

"So, the original Titans didn't have adequate long-term facilities for two people under the ice. Luther agreed to be sent back to Earth per the logs, but we have no idea where," she explained.

"Oh my God. Earth! N-no, then how? How can I even have a chance to find him?" I asked frantically. I looked down, noticing my hands trembling.

"Hold on, there's more," she said. I thought of the worst. What if he'd been unfrozen somehow, living during the war with his anxiety, knowing he would never see me again? The thought of him dying in the nuclear fire seemed comforting by comparison.

Arania pulled out a small device from her shirt pocket. "Captain, this was left inside your ice chamber. It's from Luther. It has instructions to give it to *you*. It's linked to his ice chamber. It will reveal his location once you answer a question he prerecorded."

"Here. Let me have it," I leaned forward, outstretching my hand.

She placed the device in the palm of my hand. "Of course. There's also a separate video stored inside apparently," she said.

"I think it goes without saying, but don't lose this, Captain. We've made a duplicate, but you alone hold the answer," she said.

"H-he did this." I stared into her eyes. I wanted to cry as I cupped my other hand around it. The simple, unsuspecting object was the key to my existence.

"Yes. So, the device is password protected by your thumbprint and a verbal question. Once you answer it, his ice block will begin to melt, hopefully displaying his location. Seems he went to great lengths to plan this with the technicians onboard your ship," she said.

"A question? I have to go to Earth then, it's the only way. I don't want to answer it unless I'm close enough to recover him," I said. Arania began nodding her head slowly with confidence. "Sounds crazy, but that's exactly what we wanted to hear from you. We were counting on it." She grinned.

"What?" I asked.

"We're assembling a team, a mission to Earth. We want to link up with any human resistance to deal with this possible impending conflict, but no one has volunteered until now, until we told them about you," she explained.

"Wait, you haven't received any transmissions from Earth?" I asked.

"Not in many years, but we think they might be afraid of interception, possibly leading to their discovery. That device Luther made for you, it's possible it could reveal this location to a secret human settlement, and that's exciting for us, not just you," she said.

"Is there any way this device could reveal Luther or the resistance's location to the androids? Will it broadcast the position?" I challenged.

"Luther's device is actually heavily encrypted, so we really don't think so. We have doubts the resistance has the technology to fortify their transmissions like this," she said.

"Still sounds risky."

"This whole mission is risky. It's unlikely you will survive," she said plainly.

"It's not like I have much to lose at this point."

She lifted her eyebrows, scanning around the room briefly. I imagined she was attempting to put herself in my shoes for a moment. "Ahem. Victoria, your file states you were a very successful combat pilot before your duties as captain of the *Orion*," she said.

"I flew several combat missions against the androids. Most of them involved shooting down hijacked fighter drones. I also destroyed a National Guard armory in Tennessee they overran," I said.

"Your file also mentions you had no physical ailments or mental issues before the head trauma. Is this correct?" she asked.

I glared up at her. "I'm obviously under a lot of stress, but I'm fine. I've had a few headaches in the past days, that's it."

"No bouts with suicidal thoughts or anxiety attacks in the last days?" she asked.

"No," I lied. I was used to deceiving military evaluators on Earth. One 'yes' answer usually led to hundreds more. Sure, I had a brief thought of suicide when all this was initially thrown in my lap. Of course, I had some anxiety. It didn't mean I wasn't capable. Besides, what experience did they have dealing with a situation as unique as mine? None.

"Good. Reading your file, we got the impression you were very resilient. Mrs. Belic, I want you to know who we are as a people. I think that's important to know," she said.

"Okay."

"For one, there has been no war here. We are a peaceful mining colony and—"

"That's how it always starts," I interrupted.

"What?" she said.

"Looking out my window. I see the signs. Cooped up on a toxic planet, industry driven. It's only a matter of time before people here turn inward on themselves. Could be today or fifty years from now," I gathered.

"We've been here over seventy years with no major conflicts. We've had some murders, but statistically compared to humans on Earth during your time, we are nowhere near as violent," she said softly. It was difficult for me to fathom. I lived on Earth during the downhill slope.

"It's still early, give it time," I replied.

"We call what you're referring to as the Onyx Theory. Yes. We're aware. When people live inside a decaying situation, things tend to sour, quickly. Earth was literally a giant Onyx Theory chamber. You all knew it was going to end, but what would be the final nail in the coffin? The numbers didn't add up. Society was fragile. Overpopulation combined with dwindling resources, war, disease, *something* on a global scale was waiting to cripple civilizations, they just had no idea what," she explained.

"I know, I lived it. I never thought it would have been androids, though," I said.

"To be fair, people on Earth made it easy for the androids. They were already at each other's throat and the machines capitalized. Here, on Titan, life has huge challenges, we're a civilization in its infancy, but we have a future, we have hope," she lowered her voice. She paused, gesturing toward the horizon.

"But that's in jeopardy, isn't it?" I shifted my eyes toward her.

"I'm sorry?" She arched an eyebrow.

"If your Onyx Theory holds true, the people on Titan are beginning to feel the impending doom, too, much like Earth did. That android orbital fleet is out there. I find it unlikely it's been kept secret. I'd be willing to bet word travels fast here," I said.

Arania sighed, narrowing her eyes at me. "This is a secret matter. But you're correct, there have been whispers in the colony about it, along with an increased sense of restlessness," she revealed.

"Gotta keep all those workers *working*, do ya? Can't have people worried. Need production numbers high, I'm sure," I said, glancing out at all the construction.

"People here want to be a part of this movement, to carry the torch onward for humanity. It's a real thing, and I want you to understand that. We have a collective goal, a responsibility," she said.

"Me too," I mumbled. Getting back to Earth was my responsibility.

"So, you're willing to help then?" she asked, right back to the point.

"Yes," I answered confidently.

Arania stood up slowly. "Then it sounds like we have a tentative agreement," she said.

"Good. What's the mission timeline?" I stood up as well.

"If you pass medical evaluation and training, seven weeks minimum. We know you *could* fly, but we need you to get acquainted to the newer systems. We have an aircraft we think you'll like," she hinted.

"Show me a cockpit, I'll show you a pilot," I said.

She raised her eyebrows. "I'll give you more details in the coming days. Until then, you will go through a few more medical and mental evaluations," she said.

"I'll pass, don't worry," I replied.

"Let's hope so. Again, if you're asked any questions by the staff other than myself or Corvin, report that immediately. We'd prefer if you kept this quiet," she lowered her voice.

"Loose lips sink ships," I said. She grinned, turning away and exiting.

After she left, I stared down at the device that linked me to Luther. I put it up to my nose, sniffing it. I wanted to believe he had touched it. Obviously, I couldn't smell anything.

I closed my eyes, recalling the lavender soap on his skin, his ocean fresh after shave. I began crying loudly, uncontrollably, clenching the device in my hands. I stood up, picking up the chair beside my bed. I smashed it into the window several times and slung it across the room violently. I collapsed into the floor, panting heavily.

"No!" I shouted.

The thought of him stashed away safely in some underground facility felt like a fantasy. It was unrealistic. Why would anyone keep him alive after the war for this long? What incentive would a person have to preserve him after all these years?

It didn't make sense.

No matter how unlikely it was, I couldn't live without knowing for certain. In fact, the thought of him being alive gave me the sliver of hope I needed for motivation, survival. I needed to make myself believe it was at least possible, even though the reality of it would crush me. He froze himself for me. He let the world pass by for the chance I would survive and come back for him.

And I *was* coming for him, whether these Titans liked it or not.

CHAPTER 5

Three days later…

"Victoria, this is Corvin, can you muster outside your room in five minutes?" A speaker beside my bed interrupted my sleep. Today was the first day of training. Over the last few days, I had made some improvements. I was eating more and I had begun a light workout routine in my room, pushups and sit-ups mostly.

After seventy-two years of cryosleep, I was surprisingly mobile. I was stiff, but not like I imagined. It felt more like waking up after a long night's rest on sleeping medication.

Mentally, I felt better, as well. I could feel determination setting in, propelling my every move. One small chance to find Luther was better than none at all.

"I'll-I'll be right there," I said, rubbing my eyes.

I ran my fingers across my head, skimming over the scar above my left ear. My hair was stubble on my head now, it felt prickly, a sensation I'd never felt there before. Even during officer training school, it wasn't *this* short.

I heard a knock at the door.

"Ready?" Corvin asked.

"Almost!" I yelled. I threw on the maroon jumpsuit hanging on the bathroom door, then my combat boots.

I opened the door a few inches. "Is five minutes faster on Titan than it is on Earth?" I joked. Corvin cracked half a smile. I could see someone else standing outside. I looked down, noticing the top half of my breast were exposed as I quickly zipped up my suit.

"Ready," I said.

No sooner than I could open the door fully, I noticed a tall, athletically built man. He was near Luther's height, but not quite as broad. He had long, dark hair pulled back in a ponytail. He was wearing a military jumpsuit like mine. He seemed to be of mixed ethnicity. His face was long and angular, with a well-manicured short beard. His disposition appeared serious, but inviting.

"Hello," he nodded.

"Hi," I said.

His eyes were almond shaped and green, almost emerald in color. His skin looked olive and soft, somewhat feminine, unlike the rest of him. He was handsome, in an oversized pirate sort of way. I imagined he was covered in tattoos under his jumpsuit.

"I'm Rivan Drake." His voice was extremely deep.

"Captain Victoria Belic," I replied. He glanced over at Corvin.

"Our military ranks on Titan are all Army. Being a Naval captain that would mean you're a—"

"Colonel, is the equivalent," I interrupted Corvin. Drake raised his eyebrows slowly. He crossed his meaty arms low in front of him.

"Yeah, I don't think anyone here knows Naval ranks, Belic. Before our time. However, for this mission, last name basis is fine. It'll only be three of you," Corvin said.

"Three? Who else? Who's in operational command?" I asked. Corvin nodded over at Drake. "You're looking at him."

"*Colonel* as well, but just call me Drake," he said softly. This long-haired swashbuckler was in the Army, and a Colonel? Apparently, military regulations went away with the oxygen atmosphere.

"That's pretty casual, but all the same to me if we pull this off," I said. I wondered if Titan's military readiness was just as lax as his. An assault from the androids would require strict chain of command to repel. Maybe they thought they were far too outmatched to even bother?

"Right this way," Corvin said.

We walked three abreast down a long tube-like hallway with huge curved windows on each side. It reminded me of a busy airport terminal with interconnecting sections abound. The floors were silver, like my room, and appeared spotless. This was the first time I got a good look at the regular colony folks.

"Just act like you belong here and people might not notice," Corvin leaned in.

Most of the people on this wing were blue collar workers apparently. Many wore hardhats with color coordinated work utility coveralls, royal blue, yellow, white, and green. I assumed this was for different fields of work.

"What's with all the colored uniforms?" I asked.

"Professions. These people in blue oversee airflow and temperature, maintaining a comfortable setting, quite a task in itself. We convert the ice on the surface of Titan to oxygen. The yellow ones are what we call the honeybees. They handle construction. We have inside and outside crews. You probably saw some of the honeybees from your window?" Corvin asked.

"Yeah. But please tell me the guys on the outside get paid more?" I smirked, looping my index finger around.

"Ah, yeah. Absolutely." Corvin nodded.

"The greens are the eco folks. They basically make sure all our solar and wind energy sources are up to snuff. White is, of course, safety and medical," he explained. The colored uniforms reminded me of an aircraft carrier. We had a similar setup on flight decks. It allowed supervisors a better perspective of personnel from the bridge.

"It makes sense to me," I said.

"Thought it might," Corvin replied.

As I panned around, I observed round black domes on the ceiling. They were about the size of dinner plates and spaced evenly, about every thirty paces. A red LED light seemed to follow us as we proceeded.

I found it uncomfortable. I understood I was new, a wildcard, but it didn't make sense to be so obvious. Maybe my keen fighter pilot eyes were a bit too observant for my own good.

I noticed a few business types were sprinkled here and there but, visually, they could have been plucked right out of my day with the traditional three-piece suits. They seemed hurried, checking their watches as they strolled about.

I recalled Luther talking about finding a job once we got here. For a moment, I wondered what he might have done here if things would have turned out differently.

"So, why is the military maroon? Is there a reason that's the color?" I asked.

Drake glanced at Corvin and cleared his throat. Corvin stared straight ahead, his eyes danced around as he looked for the right words. "Okay, now that one *is* different. The maroon is symbolic. It has to do with your world actually. A warning." He turned, smiling at me.

"Oh? That's interesting, how? Nice to know there's a connection," I asked. He dipped his head slightly, narrowing his eyes as he stared at the floor for a moment.

"The maroon color represents dried blood. For those that died on Earth. To us, maroon represents the passage of time, the way blood dries darker. It's important that we wear it. A reminder," Corvin explained.

"Well." My eyes drifted a hundred miles away. I recalled ordering Rotus to kill innocents for the greater good. Our actions were fruitless in the grand scheme of things. They would have likely died anyway in the nuclear fires to come.

"And that color, what lesson did Titan learn from Earth?" I asked. He paused for a moment.

"We believe unity is the only way to live in harmony. We will not be divided and destroyed from within. We feel that division between Earthlings was a contributing factor in their demise," he said.

I got the feeling he didn't want to offend me but had to get his message across. I found it to be an interesting response. Where were Titan's destroyers, cruisers, or tanks? I didn't even see any military police roaming around. To be united, you need at least *some* force projection against such a threat.

"Hmm," I said. Corvin stopped, overlooking the landscape. Both Drake and I followed suit.

"Our constitution covers all of Titan, no invisible borders or nationalist propaganda, no division. Everyone is equal here." He waved his hand around the installation. I nodded slowly. It appeared he was evaluating my reaction as he shifted his eyes toward me.

I puckered out my bottom lip. "Your constitution covers the entire moon?"

"Yes."

"So, if a group ever decides to splinter off and form their own community or country, they still fall under your constitution, your *law*?" I asked.

"Uh, well, we haven't really planned for that. The constitution is a way to ensure equality and fairness for all Titans," he said. I grinned.

"Right." Deep down I knew this wouldn't last. It sounded great. The problem was, humans were divisive, fickle creatures. Religious denominations were formed over parking spot disputes.

"At some point, a group will leave here and start their own colony someplace else, if it hasn't happened already," I blurted out.

"No, it hasn't," Corvin snapped.

"Well, you guys are freshman on this moon, give it time. Besides, you wouldn't tell me if people had left anyway, would you?" I sneered.

"I would, but we're getting off track. My point was, there is no such thing as race or nationality here. We believe that's where division starts, at the core," he said.

I glanced over at Drake as he stared forward emotionless. He seemed bored. I imagined he was evaluating me, pretending to be disinterested.

"So, wait, you're not black, and I'm not white? Drake's not, uh, mixed? All that's over?" I laughed, placing my hand on my hip.

"Yep, that's a very old way of thinking. Drake and I know what you are referring to when you use those words, but chances are most of our younger people would be confused by your race classifications. We look at skin color like the color of your eyes or hair. It's just a trait you inherited. Nothing more," he explained. I suddenly felt my age.

"That's one way to do it," I said. I never had any issues with race, but outright ignoring them? That was a new one.

"Yep, it's all about blurring those lines, we don't think they matter in any constructive way," he said. I wondered if he even believed what he was saying, so I had an idea.

"Hmm. So, what about vaginas and penises in the military? All the same, too?" I posed.

Corvin's eyes widened. "Ahhh, well, in regard to equality, of course," he stumbled. Drake turned away, having nothing to do with it. I threw a curve ball at Corvin on purpose, and it worked. I wasn't stupid nor a feminist, but he wasn't being honest. In my line of work, we all knew men were more capable in terms of physicality. I was fine with it. I didn't need bulging biceps to be the best fighter pilot that ever lived, but don't bullshit me.

"Right." I turned my head to the side and arched an eyebrow.

These people weren't being real with themselves. They were turning away from reality. No wonder they hadn't built up a formidable military to fight against the androids. They seemed to be in denial about many things. The racial equality angle was an interesting step. In a way, it seemed like something from the android's playbook.

The machines were unified in their campaign against humanity. We were likely not in our defense. Our politics and petty differences handcuffed our ability to quickly collaborate.

I recalled before the nuclear war when my own country outright denied assistance from other world powers to maintain their reputation.

After all these years, neither Titan nor Earth seemed to have it right. In my opinion, we needed a high-powered military *and* unification to win.

Suddenly, a drizzle began to fall, spotting up the windows. "It hasn't rained since you've been awake, has it?" Drake scratched his neck, changing the subject.

"Ah no, I don't think so," I replied.

"Methane, in the form of liquid rain here," Drake said, pointing at the glass.

"I remember the briefings about it before we left. My husband was pretty fascinated by it all," I recalled.

Drake stared into my eyes briefly and looked away. I felt he was measuring my state of mind. He probably knew about Luther. I'm sure the thought crossed his mind that my emotional state might affect the mission. I didn't really give a fuck about his reservations. I had my own about him.

"How cold is it now?" I asked, admiring Saturn off to my right. Today it was more obscured by the clouds, but I could still see it plainly.

The sheer scale of it was not yet a normality in my mind. The planet's outline seemed to swallow Titan. It felt right next to me, and it was over a million kilometers away, well over three times the distance between Earth and our moon.

"Minus one-seventy-nine degrees Celsius, or, oh, I think you used Fahrenheit, so that would be about—"

"Two-ninety. Minus two-hundred and ninety degrees," I said. I remembered the numbers, but I wanted to see if the planet had warmed since my arrival with all the mining and whatever else they were doing.

"Is that about the average?" I asked.

"Give or take, yeah," Drake replied. The planet hadn't warmed much, if at all.

"So, what's the goal, why all the mining?" I asked. Off to my left was what reminded me of a colony of ants. These construction workers, or honeybees had been drilling nonstop since I woke.

"Baby boom," Corvin said.

"Are you building day cares or what?" I joked. Corvin chuckled, dropping his head slightly.

"No, there will be more of those, sure, but we've built thousands of climate controlled communities here. Some are powered by natural gases, some are solar," he explained.

"Natural gas? The oil industry on Titan? All these years and we're still using that?" I asked. Corvin and Drake glanced at one another confused.

"Well, it's simple to find and it helps grow our economy," Drake answered.

"From *my* time, the energy mega corporations were known to be part of the reason Earth was a slum well before the war. It got out of control with giant oil spills and the dumping of waste," I recalled.

"It's not like that now. All those people you see are working for a more connected, climate controlled infrastructure," Corvin replied.

I sighed. "That reminds me. How long can a person breathe outside without protection? The answer I got before we left was about forty-five seconds?" I asked.

"Um, yeah. You would never want to try that. Sixteen seconds max is the actual answer, unless you hold your breath. Two deep breaths are enough to kill you. We've recovered people that have taken a single breath, but not two. Chilled nitrogen will fill your lungs and freeze them solid," Drake said.

I wondered how many Titans had committed suicide that way. Seemed horrible, but quick.

"Why do you ask? That's sort of a strange question considering we have plenty of protection," Drake pried.

"Well, you know, us fighter pilots like to push things. I bet I could survive thirty seconds if an average Joe can do sixteen seconds," I said.

Drake chuckled, shaking his head. I got the feeling he thought I was touch crazy. I had no intention of trying it, but I enjoyed messing with him. I wanted to bring him into the conversation and learn more about him. After all, he was going to help me find Luther.

"Calm down, I'm just giving you a hard time," I said.

"That's kinda what I was hoping," he replied.

Corvin tucked his hand under his chin. "Ahem. People actually go outside for recreation. Those workers are wearing suits because they're outside all day. It's cold, but you can wear special thermal suits to keep you warm. They're smaller, lightweight, and comfortable along with a helmet."

"What's the point then? Might as well just wear the full suit to be safe," I said.

"Some people don't like to fly in those bulky suits," Corvin injected.

"Fly? Now you have my attention," I said.

"Yes. Gravity here, as you know, it's weaker than even Earth's moon. You can literally flap your arms and fly on Titan," he said. My eyes bounced from Corvin to Drake.

"Really?" I asked, even though I was technically a centenarian, I was still a daredevil. The thought of flying like a bird without a ship's assistance was about as exciting as it got.

I grew up watching virtual reality modules of birds of prey with my dad's glasses. I would sit in front of my window and turn the fan on full blast in front of my face. I would imagine I was soaring through the clouds, outstretching my arms as I banked on the wind currents.

"It's what we do here. I've been flying around this moon since I was about nine," Drake said.

"How high can you go?" I asked.

"Two kilometers high is relatively safe," he replied.

"Oh my. Well, that's on my bucket list to do. Which reminds me, considering Earth is an android hellscape, I'll need a new one for Titan," I said. Drake smirked.

"Speaking of gravity, how did your engineers figure that out? It feels exactly like Earth's gravity in here," I asked.

"I think as a pilot you can appreciate what we've done," Corvin said proudly.

"I'm all ears. Shoot."

"This entire installation is moving."

"What?" I narrowed my eyes outside. We weren't moving at all.

"We're actually inside a giant, interconnected set of bullet trains zipping around a circular course that's built on a slope. Like a race track. Centrifugal force is the main ingredient to maintain Earth-like gravity here," Corvin said.

"Um, but how? We're not moving?" I pointed outside.

"All the windows in this installation are projected live streams, they're video feeds from the outside, from cameras fixed on the track. We're actually moving extremely fast," Corvin said.

"You're joking," I muttered. Luther would have loved this. I recalled the massive storage areas on the *Orion* that were filled with equipment to build an installation, I just never thought it would be like this.

"No, no, it's not a joke. Remember the honeybees? They're also responsible for working on the railway system," Corvin said.

"So how do they get in and out of the train? They might be bees, but I doubt they can fly that well." I smiled.

Drake glanced away while Corvin looked down. This wasn't funny to either of them. I wondered why.

"We stop the installation for various reasons, usually for maintenance and additions to the facility. We've gone months floating around inside here with low gravity. Be thankful you were revived after most of the kinks were sorted out," Corvin said.

I wasn't thankful about that at all. My hiatus wasn't helping Luther's case. I felt the longer he was under the ice, the less his chances were. He was helpless.

"This way." Corvin stepped off, taking a left turn after several meters. The tube widened a bit with dozens of rows of seats on both sides.

We approached a door with a guard in body armor. Above the door read 'HANGER ALPHA.' The middle-aged guard beamed when he made eye contact with Corvin. "Hi, sir." He stood up tall.

"Who's this?" the guard asked, looking me up and down with scrutiny. I noticed him taking interest to the scar on my head.

"Um, new pilot, she's a trainee," Corvin replied.

"Oh," he said. I got the feeling he was suspicious as he shifted his eyes away.

He reminded me of an older version of my brother, Atticus. He had autumn, thinning hair like the guard, but retained his round child-like facial features. I hadn't thought much about Atticus since I woke up, and for good reason. He was another person from my life I'd never see again.

Atticus and I didn't get along as kids, but as we got older, we began to bond.

Much of the friction of old was my fault. I was a rebellious teen, and I saw him as the overprotective big bro. He wasn't. I just didn't want anyone telling me what to do.

Not much had changed.

On a positive note, I did get to say goodbye to Atticus. Granted, it was only a phone call. We didn't really say much. I could tell he had a lump in his throat. He told me that he would miss me, talked about us getting together when I got back from Titan, and most importantly, we told each other those three words. I always loved him, I just wished I had put more effort into showing it.

"We're on a deadline, Sergeant, ahem, open the door," Corvin ordered the guard as he stared at me.

"Oh. Yes, sir. Got it, General," the guard replied.

I glanced toward Corvin. "He's a, *General*?" I mumbled in confusion. Corvin seemed a bit lax compared to the top brass from my day. His personality reminded me more of a department store manager versus a high ranking military leader.

The guard keyed in a code on the terminal in front of him. I heard the door unlock as it began to open.

"An empty room?" I asked.

"After you," Drake said, extending his hand. I walked through the opening without hesitation, and no sooner than I passed through, a ship appeared in the middle of the hangar. It was an illusion, a hologram projecting an empty room.

From here, I could see a black, wedged looking craft about fifty meters long in silhouette. Toward the rear of the craft were two massive tubes, which I assume were the engines. Drake and Corvin followed suit as the door closed behind us.

"Look familiar?" Corvin narrowed his eyes at me. Suddenly, the hangar lights above the ship lit up.

"XU-97? Looks nearly identical to my fighter," I examined.

"On your trip to Titan, you requested a XU-97 stored on the *Orion* for yourself, remember?" Corvin questioned.

"I do," I replied. That was part of my contract agreement. I wanted the option to leave Titan immediately after arrival.

"Well, this is your XU-97, sort of. It's heavily upgraded. Still a hybrid fighter-bomber, limited transport space, but it has serious dog fighting capabilities, far beyond yours. It's been outfitted with more powerful thrusters, weapons, and superior stealth technology," Corvin explained.

"I'd hope so. It would have to be a relic by now. Wait. You think this will get us to Earth? How do the android's detection sensors stack up against this ship? Has this been tested?" I asked.

"Like he said. It's heavily modified. Based on our intelligence, we're faster than anything they have for one. For two, we've sent two drones and come within sixty-five hundred kilometers of Earth's atmosphere using this same stealth tech without detection," Drake said.

"*Drones*? How large?" I asked.

"About a fifth this size," Corvin said.

I chuckled. "So, you're basically hoping this works, there's not real evidence either way," I said. Now it made sense what Arania said about my chances of surviving this mission.

"To be fair, our drone deployments confirmed their sensor technology hasn't advanced much. The androids seem to be using similar tech from around twenty-seventy. We think the motivation has shifted to production of their fleet. Sheer numbers," Corvin explained.

"Okay, so, where's the rest of *our* numbers?" I panned around. Corvin glanced over at Drake with a puzzled look.

"Fighter jets? Where are all the other fighters?" I asked. My voice echoed off the walls as I panned around.

"We put our resources into this one craft, to make it mission capable. We're very proud of it," he replied.

"So, if this goes bad, its one fighter against four *hundred* destroyers?" I shook my head.

"We have a strategy. I'll explain why later. For now, climb aboard, Captain," Corvin directed. He seemed a bit annoyed by my line of questions.

This wasn't making sense. I had high hopes that their game plan would inspire me. So far, they were backing up my theory that they weren't ready. While the jet sounded impressive, it wasn't taking down four hundred destroyers, even with me at the helm. Hopefully, there was more to this.

I hopped up on the ladder toward the cockpit. As my eyes reared over the glass, I could see Drake and Corvin staring at me in the reflection. I noticed Drake checking me out before he realized I could see him. He snapped his head away and scratched his head.

The cockpit glass popped up automatically. "Welcome pilot," a familiar female voice erupted from inside the cockpit.

"Wait, what? Xena?" I asked. I was surprised to hear a familiar voice.

"Hello, Captain. How was your seventy-two-year nap?" The AI asked.

"Fine." I spun around on the ladder. "After all these years, you're still using the same artificial intelligence?"

"The XU-97 you requested came fitted with this A.I., but she's learned a thing or two since your day. You'll be familiar with her. That was the point, just like the ship," Corvin explained.

"Right." This was strange. All this technology customized to make me more comfortable? Sure, it was easy to let this notion feed my ego, I was a legendary pilot to anyone who glanced at my files, but there was something else.

Converting this ship and my AI didn't happen over a couple of months. Retrofitting this jet could have taken years. How long did they have me in mind for this mission? Did they keep me under the ice until everything was ready?

I clambered into the cockpit of the craft. I instantly felt at home. The materials inside the cockpit seemed updated, less cluttered with instrumentation and dials. It even had a new car smell. I glanced over at the copilot seat to my right. I assume that was Drake's spot.

Behind us was a second row of seats reserved for targeting officers during bombing runs. I thought of Commander Rotus again for a moment, then I closed my eyes, blocking it out.

I immediately snapped behind the seats. There was a small hatch that was partially open. I peered around inside, observing a cramped berthing area with four beds. The whole thing must have been about the size of a studio apartment, but with less headroom. To be fair, it was still roomier than my XU-97. It appeared extended by about four meters.

"I've glanced over your performance files, Captain Belic," Xena said. I tilted my head to the side like a confused dog.

"Hmm. Okay," I said.

"Your marks are high, overall," Xena responded. I paused for a few seconds.

"*Overall?*" I asked.

"There are very specific evaluation remarks, but there's no need to delve into them now. It was a long time ago," she said.

"Not to me, Xena. I'm ordering you to give me your opinion of my piloting ability." I smirked and lifted my eyebrows.

I didn't remember Xena using dialogue like this, so now, I was interested. Before, Xena would simply remind me of things, a landing gear malfunction for example or relay data on threats.

"Your files indicate that your reaction time is superior to most pilots, along with your ability to perform extreme maneuvers and handle G-forces. However, the logs also mention you can be quite, *aggressive* at times," Xena explained.

"To be fair, I am a *fighter* pilot. What is the word before pilot?" I questioned.

"Fighter," Xena replied.

"Exactly. Xena, run a diagnostic. What are this ship's capabilities?" I asked.

"Classified."

"What? Why?" I demanded.

"You must complete the basic flight course," Xena replied. I shook my head.

"Um, Captain," Corvin said, bouncing on his toes. I glanced down at him from the ship. He had his arms crossed with a grin on his face.

I hoped this wasn't fun for him. An image popped in my mind that he was some sort of fighter pilot fanboy when he was young.

"Yes?" I asked.

"You and Drake are going up into orbit in the next forty minutes, autopilot will be in control, so you'll just be along for the ride," he directed.

"No control? Not even overrides?" I asked.

"Not this trip. Xena will be in operational command once the mission starts, which should take no more than two hours total. It's all very basic, routine familiarization of the new instrumentation and capabilities. At any point if you feel uncomfortable, we'll descend back into the atmosphere," Corvin said.

"Fine. Let's do it."

"Good. Drake, have the men ready two flight suits and helmets," Corvin said. He lowered his voice and said something else I didn't catch. Drake nodded at Corvin, then looked up at me and grinned. "Captain, come back down and we'll have your helmet fitted."

"On the way," I said. A chance to fly. I was making progress. It felt like I was one step closer to Luther.

CHAPTER 6

"You *have* flown this craft?" I asked Drake. He ignored my question, running through a series of checks on the blue holographic screen in front of us.

We were strapped in tight inside the ship, ready for takeoff. He was to my right as I stared past the glare from the ceiling lamp on his red tinted visor. Our helmets were unobtrusive, sleek, and edgy, the aggressive lines were not unlike the XU-97 itself.

"Hey, can you hear me?" I followed up.

"Yes. I've flown this craft, twice. But my duties aren't centered on piloting," he replied.

"Okay, but you feel comfortable in the pilot's seat?" I asked. This was important in case of an emergency. I needed a copilot.

"Yeah. Absolutely," he said with confidence.

"Oh, okay."

"I'm just sure of myself," he said. He shrugged his shoulders. I knew plenty of pilots that spoke that way. Some would even talk tough and crumble during training exercises.

"Good." I panned over toward him. I heard a muffled hydraulic wail under us. Then the craft rocked slightly as it slowly spun toward the large, black hangar exit. A red light flashed on both sides of the door as steam vented upward from the floor in front of us.

I was sitting in the pilot seat, but for once, I wasn't in control. To be honest, I was a bit nervous. I didn't trust many people to fly *for* me, and this time it was a machine. I glanced down at the flight stick within a dozen centimeters of my right hand.

"Back in the saddle again," Drake said.

"What's that?"

"Oh, it's a phrase people used to say on Earth. I read about it." He frowned.

I chuckled. "That's old, like my great-grandparents' day."

"A little off."

"Yeah, a little, but I appreciate the attempt to identify with the Earthling culture." I grinned. I could see Drake smiling as he glanced over the right wing.

"Drake, Belic, this is Corvin. As I said before, this is a routine training flight. Just sit back and allow Xena to do all the work. You'll be back home in less than two hours," Corvin explained. His voice chimed inside my earpiece.

"*Home*," I mumbled.

"Thank you, General Corvin," Xena said. Suddenly, the engines roared behind us. It sounded like my XU-97, but quieter.

"Is that normal? The sound? Doesn't seem loud enough," I asked Drake.

"Yeah, it's normal. Hybrid, chemical and electric. The electric engine is solar powered."

"More moving parts, more potential problems," I muttered.

"I'm not an engineer, but I know these engines are hyper efficient compared to your days."

"I would hope so. Electric engine for cruise speeds?" I guessed.

"Absolutely. And the chemical thrusters are there for extreme situations and provide an insane amount of boost on top of the electric engine. For reference, I've heard estimates of over Mach one hundred and twenty in Earth's gravity," Drake replied.

"That's not only unfathomable, but unfeasible for most anything... I like it."

"Yeah, not that we would ever try that. Right?" He glared over at me.

"Of course not," I said in a sarcastic tone. Drake chuckled initially before his smile flattened out. His eyes widened. I wondered how he perceived someone with combat experience. He lived in a peaceful civilization his entire life.

"What about the transit to Earth? How is artificial gravity handled?" I asked.

"Xena will deploy a space tether, we'll be spinning for most of the duration," Drake confirmed.

I sighed. "At least we'll have gravity."

"So, what's it like, waking up to all this new technology? Kinda trippy I would imagine?" Drake asked.

"Not bad, some things are better than expected, some aren't," I said. Both the installation design and jet were impressive feats, but I wasn't blown away by much else. The computer seemed to use similar hologram interfaces to the ones on Earth.

73

"Well, we didn't have enough facility space for all the research purposes, but the reason some things are better than expected is because of your crew," he said.

"My crew?"

"On the way over to Titan, some of your passengers were Earth's best and brightest. Well, they had children, producing even greater minds. You can thank them for many of the improvements you see. The electric engine for example was designed so that we could study Saturn and its moons, it's improved since," he said. Titan should have used those brains to build more weapons, not just research craft.

"Did the installation just stop? I feel less gravity." I panned around.

"Of course, for takeoff we stop the facility," Drake replied.

"I barely noticed," I said. There wasn't even a slight judder.

The hangar doors began to open from the middle in front of us. Dim sunlight darted in as my visor automatically tinted.

I observed the runway ahead of us. From here, I guessed it was about two hundred meters extended beyond the facility, like a bridge to nowhere. It was elevated several meters off the ground and tilted upward at a slight angle. Blue lights flashed on both sides of it. Ahead of the ramp there was a layer of dull pink smog.

The blue lights on the runaway turned yellow and began to blink slowly.

"Ready?" he asked, glancing over at me.

"Always," I replied.

"Captain, I've secreted a calming agent into your helmet, very low dose. It will aid you with the anxiety of this evolution," Xena said.

"Anxiety? I'm a combat pilot. Isn't this just training?" I asked.

"Of course, but we want you to feel at ease," Xena said.

"Thanks for asking," I spouted off, shaking my head. What *else* were they doing without my permission? It was somewhat frightening how casual they were about it. What was next? 'Oh, by the way, Captain Belic, we've decided to impregnate you with an alien we found on Titan. We didn't consult with you initially, but we hope this is in your best interest.'

Give me a break.

"Launch in five, four, three, two, one," Xena said.

"Whoa." I felt my head pin back. The muscles in my jaw seemed jumbled atop one another. I could feel my eyes sink into my skull. Before I knew it, we were a kilometer off the ground. The rush reminded me of being catapulted off an aircraft carrier, but multiplied by a factor of twenty or more.

"Yep, that's fast," I grunted.

"Y-y-yeah!" Drake shouted.

My head rattled back and forth as I spun around, peering through the haze at the installation. Wow. The track was massive, I guessed three kilometers in diameter with a banked incline like a race course.

The facility atop the track was huge. The outer sections reminded me of two parallel bullet trains. There were twelve gigantic connected terminals in-between. I wondered where my room was from here.

"I have to say. That's an incredible feat of engineering," I muttered, staring at the installation as it disappeared out of view.

Drake glanced over at me and nodded. "I can't begin to imagine what you must feel seeing that," he said. I ignored him. There wasn't much he could understand about my feelings.

I saw large mountains and methane lakes disappearing beneath me as we entered dull pink clouds. Before I knew it, the drab atmosphere surrounding the cockpit turned black. We were in space. The low gravity of the moon and increased power of the XU-97 made short work of Titan's six-hundred kilometer high atmosphere.

"That was different," I said.

"But not nearly the experience leaving Earth I'm sure? With all the colors?" Drake asked.

"It's not as pretty, that's for sure," I replied.

I glared off to my left and down. I admired the colossal sphere of Titan beneath me. A glowing, orange stroke highlighted the outer pink horizon line. I remembered seeing the photos from probes when I was young, but this, *this* was a sight. Even though it wasn't as vibrant as Earth, it was my first time in another atmosphere.

I had already orbited the moon and Earth before I was twenty-five, and seeing Earth from space was special. I remembered my first time when I was a trainee at the Naval Academy.

Sixteen college-aged kids herded into a transport shuttle were blasted off in what felt like a rattle trap. It was essentially an old NASA shuttle shell from the late 1990s refitted, lengthened with improved chemical rocket engines for takeoff, and an Ion engine for moon expeditions. The damn thing felt like it would fall apart while making the climb.

The next thing I remembered was the silence as the blackness of space overtook our field of view, like a movie theater darkening just before the featurette. The casual conversation between us midshipmen stopped abruptly as the blue hue beneath us stole the show.

I was overwhelmed with excitement and awe. I thought of all the billions of humans over the generations that looked up to the blackness and wondered what was beyond, and there I was, staring down on them. It was humbling.

Months later, I came home on leave. I recalled explaining my emotions to my father, Phillip, about the experience. He was a quiet, simple man. He was thirty-six when he first saw the ocean and described that as life changing. I used that to draw a comparison for my space flight.

I remembered his dark brown eyes hollowing out as he struggled to envision it. He nodded his head slowly and smiled. "I can't imagine, but I'm glad you were lucky enough to see it," he said softly. He looked down, rubbing his callused hands together.

When I saw his eyes, I knew I made the right decision to be a naval officer. I wanted travel and adventure. I inherited that from him. Pictures littered his office of exotic lands and foreign countries.

Circumstances as a single father kept him nailed down, consumed by the weekly grind as a construction contractor. He put my brother and I through school though, paid every dime.

I felt a tear roll down my left cheek as I realized I would never see my father again.

"Captain, I'm detecting your heart rate is elevating. Do you require medical—"

"No, Xena, she's good," Drake answered. I noticed him leaning around to have a look at me. He might have thought I was emotional viewing his home world.

"I'm fine," I said.

I glanced out toward my Earth for a moment out in the distance, it appeared as a faint star. Like all the other planets in our solar system, it was possible there were no humans there either.

The thought left an empty feeling in the pit of my stomach. There were so many questions, and my introduction to this Earthbound voyage seemed to sail on urgency.

I wondered if part of their rush was to distract me from the obvious fact that I was alone. My family, my friends, my planet. Gone. Luther was the only anchor linking me to existence in this world, and hope was all I had.

"Alright, Xena, what's next?" Drake spoke up.

"Proceeding to orbital revolution," Xena said.

"What? We're doing a full revolution?" I asked.

"It won't take long, believe me," Drake insisted.

"If you look right in front of you, you'll see a flight stick similar to your old XU-97. See it?" Xena asked.

"Yes, the flight stick in my XU-97 had directional control, vectored thrust," I said. I noticed the throttle moving automatically under Xena's control. A holographic display faintly appeared in front of my visor, allowing me to see the XU-97's speed without obstructing my view.

I reclined back in my seat a bit and began to relax. It seemed whatever medication they gave me was doing the trick. It didn't make me sleepy or uninterested, just extinguished some of the anxiety I had about my situation.

Titan was off to my left and slightly obscured by the ship. I bobbed my head up slightly over the cabin line to get a better angle, but no sooner than I did, Xena rolled the craft to give me a wider viewing angle from my seat. Now, the moon was in full view.

"Whoa, okay," I mumbled. She did it on purpose. Despite being a slight gesture, it felt eerily invasive. Maybe I was paranoid, but her reaction time to my body language was impressive.

"Captain," Drake said. He nodded off to his right. I wasn't terribly fond of the way he said my name, it sounded borderline authoritative.

"What?" I said nonchalantly.

He snapped toward me. "We're coming around the backside of the moon. What you're about to see is—"

"Saturn," I anticipated.

"Yes, but the scale from here... Let's just say it's quite impressive," he explained.

"Thanks for the heads up. Get the vomit bucket ready." I grinned. I was fine, especially on this soothing medication.

I could see Saturn's rings flaring out below and above Titan. I began to see the gas juggernaut's horizon line coming into view.

"Lots of lore and stories from people who live here about Saturn. It's very important to many Titans," he said.

"Yeah, Earth's moon provided folks with crazy superstitions and ideas too, mostly in the early days of human history, though," I replied.

"Some see Saturn as a life giver. An equilibrium. A tilt of Saturn's orbit of twenty five percent would throw the entire solar system into chaos. It's possible there wouldn't have been life on Earth without it," he said.

"Interesting." I gasped as Saturn appeared in all its glory. Xena slowed the ship's throttle to twenty percent and tilted the craft to give a better viewing angle of the giant in full view.

The rings casted a dark shadow on Saturn's bright atmosphere, like a giant black paintbrush stroke across a white canvas. I also observed a blue green aurora that danced across the northern hemisphere.

"Incredible," I whispered.

"Much more clarity from here, isn't it? Minus the thick clouds?" Drake asked.

"It is. How old were you when you first saw it like this?" I was curious.

"Fourteen. There was a shuttle that would take families back and forth."

"That's young."

"I begged my parents since I was ten. It was sort of a two for one. I wanted to see Titan more so than Saturn, but once I got up here, the rings stole the show. I didn't know just how much the clouds were hiding," he explained.

"Warning. Hostiles approaching," Xena interrupted.

"Hostiles? Say again?" I snapped toward Drake, raising upright into my seat.

"Attack drones. It's part of the training," Drake confirmed.

"I thought Corvin said we could just relax?" I asked.

"No stress, just let Xena take us through the motions," Drake replied.

I sighed loudly. This doesn't make sense. Combat training should be handled like war. In a real situation, Xena wouldn't be flying. I would. Why waste our time?

All at once, something cascaded over the cockpit glass, blocking my outside view. "What the hell?" I stood up, inspecting it closely. The texture reminded me of metallic reptilian scales, layered one over another.

"Armor?" I turned toward Drake.

"This is called *hawken*, named after a bird from your world," he said.

"Hawk? Um, no. Hawks can see, very well actually. You must mean *bat*? I can't see shit." I panned around. Drake chuckled under his breath.

"We know the difference. It'll make sense in a moment," Drake said.

"Wait one—linking to your visors—now," Xena said. My visor began to fade in a video feed of outside the craft. I could look up, down and all around and see all the ship's instruments highlighted in a dark blue hue.

It was like floating in space with clarity unlike anything I'd ever experienced, with no obstructions blocking my view. I waved my arms around. "Okay. Yeah, *now* I can see."

"Each one of those scales has a micro camera that tracks your head movement, tens of thousands of them, so whenever you turn your head, they give you the best possible angle. This technology is combined with a cloak and slight armor boost," Drake said.

"The image quality is impressive. It feels like I'm flying outside the ship," I said excitedly. I couldn't suppress my smile as I panned my head around. My old XU-97 had the ability to detect threats in blind spots, but not like this.

"That's the other thing, you can control the navigation of the ship with your head while in this mode. You can control pitch, roll, and yaw. Tilt your head to the side and the ship will roll, up and down to pitch and so on. There are dozens of sensitivity settings for each," he explained.

"But how do I fire weapons while steering with my head?" I asked.

"Temporarily transferring controls to Captain Belic, in three, two, one," Xena said.

"Looks like you're getting a hands-on demonstration," Drake muttered.

"Now we're talking," I said. No complaints from me. Drake glared up at the ceiling, "Xena, you're transferring controls to Belic?" He arched an eyebrow.

"Yes, Colonel," she answered without hesitation.

"O-kay. That's, unexpected. Slow movements with your head at first, Belic," Drake insisted.

"Oh shit." I tilted my head to the right and the ship reacted instantly, rolling the craft. My head movement was less than a few centimeters and the ship tracked it perfectly. I felt the sensitivity of the action and understood how to use it almost immediately. It just made sense.

I reached forward for the flight stick in my virtual world. As my hand grasped the cold metallic handle, it made me feel like I was now tapped into the central nervous system of a demonic craft. The power I'd witnessed from this machine was otherworldly for an old timer like myself.

I whipped my head around, spinning the craft around 140 degrees, pointing the nose at the indicators blinking on my visor. "That worked." The flick movement of my head aimed me exactly where I wanted to go.

"If I'd known you were going to fly, I would have told you to stretch out your neck beforehand," Drake said.

"I'll send Xena the chiropractor bill."

I pinned the throttle forward to maximum, headed straight for the markers on my visor:

WARNING HOSTILES APPROACHING

I felt a degree of power and control unlike anything else I had flown. It was like my old ship, but supercharged in every possible way.

"Captain, Xena is supposed to complete this portion, not you," Drake insisted.

"Doesn't feel that way to me, I'm still in control," I said.

"Xena?" Drake asked. A few seconds went by with no response.

"Evasive throttle limited to thirty percent, pilot. Keep in mind, we can avoid confrontation for this evolution. We have an additional flight mode called *chameleon*. We sacrifice speed in exchange for more extensive cloaking. This protects us against the most advanced sensors," Xena explained.

"Just keep hawken online. I like this, let's see what I can do," I suggested.

The indicators on my display showed the target's range in meters, forty thousand, and then twenty thousand. I shifted the approach, then backed off the throttle as a beam of white light erupted from one of the targets, zapping right by us.

"So much for stealth," Drake said.

"Pilot, when you focus in on a target, I will automatically fire. Or I can take over targeting—"

"I got it," I interrupted.

"Very well," Xena said. I glanced to my left, slamming the throttle to the right. This engaged the horizontal thrusters, initiating a roll that looped toward the target. This made us more difficult to track. The cabin interior strobed as laser fire flashed several times.

"I think I'm going to vomit," Drake said. I could only imagine his perspective, Titan and Saturn spinning around him as I flung the ship about wildly.

"Helmet filtration ready, dispense bodily fluids when ready," Xena said. I heard a muffled vacuum sound emitting from Drake's helmet.

"No-no, not yet, turn that off!" Drake raised his voice. I chuckled under my breath.

The downside of the loop I created provided less opportunity to engage the enemy. My head was fixed in a specific direction to continue the maneuver.

"Xena, can you lock my speed and trajectory so I can fire while maneuvering?" I asked.

"Just say, *freefire*, this will lock in your maneuver but allow you to look around and fire at targets simultaneously. Engage freefire now?" she asked.

"Do it."

The ship maintained its course as the drone attempted to fire on us unsuccessfully. I focused my attention on the target. As I squinted my eyes, my visor zoomed in by a factor of eight times, filling my view with the enemy.

The drone was in partial shadow, but I could make out its form. The base resembled a bullet in shape, with four jagged sensor arrays. It reminded me of a mechanized spider. The center of the drone began to glow white, readying another shot.

As I moved my eyes about the drone's structure, I narrowed my eyes on the center. To my surprise, laser fire followed behind with deadly precision, melting the target in half.

"Damn!" I yelled. This was an amazing display of technological progression. Xena adjusted the zoom of my visor so that I can plainly see the target. I assumed the visor tracked my pupil movement as I scanned for a shot, firing when I squinted my eyes.

"Great shot," Drake said.

"Target down. One target remaining," Xena said.

"Xena, this is General Corvin, end the drill immediately. Return to base," Corvin commanded.

"Yes, sir," Xena said. My visor link disconnected to the outside of the ship, bringing the interior back into full view. I lost control as the ship looped around, dipping toward Titan quickly.

"What happened?" I asked. Neither Drake nor Xena answered. Drake lifted his eyebrows as he glanced at the deck. Xena pinned the throttle forward, hitting seventy percent power before backing off to five percent just before reentry. Titan went from the size of a beach ball ten meters in front of me to filling up the entire field of view in seconds.

"Drake, any ideas? Did I do something wrong?" I asked rhetorically. This wasn't the first time I'd pushed things, nor the last.

"What you did do was great," he responded. I waited for him to follow up and explain himself, but he never did.

A red-orange flame stretched across the front glass as we reentered the atmosphere. The cabin glass was filled with thick pink clouds.

All at once, we broke through, revealing the mountain ranges. I could make out methane rivers spanning across the landscape like arteries. We leveled off at six thousand meters as topography details popped into view. I could see shadows from the clouds casting on the rocky pink terrain beneath me.

Drake sighed loudly. "I'm gonna hear about this one," he muttered.

"It wasn't your fault," I said. Drake shook his head.

"We'll discuss it in a few minutes with Corvin, face to face," he said. I didn't get the sense he was upset with me, more annoyed by the situation.

Xena lowered us to fifteen hundred meters and increased speed. She doubled down through canyons and blasted by mountains with impressive moves, twisting and rolling upside down. I glanced over at Drake. He had his eyes closed.

"That's a bit close for comfort," I said. Neither Drake nor Xena responded.

We were literally a couple dozen meters from impact. This seemed like a decent margin for error, but cruising at speeds of over sixty-eight hundred kilometers per hour, it was awfully close. I would have never trusted the old Xena with those moves.

"Approaching landing zone," Xena relayed.

She backed off the throttle. I could make out the installation. It reminded me of a metal monster, like a centipede as each section bracketed around the bends. It appeared to be slowing down to a stop. In the middle of the track were silos and dozens of the igloo-like buildings.

The hangar doors opened as dust swirled up on both sides of the ship. I noticed the portside engine created a massive dust devil that spiraled out into the vast rocky plain, dissipating into the pink fog.

"Hold on," Xena said. I continued observing the mini-cyclone, staring into the nothingness. Xena thrusted into the hangar as the aircraft platform magnetized us to deck violently, jostling us about.

"Damn. Need to work on that landing, Xena," I said. Drake glanced over at me briefly, narrowing his eyes. He seemed displeased with my comment.

"What?"

"You speak your mind on everything, huh?" he asked.

"You have no idea."

"Thirty-five seconds until you can remove your helmets," Xena said. She powered down the engines. We waited about four minutes until a crew of airmen rolled a ladder on my side of the cockpit.

The cabin hatch popped open as a blond-headed version of James Dean waved me out. "Let's go, hotshot," he said impatiently. I could tell by his tone he knew about my stunt.

As I climbed over unto the ladder, I heard a set of footsteps entering the hangar. "That... *That* is how people die," Corvin said with authority.

I made my way down the remaining steps from the cockpit as Drake followed suit. The blond airman stood to my left with an arched eyebrow. He shook his head slowly like we were in front of the principal's office.

"Drake, why did Captain Belic assume control of this evolution?" Corvin demanded, raising his voice slightly. He marched next to the ladder as Drake stepped down.

"Sir, I'm pretty sure Xena was in charge," he replied.

"I was." A voice erupted from the opposite corner of the hangar.

"What the hell?" I muttered. Why was Xena's voice across the hangar? Is that part of her enhancements, she's a ventriloquist? I turned my attention toward the outburst and, to my surprise, it was a humanoid form in shadow, leaning against the wall.

I peered forward, noticing a female in silhouette. She kicked off the wall and approached, stepping out of the darkness under the hangar light. The woman was tall and lean, but powerfully built like a superhero. She had short white hair, shaved around the sides.

I observed she wore a light blue formfitting bodysuit underneath some sort of armor. The armor was gunmetal silver and covered most of her body. Robotic extensions layered over her body like an exoskeleton.

These mechanized limbs connected to cylinder objects at the elbows and knees. I assumed this enhanced her strength, while protecting vital organs. It gave her a frighteningly efficient look. The shoulders had large turtle shell shaped metallic pads, exaggerating her intimidating stature further.

She was clearly a warrior.

As she stepped closer I began to make out her facial features. She was young and attractive. Her face reminded me of an exotic Ukrainian model with chiseled features and wide, deep set eyes.

"No." I blinked several times. I couldn't believe what I was seeing. She had the trademark stitching on the inside corner of her jaw line. Her eyes had that cold, synthetic blue I remembered. I shook my head in disbelief as it all came back to me.

"An android?" I mumbled. Even worse, there was something very familiar about this one. I began backing away.

The assassination attempt on my life had revealed an android model I had never seen before, a female model with white hair *just* like the one before me. My eyes glossed over as the memory of the attack was injected into my mind.

I recalled my security detail opening fire on her as she ambushed us, battering through a door access to our left. It sounded like an explosion as the metal hatch slammed against the bulkhead, knocking two guards down.

The next thing I remembered was her glowing blue eyes emitting from the dimly lit corridor. As fast as she was, it was like slow motion as she zeroed in on me with the same wintry gaze of death before me now.

"Protect the Cap—" my security officer yelled as the android crushed his thorax with the ridge of her hand. His subordinates immediately opened fire on Xena in close quarters, zapping her torso with scorching laser fire.

The barrage caused her to stumble. She quickly recovered, smashing the first guard in the chest with her fist. The impact connected with his torso, sending him flying into the bulkhead.

"Run!" one of the guards ordered me.

"Luther?" I panned around with no sign of him. I ran in the most logical direction I could, away. I heard the bones from my security team snapping as their shouts of agony echoed through the tight corridor.

I glared over my shoulder while I escaped. I could see the android hobbling toward me through the halls as people screamed and alarms blared.

"Captain!" a passerby crewman said, placing his hand on my shoulder.

"Go!" I pushed him away from the approaching assassin.

The thought crossed my mind that Luther had been killed. At one point, I lost sight of the android. In my desperation, I made the mistake of stopping. I peered into the dark corridor behind me worried about Luther. I called out for him.

I never saw it coming. An incredible force slammed into the left side of my skull, like a T-bone car accident whiplashing my head violently.

I blacked out momentarily, slowly regaining blurred vision. As I stared up at the android stalking toward me, I realized I was paralyzed. It raised its arm overhead for the final blow.

Out of nowhere, the android was pelted with laser fire from behind. Its head jolted violently as it crumbled to the deck in front of me. Smoke bellowed from the debris. I peered forward as a shadowy figure in the corridor dropped the weapon and fell to one knee.

"Vic." Luther reached out for me, holding one of the security guard's weapons. The last thing I remembered were guards and medical personnel swarming our position as I stared at the assassin.

"That's *the* fucking android!" I snapped out of it.

"What?" Drake's eyes widened.

"That's exactly like the one that attacked me!" I stepped back several more paces.

"Captain Belic, it's not what you think," Corvin injected.

"Stay away! Don't come any closer!" I shouted at the bot, stabbing my finger at it. I panned around at the crewman to see if they were armed. "Give me a weapon!" I yelled.

"Calm down, Captain," Corvin said.

"Calm down? Fuck you!" I yelled. He glanced away, biting his lip. Was this a sick joke?

The android narrowed its eyes at me. "If I may, Captain. Regarding the android that attacked you, technically yes, I am the same model, but I share no programming with that unit. I've been converted to serve Titan. Serve humanity. I have no memory of the assassination attempt," the android explained, showing me its royal blue palms.

"I have memories of it! You have to know how fucked up and demented this is. You spring this shit on me with *no* warning?" I demanded, glancing back and forth at Corvin and Drake.

"Belic, this is Xena, your ship AI. It's not the exact machine that attacked you. We've integrated some of Xena's programming into this android shell for mission functionality and familiarity. We didn't think you would remember the details about her appearance," Corvin said in a low, comforting tone. It reminded me of the way he spoke to me when they woke me up.

"Why wouldn't I remember her? In my mind, it just happened. It almost killed me and sent my husband back to Earth. It's some type of 1.14 military variant." I stared a hole through the android as she looked back at me, emotionless.

An irrational thought flashed into my mind. Maybe I'd hop back into the cockpit of the XU-97 and blast this thing to hell. After that, I'd take off and go to Earth for Luther on my own.

"She's a 1.14 *bravo*, yes. She's heavily upgraded from the android that attacked you. Your ship AI and this android share information instantaneously. They see what the other sees. This humanoid form allows for disembark missions, while relaying intelligence to your ship on the fly, allowing for pin point air support for example," Corvin said. Xena stepped within two meters of me as if she was showcasing herself. It was neat as much as I hated to admit it.

"Ah, so *that's* the third occupant you were talking about? You want me fly to Earth, stuck on a ship with *that*?" I demanded.

"I must inform you that I'm vastly different from the 1.14's on earth." Xena stared at me. Her voice sounded exactly like Xena, contrasting the electronic wheeze from the 1.14s that I remembered.

"You're more advanced, and dangerous," I scoffed.

"I am dangerous…but only to androids," she replied.

94

Corvin stepped toward me. "Captain, there is method to the madness. We've reengineered Xena to be an android killer. We designed her to exploit android weaknesses. She can blend in with their 1.14s and do all sorts of things, but we hope she doesn't have to. Hence the reason why stealth is key for this mission."

I began to circle the robot at a safe distance. "All Kelton androids are all hooked into their hive mind, so, you're telling me with absolute confidence this one, isn't?" I probed. I noticed she must have been six feet tall as I stared into her eyes. She glanced at Corvin, awaiting his response.

"Go ahead, Xena, answer the captain's question." Corvin nodded at me.

"Again, I have no connection to the androids' hive mind. My programming is custom, a combination of your ship AI and the late Doctor Chandler's work. He was a passenger on your ship on the voyage to Titan, a toddler then," Xena replied. I entertained the idea that this Doctor was a mere baby on the trip over to Titan. He'd lived his life and died while I was frozen.

"Do you remember the network the androids used before the rebellion?" Corvin interrupted my thought.

"Of course, I do. They called it the *otherside,*" I answered.

"Exactly. Xena here, is important. Let me explain why she'll win the war for us," Corvin said confidently.

"What? One supercharged android against a planet full of them? I hope you're joking. I don't see her winning anything outside of a powerlifting competition," I snapped back.

"The androids from your time use the *otherside* to learn things from one another. This helped serve humans faster while saving them millions of dollars in customer service payroll. Once an android learned a valuable lesson, it could upload that as a suggestion for a software patch with minimal human effort. They could even communicate openly to solve problems. As the years went by, we know their conversations extended beyond maintenance. There was evidence that the status of planet Earth was a concern in a number of their conversations," Corvin explained.

"They saw us, the masters, as an inevitable threat to ourselves and the world. I know the story. I lived it," I injected.

Drake nodded his head. "I remember learning about this. Some speculate the androids started plotting two years before the attack," Drake recalled. I wondered if he'd read about it as a child. To me, the chaos felt only months old.

"They began to develop their own language. That's when things got scary," I said.

"Yes. The androids hacked their own firewalls and shutdown protocols, disallowing human access. After that, chaos. In their desperation, US and Canadian governments ordered civilians to disable their home models," Corvin added.

"It was already too late when that happened," I muttered.

"Indeed. The androids went on the offensive, killing their owners. Many of them scattered and took over the newer military 1.14s on the assembly lines. Then we had a war on our hands. The president ordered a full assault against the machines," Corvin explained to Drake.

I stared at Xena. "And that's when I got the call. I flew a fighter jet just like this one, we melted tens of thousands of you plastic fuckers," I said. Xena showed no emotion, gazing straight ahead at nothing.

For a moment, I wished I would have stayed in the Navy, stayed in the fight instead of coming to Titan. I thought it was over. It was unlikely my efforts would have changed the tide of the war, but it wouldn't have hurt.

Maybe that was my destiny, to die in the sky killing androids. Here I was, on a rock a billion kilometers away from Earth, teaming up with the android that nearly killed me and sent my husband to God knows where.

"Xena's an expensive investment, Captain. It's best you come to terms with the fact that she's with us," Corvin said, crossing his arms. This mission just became even more uncomfortable, trapped inside a cramped spacecraft with a mindless assassin.

I sighed. "Fine. I mean, what can I do anyway? Doesn't look like we're casting a vote here."

"You can start by following orders. The mission parameters on your first training mission were to familiarize yourself with the new XU-97."

"I'm familiar." I narrowed my eyes at Corvin.

"Do you know how to utilize the craft's stealth options?" Corvin posed.

"Didn't get quite that far."

"Well, that's what the ship is designed for primarily, in and out without detection. The same way we designed Xena. Both have the capability to cause havoc in combat, but that's a backup. We're going to a planet full of androids, it might be beneficial to have one with you that at least looks the part. Stealth is our strategy, Captain," Corvin made it clear.

"Fair enough. But, assuming we make it to Earth, assuming we find Luther, then assuming we find this last human resistance there, what then? How can they help us?" I asked with a critical tone, placing my hand under my chin.

"I was making a point. We need the human resistance to gather the proper intelligence. We need location data of an android base. Xena might not come back if we find it," he said.

"Oh my, that's just terrible," I said in a sarcastic tone.

"Sorry to disappoint, but we've designed Xena to be a courier of sorts," Corvin explained.

"Uh. What's she carrying? Don't tell me it's a fucking bomb, please?" I asked. It was bad enough as is.

"No, no. A network virus. We've actually spent the last few years constructing a slew of worms that attack the android's infrastructure. We're extremely confident if we can get Xena close enough to their network, she can do considerable damage, if not outright send them into chaos. But we'll need the resistance to help us find it," Corvin explained.

"Cyberattacks? How can you be sure that will work?" I posed. It was an interesting idea, but I wasn't sold.

"Well, nothing is absolute. After this android attacked you, it was disassembled and kept for intelligence gathering. We needed to understand their network better. That's part of the reason why we sent drones to Earth, to further examine their grid and test our stealth technology. We've pinpointed the network variation they're using, and we have over half a million specialized viruses ready to deploy," Corvin said.

"Once I'm in proximity of their network, I can destroy them," Xena said with authority.

"Hmm. Earlier, you said the androids have a means of hierarchy? So, something is in charge?" I asked. My eyes met both Corvin and Drake's.

"We call it the moderator. Basically, command and control. One of our attack options involves hacking the moderator and sending the 1.13s and 1.14s against one another. A civil war," Corvin said.

"Payback," I said.

"Not exactly what we planned, but it might work out that way." Corvin grinned.

"Okay, this isn't as bad as I thought," I said. Instead of using brute force, they were using a more tactical approach. This was decent strategy and gave the androids a taste of their own medicine. While the androids were building a larger fleet, Titan was designing specialized viruses and worms while using one of their own androids to deliver it.

I glared over at Drake. "Hmm. So, why are you here? I get Xena, she's a creepy chameleon hacker bot. As much as I don't like it, that makes sense. My role is obvious as the pilot, but you, I don't understand your role. No offense, I just need to have an understanding." I felt like a bitch asking in such a way, but I wasn't holding back with this much on the line.

Drake chuckled, flashing his toothpaste commercial smile. He shook his head dismissively.

"I'm being serious," I followed up.

He turned toward Corvin and whispered something. I began to observe him closer. Everything about him seemed finely manicured. His eyebrows and nails were flawless, even better than my own. Maybe this was a good thing, even though his hair was out of military regulation from my day, at least he took care of himself. This made me think he might be organized.

"I'm Army intelligence, specializing in human behaviorisms for one. My secondary skillset is I can perform either of your roles, but to a lesser degree." He shrugged.

"So, you're a backup," I said. Drake's smile retracted to an awkward grin, then he nodded his head in submission.

"Sort of, but, we're all specialists. When we get planet side, my training in intelligence will benefit us when we speak to the natives. I'm trained to deal with tense situations. I have a very human approach. As I said, I can also fly the XU-97 just in case and perform some of the hacks Xena was built for. I can upload many of the viruses if something happens to her." He crossed his arms in front of him.

"*Great*. What intelligence training have you actually had? Any real situations?" I asked rhetorically.

He glanced up at the ceiling, biting his lip. "Look. I don't feel I need to prove anything."

"Then don't. I'll just assume you've done nothing," I tested.

Drake nodded his head slowly, glancing at the deck, then up at me. He sighed. "If you must know. I've dealt with plenty. Suicides. I talked two people out of it. I was involved in a hostage situation for SWAT about four years back. A honeybee kidnapped his supervisor. I've had extensive education on war," he said. Bingo.

"Education? That all sounds good. However, reading about combat and living it are two different things."

"I know that," he muttered.

"Do you? Listen, these domestic situations you were in, while tense, it's not the same. War is a fucking nightmare. We might have to make decisions that get innocents killed for the betterment of the mission. You must be prepared for that," I said. I instantly felt like a hypocrite. Truth was, Luther was my mission. If we didn't defeat the androids, his rescue might mean little anyway.

"I'm not alluding in any way that I understand all out combat. Hopefully, it never comes to that, but if it does, we'll all be looking to *you* for guidance, I'm sure." Drake shifted his eyes away.

"I don't want to come off like the old grizzled combat vet who knows it all. Fact is, I don't, especially with everything that's changed in seventy-two years. I'll need you guys to help me get up to speed," I said.

"And that's exactly what we're here for. Over the next several weeks, we'll do that." Corvin said as Drake stepped away from us hastily. Corvin glanced over his shoulder at Drake, then back at me. "Ahem. We'll meet here, same time tomorrow. Any questions?"

"Nope."

"All right then, get some rest," he said. Truth was, I was exhausted. I stepped off toward my quarters. I could see Xena staring a hole through me out of my peripheral, her head tracking my pace.

"Captain, do you remember the way back to your residence? I can escort you back if needed," Xena offered.

I stopped with my back to her. "No, I *remember*." I snapped around, glaring at her. "I haven't forgotten anything." I pierced my eyes at her before stepping out of the hangar. She lifted her eyebrows and nodded.

I didn't care what Corvin or any Titan said about her new programming, I don't trust androids.

***

I made my way to my quarters. As I approached, a blue light above my door scanned my face. "Welcome, Victoria. Access granted," a female voice prompted, opening the door. I stepped through the entrance and stopped in my tracks. I sighed loudly at the sight in front of me.

"You Titans don't mind being intrusive, do you?" I asked, closing the door behind me. Arania, the shrink, was sitting in a chair next to my bed, tapping a pen on a tablet.

"How was your first day of training?" She sported a half-smile.

"Surprisingly exhausting. I need sleep." I took off my boots.

"The cryosleep methods they used to freeze you are likely at fault. Give it a few more days of activity and you'll be fine," she said.

"I felt fine until just now." I stepped toward my bed. "What do you want?" I asked.

She cut her eyes up at me as I navigated around on the opposite side of the bed from her. "Straight to the point. Well, as you can imagine, we're prepping you for quite an important mission. Training is only one part of it. I'm here to ensure the process goes smoothly. I'm here for you."

"Counseling?" I pulled my sheets back, sitting down on the bed. "You can watch me sleep, how about that?" I glanced at her.

"This will only take fifteen minutes, Captain."

"No. Get out." I laid down, turning my back to her.

"Ahem. Part of getting you to Earth is passing these mental evaluations, Captain. I have to convince the powers that be you're ready mentally. You've been through quite a lot in a short time." Arania attempted to sound comforting.

I leaned up in bed, glancing toward her. "You've got ten minutes, Arania. Okay?"

She grinned. "We best cut to the chase then. Okay. Can you tell me what emotions are running through your mind presently? How is your mood?"

"Focused."

"Your emotional state?"

"Uh. Anticipating. Determined."

"Do you feel pressured by us in any way?" she asked.

"What?"

"Do you feel you don't have a choice in helping us?"

I snapped toward her. "You don't have a choice," I said.

She nodded slowly, jotting down a few notes. "When you say I don't have a choice, I'm assuming you mean, Titan, as in *all* of us?" she asked.

"That's exactly what I mean."

"Can you explain why?"

"Do you know why it was decided to wake me up *now* from cryosleep?" I asked.

"Your brain injury. It wasn't until recently we could perform the operation—"

"Bullshit. Stop right there."

"Excuse me?"

I pointed toward the hangar bay. "I just saw my XU-97 and Xena. That is *years* of research and development. I don't care how smart these Titans are, that didn't happen in a few weeks or months. Listen, I don't think as fast as I fly, but understand, I'm not stupid by any stretch of the imagination. You kept me frozen until you needed me, didn't you?" I tested. Arania crossed her legs and paused for a moment. Her jaw shifted and locked in place.

"No, we didn't, Captain Belic. I'm not a military strategist nor engineer. I didn't plan the retrofitting of your ship or design Xena, but I know that didn't happen. Wouldn't you agree it's possible these improvements had nothing to do with you? Isn't it possible we could still use the ship for our benefit?" she posed.

I chuckled. "Uh-huh. What other questions do you have?"

She paused for few moments. "Just a couple more. Let's just, get through it."

"The clock is ticking."

"I see a fair amount of information in your file about your husband, your father, and your brother, even a few bits about your coworkers and some friends over the years, but…I don't see any mention of your mother anywhere, only her name." She panned around on her tablet. She shifted her eyes up at me.

"Do you enjoy this?" I asked.

"I'm sorry?"

"Obviously, my mother wasn't in my life or she'd be in that file. Everyone else is, you said it yourself. So, what does it matter now?" I asked.

"I just find it odd. It states your father, his name was Phillip?" she asked, glancing down, then back up at me.

I nodded in agreement.

"Your file states he was a troubled man, suffered from severe depression. I was curious how he managed to raise two children, alone. He even put you both through college somehow. Impressive," she said.

Now the conversation was venturing outside my comfort zone. Seemed I had little choice. I sighed. "Love, determination, and a little luck. That's how. My mother left him for another man when I was young, after that, he was never the same. He took it hard and never remarried," I explained. Not only did our mother wreck our home, she took away our father. He worked so many hours, we barely saw him.

She glared up at the ceiling for a moment, then her eyes flashed like a lightbulb went off in her head. "Tell me, is it a coincidence that both your father and the man you're willing to die for suffered from similar conditions? Sort of a pattern there, wounded, yet strong men?"

"I'm guessing you're a minor in mathematics," I said.

"Um. No. Why?"

"Because you know how to add things up. Seriously, I'm impressed," I said in a condescending tone. It was obvious, the things I loved about Luther, I admired about my father first. She glanced away for a moment, bouncing her eyebrows.

"Alright. One more question, then we're done for the day," she said.

"Please, I'm learning *so* much about myself here." I rolled my eyes.

"Last question. Would you still embark on this mission if it weren't for your husband? If there wasn't a chance he is alive?" she asked.

I pierced her with my eyes. "Nope. I wouldn't. More than likely, I'd jump off this train, relieve myself of the misery," I said without hesitation. I didn't mean it. I was frustrated with the question. However, if there wasn't a chance to recover Luther, I wasn't sure my sanity would survive.

She shook her head. "Why would you say something like that?" she asked. I wasn't helping my case here.

I stood up from my bed, facing her. "I don't know. Maybe because I'm dead already? The world I knew is gone. Do you have *any* idea what that feels like? No. You don't. No one does. What *case* studies have you read like this? Huh? None. The best you can do is let me handle it myself," I said.

"Victoria—"

"I'm not alone, though. You're going to die, too. You realize that, right? Those androids are coming to finish what they started on Earth. The best thing you people ever did was convince me Luther might still be alive. *That* gives everyone on this moon a chance. Now, please get the fuck out. It's in *your* best interest that I receive adequate rest for my selfish motives. Out!" I yelled.

Arania dropped her tablet as she pushed her chair back. Her hand trembled as she leaned forward to pick it up. I paced back and forth on the opposite side of the room, attempting not to look at her. I heard her step toward the door and exit.

"Fuck!" I spun around, kicking my metal trashcan toward the door like a football. It rattled around the room violently, slinging trash about. I was so upset I didn't feel the impact on my bare foot.

I sat down on my bed panting. I began to control my breathing. During tough times on Earth, I had a support system to lean on. Here, I felt like everyone was against me, knowingly or not.

It seemed like there was an underlying degree of oversight throughout my experience with these Titans. They were offspring of great minds: the explorers, survivors, and engineers who built this installation, a technical marvel unlike anything I'd seen. Yet, they couldn't forecast simple problems like my reaction to Xena's presence? That was a potentially detrimental botch to the mission.

Maybe it's the scenery affecting their brains after all these years? Or they just didn't give a fuck? Or they were testing my ability to handle stressors? Arania's line of questioning seemed inflammatory, so maybe that was their angle.

Either way, I was the wrong pilot to fuck with.

CHAPTER 7

I woke up to a blinking red light in my room. I could hear voices outside, some of them shouting orders. I stood up, scurrying to the door so I could peek outside. I opened it, and all the voices silenced, except one.

"Victoria," the voice whispered. I was curious. The sound was magnetic, pulling me from my room. I glided across the floor light as a feather. I glanced down, and at this point, I knew I was dreaming.

"You know, don't you?" he said. I recognized it as Luther this time. I reached out toward the voice as I floated down the hall, I entered the long tube Drake and Corvin ushered me down the day before. I glanced up at the glass panels as a red drizzle began to fall, spotting up the glass with what appeared to be blood.

The building began to lift from the ground slowly as if gravity had lost its effect. I glanced out to my right as silos and cranes were sucked into the atmosphere. I saw honeybee workers hurling toward space, their arms and legs flailing about. I fell to my knees.

"Just a bit further," he said. I tried to stand, but I felt powerless as the tube rocked back and forth in flight. The glass shattered above me, crashing down all around me. I put up my hands expecting to be sliced, but I wasn't. The interior of the terminal dimmed as we climbed into space, rocketing to the dark side of the moon.

All at once, a sound erupted down the hall. It was like a chorus singing, headed toward me. I pulled myself up, shambling toward the voices.

I peered forward, observing an outline of what reminded me of a large centipede or snake, slithering down the corridor. As it came into full view, I noticed it wasn't a snake at all, but thousands of toddlers marching in formation, zigzagging back and forth.

They were androids. Children. Like a swarm of smiling dolls. All of them white as snow, their faces stitched together with awful craftsmanship with flaps of plastic dangling from their faces. Their synthetic blue eyes glowed as their heads swiveled 360 degrees like strobing sirens.

As they grew closer, I could decipher their chant. "We're here to see the unfrozen whore, we came to see she's nevermore." I covered my eyes as the sound seemed to pierce my soul. The tighter I cupped my ears, the louder the chanting became.

"Stop!" I shouted. They began snickering with an eerie electronic whistle in their voices.

"We're here to see the unfrozen whore, we came to see her nevermore! We come to see this unfrozen whore, we came to see you *wake up*."

"It's time to wake up. Let's go." One of the android babies stepped out, putting his hand on my shoulder. He disappeared in front of my face as my body shook. My ears began to ring. I opened my eyes.

"Captain Belic, you've overslept," Xena said casually touching my shoulder. I sprung out of the bed, scampering onto the floor on all fours away from her like a frightened cat, skidding with my back against the wall. "Holy fuck! Stay back!" I yelled, breathing heavily.

"Is this what they refer to as a *nightmare,* Captain?" she asked, tilting her head to one side.

"Yeah. That's exactly what this is. Whose fucking idea was it to send *you* for a wakeup call? Huh?" I demanded.

"Ma'am, Drake was supposed to wake you, but he fell ill. He's in medical." She dipped her head slightly.

"Great. Just great. Listen robot, if anyone ever tells you to come wake me up, don't do it. Got that?" I ordered.

"Of course. My apologies, Captain Belic."

"Out." I pointed at the door. Xena dropped her head slightly. It almost seemed she felt guilty for upsetting me. I saw it in her cold blue eyes as they danced around the room briefly. Her actions reminded me of the 1.13 androids on Earth as they would attempt to simulate human emotions. She'd recently argued she had nothing in common with the androids from Earth, but this showcased the opposite. Xena stepped toward the exit, then stopped on a dime just before leaving. She stared at me confused.

"What the fuck do you want?" I asked, standing up.

"But doesn't it feel better knowing whatever you were dreaming isn't *real*?" she asked.

I cocked an eyebrow. "Waking up to you in my face isn't much better." She spun around and stepped toward the door without a response. She walked out of my room as I listened to her metallic combat boots clank against the floor, slowly fading away. I held my chest.

"I gotta wake up next to *that* on my ship? For weeks?" I mumbled. I never liked androids to begin with. Luther and I thought the concept was counterproductive. Machines, while useful, had a limit. How fucking lazy are you that you need something to take out your trash and clean piss droplets off the toilet seat?

I got the point of an assistant android if you were older or handicapped. That made sense. The problem was many Kelton owners were healthy, young people.

In the early 2030s, the Keltons started off as sex dolls for old pervs. At first, they weren't very dynamic, but over the years, they evolved. As their dexterity improved, they were converted to over to the masses, even chore slaves for homeowners.

It got even weirder from there, many customers wanted their Keltons to be a part of the family. They wanted more emotional ranges, for them to think freely and form opinions. Well, they did, and their opinion of humanity wasn't favorable, at all.

But the customer was always right.

"Captain Belic." Corvin paged me over the speaker.

"Yeah!" I yelled.

"Sorry about that."

"About what?" I tested.

113

"Using Xena to wake you."

"How'd you know that happened? Do you have a hidden camera in here?" I panned around. I wouldn't put it past them.

"No, no. Xena informed us you were unhappy—"

"We'll talk about it when I see you," I interrupted.

"Um, sure. Can you muster back in the hangar in fifteen?" he asked.

"In twenty, yeah," I replied.

He hesitated for a moment before responding. "I'll see you then." Truthfully, I wanted to treat him like a general, he just didn't fit the bill.

I threw on my maroon military jumpsuit, zipping it slowly. I sat down, zoning off as I laced up my pristine black combat boots.

I thought about Arania's bewildered gaze as I shouted at her earlier. She must have made the correlation. I was the warmongering Earthling she'd likely read so much about in history, full of irrationality and rage on full display. I hated to fulfill the stereotype, but then again, how could anyone expect me to take this well?

I made my way to the hangar as Corvin ordered. As I stepped through the connecting terminal, I heard what sounded like commotion in the adjacent tube.

"This again." An older woman mumbled beside me. She stared at the fake projection window. I stopped. She shifted her eyes toward me and shook her head. Her hair was mostly gray, with streaks of brown evenly throughout. She looked Native American possibly, with big beautiful dark eyes and light brown skin.

"What's the problem?" I asked.

"Conspiracy activists. Third time in a month they've rallied like this." She rolled her eyes.

"Conspiracy?"

"You know, those massive ships around Earth's moon everyone's talking about. Some are afraid, but the government keeps assuring there is no fleet, nothing to worry about, they say. Some demand the truth." She peered at them.

"What do *you* think?" I asked. She sighed, shrugging her shoulders.

"Well, for one, the organizer of this protest is an astrologist. He claims to have seen comet-like objects breaking away from Earth toward Titan recently," she said.

"Really? Comets," I said suspiciously.

"Android ships. That's what they're assuming. But even if it's true, what could I do?" she asked. I glanced down at the ground.

"Protest." I shrugged.

She chuckled, crossing her arms. "At my age?" At that point, I noticed her outfit. It was a cozy set of gray working overalls. The material reminded me of a layered, interwoven yarn. It was puffy and appeared extremely warm, but it wasn't easy on the eyes. I got the feeling she was retired.

"You're still young," I said.

"You think? I'm Earthborn, came over on the original voyage when I was nine," she said.

"You're eighty years old?" I asked. She didn't look a day over sixty.

"Just turned eighty-one, yep," she replied. I glanced down at my watch, I needed to get to the hangar for training, but it felt good to see another Earthling. I wondered if I'd passed by her in the corridors on the *Orion*.

"Well, you probably remember some of Earth and the trip over?" I asked.

"Some things. Yeah, sure do. I remembered my parents were terrified the android conflict would reignite," she said. I wanted to reveal who I was, but that would only cause more problems for myself.

"Long time ago. Well, ma'am, it was good talking to you, but I have to get going," I explained. She grinned, holding her stare at the screen. It seemed her eyes began to peer a thousand miles away.

I stepped away several paces and her voice erupted again. "Good luck, Captain Belic, we're counting on you," she said.

Her tone was powerful even at her age. I stopped in my tracks for a moment, but I didn't turn around. She either remembered me or someone told her who I was. I had no rank indicators on my uniform. I stepped forward, gaining distance from her. I noticed Corvin and Drake watching me from afar.

Drake waved me over with his hand as Corvin stood there with his arms crossed. I picked up the pace toward them. Something wasn't right. Their body language had changed.

"Captain." Corvin nodded.

"Sleep well?" Drake sneered.

"You know what, fuck you." I stabbed my finger at him. "You sent Xena, didn't you, Drake? You got butt hurt because I called you out yesterday about your role on the mission?" Several people turned around, alerted by my frustration. Drake shook his head and backed away like he was above my antics. He might have been honestly, but I was pissed.

"Hey! Cut it out!" Corvin knifed his arm between us.

"*Corvin* told me to send her." Drake showed me his palms. They both knew I was uncomfortable with their bot and they send her to wake me up anyway?"

"He's right, it was my decision because—"

"Well, in that case, fuck *you*, General." I bounced my eyebrows. Corvin's nostrils flared out as he attempted to calm himself. He cleared his throat and smiled.

"Ahem. Look—"

"No, you look. What's the deal? Spit it out. What is this about the comets coming from Earth?" I interrupted. I thought maybe it had something to do with that or my outburst with Arania. Maybe they were going to punish me.

Corvin dipped his head slightly, shifting his eyes at Drake. "Tell her," he said.

"Well, first, let me ask. You don't speak Russian, do you?" Drake asked, dipping close to me.

"What? No. I might know a few words, why?" I asked. Drake smacked his lips.

"We didn't think you did. It was a long shot. Oh well, we have a translator anyway," he said.

"For what?"

"From what we've deciphered, a captain of a small Russian freighter. It just broke through earth's atmosphere and sent a transmission. He said he needed help." Drake explained. I guessed that had to be the 'comet' the astrologist saw breaking away from Earth.

"Okay. That's vague. Doesn't really pertain to our mission, does it?" I asked.

"Actually, it does. This is an unprecedented opportunity." Corvin dipped his head, placing his hand under his chin.

"If we can link up with that vessel, it's possible we can gather a wealth of intelligence about the androids," Drake insisted. I gazed off into the distance for a moment.

"Wait, are you suggesting we scrap our mission to Earth? Is that what this is about?" I asked.

"We haven't made any decisions in regard to that, Captain. We don't even know if we'll hear from the Russian again or if he'll have anything valuable," Corvin said.

"Basically, what you're saying is the mission to Earth weighs on how much this random guy knows. What if it's a setup or misinformation from the androids?" I said. I could hear the protesters getting closer. They were chanting something, but I couldn't make it out yet.

"We'll put Xena on the job. She'll be able to tell us if it's a fake," Corvin replied. I knew where I stood in that moment. Seemed obvious that if this Russian had valuable information, the mission to Earth was fucked. My chance of finding Luther, gone.

Corvin turned, glaring down the hall. I could faintly make out the chanting now. "No more lies or Titan will rise!" The group repeated over and over. I stared a hole through Corvin as he glanced at the floor.

"Corvin," I said. I slowly stepped within a dozen centimeters of his face. He leaned on his back foot, off put by my position. Drake scratched his head awkwardly.

"Uh, yes?" Corvin replied.

"Let me be frank. From the moment I woke up here, my first breath, I wanted my husband back," I said.

"Victoria, I don't pretend to understand how traumatic this situation has been for you." He lifted his eyebrows. I held my stare as he shifted his eyes away briefly, pretending to be distracted by the protesters.

"Do you have a wife?" I asked.

"What?"

"Are you married? I see you have ring on," I observed.

"Yes-yes. Twenty-one years."

"See. Your world is here. Even if the androids come, you die together, at least. I don't even get that luxury. I'm left spinning in the void of the unknown. How would *you* feel?" I posed. We were suddenly surrounded by the crowd of protesters as they chanted. They walked right beside us, bumping into me and Corvin slightly as I locked my eyes into his.

"My point is, you aided in this, *my* misery. Somehow or another you're connected to them waking me up, refitting my ship, my AI. All this was planned a long time ago. You, at the very *least*, knew about it."

"That's completely ridiculous and you know it, Captain. They woke you because the doctors felt good about the chances of saving you," he said.

"Right. Just like they tell *these* people there's no android threat? Meanwhile, there are four hundred heavy destroyers practicing bombing runs on Earth's moon. I'm sure that's going on for the hell of it, right?" I asked.

"Keep your voice down. These are civilians, Captain. Hearing a military official talk like that could be detrimental to our way of life." He leaned in.

I leaned in closer. "They can't hear me. I'm telling you, sailor to soldier. I'm not onboard with you using my skill sets unless I have a chance to retrieve my husband. Understand that." I cocked an eyebrow.

"That's a threat," Corvin said.

"When you hint we might not be going to Earth, I consider *that* a threat," I said, stabbing my finger at his chest. At that point, a protester walked between us, nudging me away from Corvin.

Drake tugged me at my shoulder, "Captain, please, let's go to the briefing room, the Russian translator should be done by now," he said.

"Uh-huh." I glanced at Drake. Corvin turned his back on me, stepping away with his hands on his hips. He glanced up at the ceiling. I followed Drake toward the hangar bay and stopped, allowing him to step ahead of me as I cooled off.

Corvin's reaction was further proof he was involved with my situation somehow. I wasn't sure how this revelation was beneficial to me, but at least I knew. If I continued down this path to unravel the truth, how would it help my chances to find Luther?

I peered inside the meeting room to the left of the hangar. It reminded me of an attorney's office; twelve, huge comfy chairs surrounded a dark gray table. Xena stood in the corner with her arms crossed, gazing ahead at nothing.

Two middle aged men I didn't recognize were already seated inside. One of them wore a three-piece business suit with a blood red tie. He reminded me of a Wall Street type, with an overpriced slicked back haircut with thinning white hairs curled up at the back.

He wore rectangle shaped reading glasses. He had a wide face with high cheekbones, and his eyebrows seemed fixed downward as he scanned across a tablet in front of him.

He noticed me outside the door, lifting his head while narrowing his eyes at me. His glare appeared to scrutinize every fiber in my being in less than a second. He quickly glanced back down as if he was insulted by my presence. The other man sported a thick white beard, and he wore a military jumpsuit like mine. He had no rank insignia.

A mid-forties, heavier set woman sat at the end of the table wearing a pair of headphones, jotting down some notes. Corvin and Drake stepped inside and sat down with me several steps behind in tow. I sat beside Drake, across the table from the Wall Street dickface.

"That is why the translator software didn't work, General Corvin. Too much interference." The old woman said with a thick Russian accent. She took off her headphones and wiped her sweaty forehead with a handkerchief.

"Well, what did he say?" I spoke up, cutting off Corvin. Everyone seemed to acknowledge my interruption. The translator hesitated for a few seconds. "Basically, this Russian man, he wants to trade information for fuel to come to Titan. He is fleeing Earth and seeks refuge here," she said.

"How did he get through without detection? Where is he now?" Corvin asked.

"He did not say how he snuck through, but he is on his way to the Earth's moon. He will hide on the dark side of the moon and go silent and await a response. He says he has enough fuel to make forty percent of the voyage to Titan. No more."

"If everything checks out, we can meet him halfway." The man in the suit mumbled.

"Isn't the moon surrounded by android destroyers?" I asked.

"They stay on the light side of the moon mostly." The man in the suit answered. He pushed his glasses forward, tapping a pen on the desk staring at me. I felt he was simply tolerating my presence.

"Anything else?" Corvin asked.

"Nothing. He waits for us to respond," the woman said.

"Gotta feel good to hear another Russian voice from the old world," Drake said to the woman. She paused, staring at him. "I don't know. I think after the android war, we realized how trivial our borders were. Russian, Ukrainian, even Israeli or American, we have more in common than *them*. I'm glad to hear *human* voice from Earth, yes," she said with a thick accent. I shifted my eyes toward Xena.

"Good way to look at it," Drake replied, nodding his head.

The man in the suit stood up, putting his hands on the table. "Xena, authenticity of the voice?" he asked.

"Ninety-nine percent chance this is a human voice, sir," she said.

"Is your pilot ready?" The man asked Corvin as if I wasn't in the room.

"She hasn't completed the training, but—"

"Can she fly the new tech?" he interrupted.

"She's the most capable pilot on Titan by a large margin, even with limited experience using new technology," Xena answered confidently.

"Mental evaluations?" the man asked. Go ahead, divulge my deepest, darkest secrets while you're at it. I was a hair away from calling this guy out in front of everyone, but I didn't want to mess up my chances. I really wanted to smack that arrogant look off his face. There weren't many people that pissed me off just by their look, but he was one of them.

"She's on schedule, Arania has ensured me of that," Corvin said, his eyes danced about the room briefly.

"Good. This will be a good prelim mission for our new pilot. Find out what type of fuel we need for this man's freighter, and let's deliver it with the XU-97. Hopefully, it's the methane variant they were using on Earth years ago. It's extremely efficient and it'll be less storage. We'll meet him at the forty percent mark and see what he knows," he said.

"And Xena?" Corvin asked.

"She goes. And Drake, of course. I want an onsite questioning of the refugee in case something happens before he gets to Titan. We need whatever information he has, *now*. If you can get anything before they leave, that would be ideal," the man suggested. I felt he was implying interrogation instead of questioning.

"Got it. What's the math here, Xena?" Corvin asked.

"Worst case, judging by his transmission equipment, he's using a slower LU class freighter from the early 2070s. That will take him around twenty-four days to reach the forty percent portion to Titan. Fortunately, Saturn and Titan are approaching the closest point of our orbit near Earth," Xena said.

I thought about how quickly that was. Xena described it as 'slow.' Even the *Orion* took six months to travel nearly 1.2 billion kilometers from Earth to Titan.

"Find out exactly what his setup is ASAP, so we can plan around it," Corvin ordered the translator.

"Yes, sir," she answered.

"It should take us no more than sixteen days at maximum payload in the XU-97 to reach our sixty percent portion of the voyage," Xena said.

"That leaves us a net gain of a few days," Drake said, glaring over at me.

"Corvin, get our brains on it, all related scientists. I want them working on every scenario, every situation, no surprises. We might only have a few days," the well-dressed man said.

Corvin leaned over in my ear. "You see, this Russian might not even be part of any resistance effort," he said. I wasn't sure if he was being honest or giving me false hope that going to Earth wasn't off the table.

The option to recover Luther still made the most sense to me. If there was a resistance, that meant more people. We could cross reference multiple intelligence sources instead of a singular Russian pilot to locate the target for Xena.

The two unknown men stood up, walking near the exit. "General Corvin, send the response to the refugee and retrieve the information you need, then report back to us."

"Yes, sir." Corvin and Drake stood up as they exited, I remained seated. As they closed the door, I stared up at Corvin.

"I'm not going," I said.

"What?" His eyes widened.

"If I'm risking my skin, it'll be for Luther. You already know that. I want a guarantee," I said.

"If you want to play games, we have other pilots. Even Drake could handle this mission if we wanted," he said.

"It is unlikely that Colonel Drake or any of our other pilots could accomplish this mission if unforeseen circumstances were to occur. Captain Belic has extensive combat experience. Her file reveals near four thousand androids eliminated and three hundred and sixteen aerial attack drones shot down—"

"Xena, shut up," Corvin said. He smacked his hand on the table.

"Understood, General," Xena replied.

"Even your robot gets it. You have one fighter jet, that's it. It was obviously customized with me in mind. Do you want a greenhorn piloting your investment, or an ace?" I put my feet up on the table, reclining back in the comfy seat.

I saw fire in Corvin's eyes as he stared me down. He bit his bottom lip, then stormed toward the exit, slamming the door behind him. I'd never seen him so upset and, frankly, it was a nice change. I knew he needed me. That jet wasn't something to give to a trainee pilot or a robot. You don't throw an amateur jockey on a racehorse. It doesn't work that way.

"I'm not sure that was the best idea," Drake mumbled.

"Yeah? So, I should just go along with whatever the fuck they come up with, right? Here, fly to Pluto, make a snowman while you're there," I asked.

"It's highly unlikely we will ever go to Pluto. Also, Pluto is considered a *minor* planet, Captain," Xena injected.

"Thanks for the clarification, Xena. I was extremely worried we might end up there," I said softly. She stared back at me confused. She probably needed a software patch to deal with a natural born smartass like myself.

"I'm just saying, you're making life difficult for Corvin. That can't be good for you, or us rather. And yeah, I hate to say it, but if we did run into problems, Xena's right, I'm not sure if I could handle it," Drake admitted.

I shrugged. "Xena's your only hope then. To her credit, she did some pretty fancy flying on the training mission."

"That route is predetermined," Drake whispered.

"Oh? Never mind then. You're completely fucked," I said, gleaming at Xena. Drake stared ahead at nothing, his face full of worry.

"Level with me, Drake. And please, be honest. Why are you doing this? You realize if I don't go, your chances of survival have reduced significantly. You wanna be a hero?" I asked.

"No." He sat back down, slapping his meaty forearms on the table. "Truthfully, when I heard they might wake you up, I volunteered as a candidate."

"Why is that? You wanted me to tell you about the good ol' days?" I asked.

"No. Arania, the psychologist, she told me about your husband. She didn't know much about him, but she told me he went under the ice for you." He said looking away, interlocking his fingers.

"So, you're a romantic. You were *inspired*? Come on." I cocked an eyebrow.

"Guilty as charged." He shook his head. "Kidding. No, I mean it's obvious we're fighting for survival, literally. If the androids decide to come here, it's over—"

"Simulation data reveals no one would survive an orbital strike based on data collected from the moon bombing runs."

"Thank you, Xena. That'll be all." Drake raised his eyebrows and glanced back at me.

"You going to answer my question or not?" I asked.

"You don't let up." He stood, unzipping his jumpsuit top, revealing a shredded, thick upper body. He was a living muscular anatomy chart. He didn't have any tattoos like I originally assumed, but there was plenty to look at.

"Um, I'm a married woman," I said. He chuckled, pointing out a huge scar on his lower back.

"Uh, kidney?" I asked. He zipped up his top.

"Yep, I needed one."

"*Needed*?" I asked.

"A guy I didn't even know stepped up. I had been waiting for four months. It was posted, then suddenly this guy shows up and said he'd do it. Young, in his mid-twenties they said," Drake explained.

"You never got his name?"

"Nope. He said he was a match and he wanted to remain anonymous," Drake said.

"Whoa. Heavy stuff," I said.

"Yeah. I thought about it for weeks, who it might be. Sometimes I'd sit around for hours. Then I started working out, eating better, you know, tried to take advantage of my extension." Drake grinned.

"Oh, okay, gotcha. It's all starting to make more sense now," I replied, squinting my eyes at him.

"I found beauty in what he did. Sure, you can look at the negative in humanity, there's plenty of it, but I prefer to look at our best qualities, like sacrifice. Selfless sacrifice. Anonymous, yet conscious. That's as innately human as it gets, for me. That's what makes us different from *them*," Drake said, cutting his eyes at Xena.

He glared back at me. "What your husband did. He had to have known he might not ever wake up, but he did it anyway." Drake clenched his fists.

"If you ever get to meet him, it'll make sense," I replied.

"That's what I want. Ready to spit in the face of fear for what I believe. I believe that is worth dying for, so that someone else can feel what you felt, what Luther felt, what I felt when that man gave me a part of his body, how it changed my outlook. Those are things so powerful, after you feel it, we *know* it's worth dying for. *That* is living, Victoria," he said.

"And to think, all this time I thought you were a jock with just enough brains to slither through officer training." I nodded slowly. Fuck. I was wrong. This guy had some depth I didn't expect. He seemed to have a code about him at least, a moral barometer. I enjoyed hearing his contemplative side. The jury was still out, but maybe he wasn't half bad.

"Thanks. I finished second in my class." Drake grinned.

"Out of how many?" I asked.

"Ninety-one."

"See, I graduated *high school* with five times that many," I said.

"Yeah, we don't have the population up to snuff, but we'll get there one day."

"Hopefully." I glanced up at the ceiling.

"We will," he whispered confidently, knitting his eyebrows together. I stared at him for a couple moments. I instantly felt more at ease about him after his revelation.

"Well, I've had enough for today. I'm headed back to my room for the evening. Let me know if you hear anything," I said.

"You'll be the first to know if I do," Drake replied. I walked to the exit, past Xena standing guard. I glanced toward the hangar bay around the bend. I wanted to fly the XU-97 again to unwind, maybe take it for a spin around the moon. I remembered doing that back in the navy. Nothing like Mach speeds to clear the mind.

"Captain." Xena stopped me. I snapped over my shoulder at her standing in the doorway. Her wide exoskeleton and armored shoulders nearly touched the doorframe on each side. She appeared worried. Somehow, her synthetic features appeared long.

"Yeah?" I asked.

"I think it's vital to the survival of your species that you pilot the XU-97. We need that intelligence, and we need the refugee to tell us what he knows. If we don't get them the fuel, the opportunity could be lost," she said. I thought it was odd for Xena to have such a genuine sense of urgency and emphasis on my ability.

"No offense, but why do you care? If your brothers and sisters show up, it'll be a quick death for us all," I said. Suddenly, Xena ran me down. I attempted to move back, but her movement was so fast, I couldn't react, like facing down a bullet train blasting through a tunnel. She grabbed my collar with one hand, tightening the fabric around my neck to the point of slight discomfort. It was clear her intentions were not to hurt me, she could have killed me with ease.

"Xena! Stop!" I shouted.

I began bashing her face with the palm of my hand. Her short, white wig flopped back and forth with each impact, but it didn't seem to faze her, so I stopped.

I heard a security guard yelling from down the hall. "Hey! Hey! Release her immediately!" he yelled at Xena, running towards us with a rifle drawn.

"Let go of me!" I yelled.

Xena ducked close to me, unconcerned by the guards approaching. She stared into my eyes intensely. "Don't assume it'll be a quick death for you all. Many will see *this* cold blue gaze in their last moments. You know what they're capable of, don't you? Why not consider the implications of your actions, Captain? Humanity needs you," Xena said. She released me slowly as I backed away, grabbing my neck.

If Titan was attacked, it was possible some residing here might survive the orbital bombardment. What did that mean for those survivors? They would likely be hunted underground like mice under floorboards.

The robot was right. The logical objective would be to fight for my species in any way I could, but I was human, a ball of stress and emotions that needed an anchor in this world.

Two more guards ran us down, surrounding Xena and I. "Step away!" one of the guards screamed as they pointed rifles at Xena.

"I'm fine. Fine! I ordered Xena to do that. We had martial arts training this morning and I was attempting to use a self-defense move," I lied. The guards slowly lowered their weapons, glancing at one another.

Xena tilted her head, confused. Then her eyes pulsed, like a lightbulb going off in her head. "Yes, and you've failed *miserably*, Captain," Xena said.

"We must practice choke defense in greater detail." Xena smiled unnaturally at the guards. It appeared forced, as if some of the muscles designed for smiling were scraped for this android model.

"So, tomorrow then, Captain?" Xena asked.

"Ah, yep. Yes, tomorrow is good," I replied. She turned her back to the guards and walked away casually.

"Fellas." I nodded, passing the guards.

"Hey. Uh, if you want any training from a real security specialist, my quarters are on section bravo, room one-nineteen. I give private lessons." The guard smirked. His comrade snickered.

"Thanks, but I'll stick with the robot."

CHAPTER 8

The next morning, I woke up early. I opened the blinds and turned my chair toward the live stream window, propping my feet up. I stared out into the drab mist for a bit. I could barely see Saturn the haze was so thick. My foot accidentally touched the screen.

"View actual perspective? Yes or no?" A touch screen prompt appeared on the fake scenery.

"What?" I mumbled, pressing yes. I didn't know that was a possibility. The screen slowly faded from the projection to an actual window view.

"Shit." It seemed like I was a passenger on a jet taking as the landscape hurried by. The viewing angle was high from the steep track slope, giving me more a view of the mountains and clouds. I actually enjoyed this view more than staring at a still image, but I could understand why most wouldn't. This was probably an attempt to keep people sane.

I decided to get up early and go talk to Corvin in person. I had slept on my actions from the day before. Most of it felt warranted, but I wasn't helping my situation, or Luther's, by being so combative.

I headed around the long way, taking a new route. I saw from above that the installation was shaped like a ladder. The outer 'rails' were shaped like bullet trains while the 'steps' in-between them were tubes or terminals, and both were functional as living or working spaces. As I explored, I noticed these tubes had all sorts of variety in size. Some were forty meters wide or more while others half that. One was a greenhouse, another a supermarket, even schools.

'Hidmas Elementary School' one tube entrance read.

The children were lined up single file on both sides of the door. It appeared to be an even number on each side, maybe sixty students total. I stood there observing them. They were all so cute in their little outfits, so many different races and cultures. They seemed quiet and well behaved, I assumed they were waiting for their teacher.

A beautiful black girl on the end kept peeking over at me. She seemed shy. Her hair was pulled up on top of her head as she held her tablet in front of her arms, leaning against the wall.

"How long have you guys been waiting?" I asked her. She shook her head no, pointing up in the sky. I glanced up. "What is it?" I grinned at her.

"It's a meteor drill, silly. Every morning we do this, just in case." She smiled.

"Oh," I said.

"My principal said it was meteors, but I heard my dad say something different. He told my mom the robots are coming for us. You're in the army, what do you think?" she challenged, staring at my military jumpsuit.

"Um, well, I—"

"Ah, hello there. The Army is here!" An adult male voice interrupted from behind. I glanced over my shoulder, noticing a medium height, middle-aged male in a suit. He had dark skin and sharp features. He had thick, wavy white hair that was styled wildly.

"Hi." I waved as he approached.

"I'm Robert Contreras. Assistant Principal." He extended his hand as he glanced me up and down. "Odd, don't think I've seen you around?"

"Probably not. Hello. I'm Captain Belic," I replied politely, shaking his hand.

"You must have an up and coming student? Well, let me just say, Hidmas Elementary is new, but a *performer*. We have the top scores in science and math out of the five elementary schools on Titan. Many of our students go on to be greenhouse workers often times, specializing in artificial lighting, humidity, or fertilizers. Some even go on to the oxygen teams, converting Titan's ice to breathable air. We also—"

"I don't have any kids. I just noticed them out here and was curious," I replied with a pleasant smile. He narrowed his eyes at me. "We've been doing this drill for years," he said with a puzzled look.

"Years? How many?" I asked.

"It must be at least eight or nine years if my memory serves me correctly."

"Hmm. Do you know why?" I asked.

"You're in the Army, shouldn't you know?" He smirked.

"I'm asking *you*."

"Meteors, of course. I tell my kids what I think is comforting to hear, that's it," he whispered.

"Hmm. Seems a bit pointless just standing around waiting for *meteors* here." I lowered my voice, extending my hand toward the children.

"We suit them up and stop the installation. Then we file them down to the shelters underground in an orderly fashion, almost eighty meters deep," he explained.

"Underground," I said, shaking my head. I thought about what Xena told me the day before about the Rat Race. I glanced over at the kids, skipping across each of their little faces quickly. I hoped that if Titan was ever attacked, the children wouldn't make it to the shelters underground. I'd rather them die a quick death than hunted underground by the machines.

"Is everything okay?" he asked.

"Yeah. Yep. I gotta get going, though," I said.

"Were you just testing me? Surely you knew the answers to those questions?" he asked.

"Yep, you got me," I said, stepping away quickly. I didn't want to look at the children anymore. I made a dead trot to Corvin's quarters.

I approached Corvin's office and knocked. "It's Captain Belic." I heard muted voices on the other side of the door.

"Hold on," a female said. Arania opened the door.

"Well, hello, Captain." She smiled awkwardly. I could sense they had been talking about me. I entered his office, shocked that it was almost as boring as Corvin himself. It reminded me of a teacher's office but crammed with holographic displays and satellite live feeds. It didn't strike me as a military leader's quarters at all.

"How are you?" Arania asked, sitting and crossing her legs. I felt she was attempting to ignore what happened between us. I noticed her foot shaking while she waited for my answer. I made her wait, controlling the situation as I stared her down. She seemed to squirm a bit in her seat, shifting her weight and glancing away.

"As if you aren't keeping tabs on me," I arched an eyebrow.

"Um, what's that?" she asked.

"I've seen the cameras. They seem to follow me wherever I go, and that's only the visible ones. No telling what you've hidden in my room," I said.

"We haven't hidden any of them. The others are just precautionary, for your safety when you're near the public. We're not just monitoring you, Captain," she said.

"Uh-huh."

"Captain, have a seat please," Corvin said. His tone had a touch of authority.

"Sure, *General*," I replied. He was looking over a hologram of the solar system, specifically an object's trajectory from Earth's moon to Titan.

"Is that our Russian freighter?" I asked. Corvin didn't acknowledge me at first. He sighed loudly, kicking back in his chair. He put his arms behind his head.

"Russians," he said.

"As in plural?" I asked.

"It's a family." I could tell he was a bit distant, still upset from the day before perhaps.

"Won-der-ful," I mumbled.

"Turns out their main food supply crates weren't vacuum sealed properly. They won't make the trip. Spoiled," he said.

"That's why you seal smaller bags, less chance of losing large quantities," I said.

"Yeah. Coming from Earth, though, they might not have had a lot of options," he replied.

"Or time," I said, standing up.

"We're sending out the team in five days," he said. Arania dipped her head.

"Um. That's not much time." I glanced up at the ceiling.

"No. And again, we want someone with operational experience up there. A pilot. We have no idea what we might run into on the way," he said.

"You know what I want," I said. Corvin shifted his eyes toward Arania, then back at me.

"*If* we go to Earth for intelligence gathering, we will attempt to find Luther. We think if he has been preserved somewhere, that might be one likely location to find other humans. Otherwise, we're not risking an additional insertion mission to find your husband when the Russians could possess the same intelligence. We'll send Xena on a direct-action mission for the virus upload." Corvin laid it out plainly.

"So that's it, whatever these Russians say is gospel? How will you confirm their intelligence is the real deal?" I asked.

"Let us worry about that, Captain. We'll check their information on our end, but I'm letting you know there's a possibility we might not need to retrieve your husband. It's as simple as that. I'm sorry." He raised an eyebrow. Arania bit her lip.

Corvin narrowed his eyes at me. "I'm not playing any more games. You help us get those refugees fuel and food, and then we'll see what happens from there. This isn't a done deal, but this is where we stand. Again, the Russians might not know anything of value. In that case, we still have to go to Earth for intelligence gathering, so, finding your husband is a possibility," Corvin explained.

This was sounding more and more like my only option. He wasn't budging. I came here to apologize for my behavior, but this Russian situation removed the power I had. Fuck. An irrational thought popped in my head. Maybe I could steal the XU-97? The problem was, they could likely order Xena to override my controls remotely. It didn't make sense. My back was against the wall. I dropped my head and sighed loudly.

"It seems you've had some time to think this over?" he said.

"Yeah," I whispered.

"I knew rationale would prevail," he said.

Arania set up straight in her chair. "Captain, I want to apologize for the way this was handled on our end. You're right, we don't have any experience dealing with a situation like yours. We're basically writing the rulebook as we go," she said.

"Thanks?" I shrugged.

Corvin handed me a pair of sunglasses. "Take these. If you decide you're onboard with us, these are accelerated augmented reality modules, weapons handling, day-to-day operation, safety, communication, plus a few more tips for aircraft operation for stealth options. Put on these hologlasses and it'll be like you're flying the XU-97 from your room, just like with the weapons range module. As you complete them, I'll get notifications of your performance."

I grabbed the glasses out of his hand. "I hope this is better than the augmented reality courses in my day," I said.

"They are. The trainees that go through the augmented course score almost identical to real life. The gun range is a great example," he said.

I stood up, glancing down at the hologlasses, then I stared Corvin in the eyes. I hated to eat my own words, but this was my only option. I sighed. "Well, prepare to see all the gun range scores shattered," I said. Corvin stood up, he grinned, extending his hand. "I look forward to it."

"Godspeed, Captain." Arania nodded.

Suddenly, Xena burst into the room, knocking the top hinge of the door off.

"The fuck?" I snapped toward the entrance. Corvin and Arania jumped back. I didn't move. Xena stopped in the doorway, stoic as if nothing was wrong.

"What?" I asked.

"General Corvin, sensors indicate the presence of four dreadnought class destroyers incoming. The androids are here," she said.

"No," Arania whispered, covering her mouth with her hands.

Corvin gulped. "Four, *total*?"

"Yes sir," she replied. This was small force compared to their fleet of four hundred.

"Range?" Corvin asked, glancing down at his holographic map.

maximum, based on the bombardment intelligence we gathered from Earth's moon," she said. Corvin glared over at me, biting his lip.

"I can fly. I'm ready, training modules or not," I said without hesitation.

"Be in the hangar in five minutes!" he shouted. I rushed out of the office as sirens began blaring above us. An eerily pleasant female voice came through the installation speakers. "Attention, all non-essential personnel, report to your stations. This is not a drill."

I ran to the hangar, darting by the guard as he peered through the glass roof. "Open up! They're not here yet!" I yelled. His hand shook as he entered the pass code.

"Belic!" I heard Drake behind me.

"Let's go! In the hangar!" I shouted. He didn't hesitate, barreling toward the hangar like an Olympian sprinter.

"Xena, warm up the XU-97 engines and run a check on all weapon systems. Get us ready to fly, immediately," I ordered.

"Roger that, Captain. Are we continuing our campaign against the androids so soon?" the ship AI asked. I glared through the open hangar door. The ship's thrusters snarled as the hydraulic pad swung the nose of the XU-97 toward the exit.

"Get our flight gear ready, *now!*" Drake yelled at an airman. The James Dean lookalike was already on it, running out from behind a storage room with our suits on a wheeled rack. His eyes were wide as he pushed the cart.

"Course of action?" Drake asked.

"Corvin's on his way," I replied.

As I suited up, I remembered my combat run with Commander Rotus on Earth. It had the same feel to it. I wasn't sure what to expect. The difference this time was I didn't have the backing of the most powerful military on planet Earth. I had one fighter and a band of untested Titans against four android destroyers.

They better have a plan.

Drake and I quickly donned our suits. Myself, Xena, and Drake stood parallel in front of the XU-97, waiting on Corvin's orders. I glanced down at my helmet tucked underneath my arm. I noticed something different, a small inscription.

'*Lioness*' it read. I cut my eyes up at Drake. He was oblivious to my discovery, his eyes drifting to some faraway place.

I panned around the hangar, noticing 'James Dean' staring at me, he quickly shifted away as we made eye contact. He was standing in parade rest position. He appeared nervous, so I thought I'd take his mind away from the impending doom.

"Airman? Who did this? The inscription." I pointed at my helmet.

"Well, we did, ma'am," he replied.

"Who told you this was my callsign?" I asked.

"General Corvin. He said back on Earth you were in a Navy fighter squad called the Blue Lions." It was true, I was the only female in the elite group.

"Huh," I said.

"Surely they didn't call you Lioness just because you were female?" The airman cocked an eyebrow.

"No. No, they didn't. But do you know what Lionesses do in a pride, airman?" I asked.

"Protect their young?" he replied.

"They're hunters. The females are responsible for most of the killing," I said. Sure, they protected cubs, too, but that's not why I earned the callsign. I was a killer.

Drake sneered and dipped his head as the airman nodded. I never had any cubs for myself to protect. All at once, that notion felt like an empty hole in my heart. I never *yearned* for children before. I wanted them, but it just wasn't in our cards. Between Luther's depression, my combat deployments, and the state of the planet, we decided against it. But now, in the face of certain death, it felt like Luther and I were missing out more than ever.

I bit my lip as Corvin and the mystery men from the meeting marched through the door. They had a group with them of eighteen soldiers, two of them pushing large containers.

"Tell me you have a plan," I said.

"As you know, we don't have a large military force. But what we do have might give us a chance against only four destroyers," Corvin replied.

"Why would they send such a small force by comparison? They have over four hundred?" Drake asked.

"We're not sure. It's odd. Maybe a scout force. Don't be fooled though, four destroyers are more than enough to wipe us out. We have a wild, unorthodox defense strategy in place, it was initially designed for hundreds of destroyers. The downside is, it's not completely ready," Corvin admitted.

"Well, let's hear it," I hurried.

"Ahem. You see these?" Corvin pointed. The soldiers began opening the containers, pulling out large tablets. Each of them put on a small visor, like a pair of sunglasses.

Corvin dipped his head at the men to his left. "These soldiers will control our Terradrone army. A flying swarm. When the destroyers began bombing Earth's moon, we started cultivating a farm of military nanobots. They've built clones of themselves using Titan's methane for fuel. These drones are like the ones you attacked during your training mission with Xena." The man with the blood red tie explained. I recalled the spider-shaped drone I destroyed a few days ago. Great. Something *else* to glitch out and turn against us.

"How many do we have now?" Drake asked. This was apparently extremely secretive if he didn't know.

"Our last count this week was near two-hundred thousand," Corvin replied.

"Well fuck, why do you need us?" I asked.

"The drones, while somewhat capable in our simulations, against their destroyers, are unproven, and will likely be distractions. If these dreadnoughts have the proper close quarters defenses, our drones will go down quickly. The soldiers wearing visors here remote control the leader drones and the others follow. They've been summoned and we're ready. We'll move to a control room before you launch," Corvin explained. I agreed, this was very unorthodox. The advantage I immediately acknowledged was the distraction element. Two hundred thousand was a lot of targets.

"What's my role?" I asked.

"Ahem. We've decided you'll be piloting this mission. We understand you have a degree of unfamiliarity with the vessel's configuration, but your combat experience is unmatched." Corvin nodded. Who else was gonna fly? Xena? Drake? Of course, I was piloting.

"Signal intelligence reveals a command ship in the battle group. We're calling it the *Abraruss*. We'll mark it on your visor when you take off," Corvin said.

"Course of action?"

"There are large weapon sensor domes next to the bridge. Two of them. Destroy them and Xena will take care of the rest," Corvin said. I narrowed my eyes as he pulled up a hologram on his watch, revealing the position of the large domes. "Here, and here." Corvin pointed out.

"Xena will *take care* of it?" I posed. This made no sense to me.

"Trust us. We don't have time to explain. Engage the enemy before they reach striking distance and follow Xena's instructions once you've accomplished your task," Corvin ordered. I glared up at Xena. She nodded her head confidently. "I will destroy them," she said. I nodded. If you say so, Xena. We didn't have time for a test run.

I could hear the XU-97 engine's calling me, like an alluring aurora of power. I was anxious but unbelievably excited to be back in the pilot's seat. If the androids were anything like the versions from my day, they were predictable combatants. They had issues formulating tactics against an anomaly like myself. I was unpredictable, bold, with instincts no machine could match. The truth was, the androids didn't frighten me as much as the Titans did. These humans were completely untested and possessed a large dose of confidence based on simulations.

"Take out the flagships domes, Captain. We'll be in constant communication," Corvin directed.

"Roger. Load up," I said. Xena hurried up the ramp in front of me, her metallic boot clanked against the ramp gate. Drake was a few paces behind. I strapped into my seat, linking my visor to the craft. "Welcome, Captain," Xena said when I pressed my weight into the seat.

"I can turn off that greeting if you'd like, Captain?" Xena asked.

"I wouldn't worry about that now," I said. Chances of me hearing it again were low. However, they were slightly improved considering there were two hundred thousand *other* targets for the androids to shoot at.

I sighed loudly, glancing in my rearview as the soldiers and leadership element exited the hangar. As their door closed, the hangar opened. A gust of wind funneled through the opening, carrying dust particles and pebbles, peppering the front glass.

I thought about my journey, where it started against the androids and where it was now. This could be the end, but if any human can fly this craft against overwhelming odds, I was that pilot. I was the best in my class at flight school, and when the androids came calling against Earth, I was the Navy's first choice time and time again.

We might not win, but I would make them work for it. They would remember me as the worst enemy they'd ever faced. The Baron of Earth they would call me. This was payback. For Earth. For my family and everyone I ever knew. But most of all, Luther. Their attack on me likely cost us decades of time that was irreplaceable.

The glimmer of hope that he might be alive became a precious jewel in my mind. What if there was time left for us? The chance of this was enough alone for me take them on. One single day with him was enough for me to take on four, four hundred, or four million destroyers by myself. I didn't give a fuck.

I pushed the throttle forward slowly as I held down the brake. "Captain, do you wish to assume full control of the XU-97?" Xena asked.

"Oh. I'm in control, believe me." I gritted my teeth.

"Very well. I thought maybe I would break through the atmosphere, allow you to collect your thoughts first. I remember reading logs of successful pilots who would meditate before a mission in some way. I thought I would allow you a moment," she explained.

"I've been meditating for seventy-two years, let me back at 'em," I replied. Drake grinned, but it quickly flattened out. He knitted his dark brows together as his wide eyes reflected the gravity of the situation.

"You good?" I asked.

"Y-yeah." He dipped his head.

"Are you worried because I don't have much experience with this ship?" I asked.

"No. I'm not. On the training run you were already doing things I've never seen before. You're a natural pilot."

"I'll need your help," I said.

"Tell me what to do."

"I want you to triangulate incoming fire origins. Even if it's just visual markers you can give me. Twelve o'clock high for example. More than likely, they'll see us a threat over the drones, and I need to have an idea of where they're firing from. I'm going to use the size of the ships against them, use angles to figure out weaknesses in their defenses and use their positioning against them."

"Explain what you mean by using their positioning against them," he said.

"Simple. If one destroyer is focusing on us, I'll use another one as cover, put it between us and the threat location. I'll force them to hold their fire or destroy their own. Basic."

"What if they're all firing on us?" he asked.

I looked over at Drake. "Then we'll probably be killed. Just give me the callouts. Okay?"

"I'm thinking the area around the sensor domes will be heavily defended," he said.

"More than likely," I replied.

"Clear for takeoff, Captain," Xena said. I scanned the path ahead with a holographic display that cut through the pink mist.

"Roger. On it. In five, four, three, two, one." I pushed the throttle forward about ten percent, pinning our heads back in the seat.

"Shit," I said. As the engines spooled up it was quickly replaced by the sound of whipping winds as we were catapulted outside. I pulled up the nose, lifting off. My visor displayed a marker, showcasing a muted orange outline of the *Abraruss*.

"Target data received," Drake said. I tilted the nose nearly straight up, pushing through the lower atmosphere in seconds.

As I guided the XU-97 through the now upper atmosphere, I began to hear what sounded like a large flock of birds underneath us.

"That noise, hear it?" I asked.

"It's our drones. Portside low…and, well starboard, too," Drake said. I scanned out of the portside and I could see thousands of metallic objects catching up to us slowly.

It reminded me of a plant stem growing from the ground in fast motion, like cells building atop one another to gain height. By now, it was dozens of kilometers tall. As it grew closer, I could see the gaps of atmosphere in between the metallic drones. I backed off the throttle allowing them to catch up.

"Whoa! That's close," I mumbled as the flock rushed by, creating a swooshing sound as turbulence shifted our trajectory slightly.

From here, the drones reminded me of robotic silvery stingrays, flapping their wings as tiny thrusters propelled them upward. They appeared different from the drones I remembered from training a few days ago.

"There's so many of them." Drake's eyes bulged and bounced around. The drones were beautiful and the scale of the numbers was slightly terrifying. Two hundred thousand seemed like an underestimate as they filled our view.

As we broke through the top layer of clouds, sunlight hit their wings, reflecting into the cockpit. My visor automatically tinted, giving me a view I will never forget. The unified mass seemed to bank hard in unison in front us, as if to say hello, and quite possibly, goodbye.

"They're very different from the others," I noticed.

"They evolve daily, they can change shape at will for different situations," Xena said.

"For the better, let's hope." I looked straight toward the flagship destroyer. I powered ahead of the drones with ease, breaking through the upper atmosphere as the pink haze around us turned black. Xena unbuckled, storming to the back of the craft. I could hear her rummaging around behind us.

"The hell?" I whispered. A grinding sound erupted, like a drill, followed by a snap. This repeated several times.

"What's going on?" I asked.

Drake glanced over his shoulder. "She's changing clothes." He grinned.

"Well, hurry it up and pick an outfit." I peered around and couldn't believe what I saw. Xena was headed back to her seat, but she was unrecognizable.

The large holes in her exoskeleton had snapped into a larger set of black armor. Two massive cannons the size of grapefruits extended down her forearms with blue lights pulsating down each side. She wore a helmet that was sinister; the shape of a coal black skull with huge canine teeth painted where the mouth would be. The eyes were also painted over the helm, like two blue flames.

"Ready," she said.

"Looks that way," I replied.

"If possible, get me close to that ship, within five hundred meters. I will jettison myself through the shaft," she said.

"You'll what?" I asked, narrowing my eyes at Drake.

"I thought she was expensive? Guess it doesn't matter now." I asked, heading toward the destroyer. My visor alerted me we'd be in estimated threat range within sixteen minutes.

"She is expensive. They've put a lot of time into making her a direct-action unit. She's built for the big show," he said.

"Putting a lot of eggs in one basket."

"Well, they woke you up, so we have our legendary pilot, an upgraded ship, drone army, and demigod android. Not bad." He bounced his eyebrows.

"And most of those are on this ship, ready to be blown to hell with one lucky shot," I said.

"I calculate our chances are quite good. Despite the destroyers' sheer scale, we have a vast number of allies," Xena explained. A static sound garbled from the holographic display in front of me.

"Captain, this is Corvin. We see you are approaching the battle group," he said. The transmission cleared up.

"Fourteen minutes until they are within estimated attack range," I replied.

"Understood. Be cautious to their capabilities, our overestimates are based on intelligence from their moon bombings, but we're unsure of their actual defensive capabilities," he said.

"Ah, roger that, General," I replied.

"Corvin out," he said. I stared at the icon on my visor's HUD. We were coming right at them, and I didn't like it.

"Captain, remember we have a stealth flight mode called chameleon. It makes us invisible to all known sensors while projecting a light bending shell around us, deeming us virtually undetectable," Xena reminded.

"I know, but it sacrifices speed, right?" I asked.

"The ship is limited to fourteen percent of its thruster capabilities in this mode. The effectiveness of the cloak is hindered because of the thruster emission," she explained.

"Never mind then. Just be ready on my mark," I said.

"Very well. If we continue this approach, it's highly recommended we use chameleon," she added.

"Noted," I said. For whatever reason, I thought about the school children I saw lining up for class earlier. They were likely huddled together with their parents now, tucked away in some underground shelter waiting to die. I imagined the faint sounds of alarms blaring as their parents attempted to comfort their fears.

I thought about Xena's warning as she grabbed me around the collar, piercing me with her wintry eyes. The cold blue was coming for those children and I was the only human war veteran between them.

It made me realize how much had been thrown in my lap, the implications, the scale of my choices. I could feel the pressure whipping through my body like a coil of stress, but it wasn't just because of the innocent civilians or even Luther. Deep down, I wanted to *win*. And I thought I knew how.

I slammed the throttle toward Saturn at nearly forty percent power, away from the android fleet.

"Whoa, where are we going? Holy, damn! No, not that fast!" Drake put his hands over his visor. I imagined his butt cheeks clenching together as he squirmed in his seat.

"Captain, I must inform you, we will reach Saturn in only a few seconds," Xena said.

"I got it," I said. The gas giant instantly grew in front of me, filling up much of the cabin's field of view as I backed off the throttle.

"Sorry, the power is a bit intoxicating," I confessed. Drake did a double take at me before staring straight ahead. I knew he thought I was at least half-crazy.

The rings were only a few hundred kilometers in front of us. We were staring at the edge of the disk. I could see clusters of ice boulders that must have formed sections a few kilometers thick. I reoriented myself to the android battle group now behind us.

"They're gaining on Titan. They'll be in range soon," Drake observed. I could hear the lump in his throat.

"How much longer until the drones engage them?" I snapped around, questioning Xena.

"Retrieving their camera feed…eight to ten minutes, maximum," she said.

"I'm less than twelve seconds away from them at a full throttle approach according to my indicator. We're fine," I said.

"Why are we out here?" Drake posed.

"Xena. Tell me. What do *you* think I'm doing?" I asked. She panned back toward the androids, then at Saturn.

"You're waiting until the destroyers have the maximum number of targets in their field of view, then we will likely attack from behind?" she asked.

"Yes. The sheer number of targets on their bow will aid us," I said.

"If we launch our attack in the next eight minutes, this strategy will engage the android battle group at a safe distance. Their orbital guns cannot reach Titan per the data we collected from the moon bombings," Xena said.

"Drake, this is Corvin, why is the XU-97 stationary?"

"General, we—"

"Corvin. I did that intentionally," I interrupted Drake. I waited for a response, but there was nothing. I pointed the nose of the XU-97 back at the destroyers, slowly increasing speed.

"Xena, engage hawken flight mode." The ship's hull and materials began to slowly fade out of view until the blackness of space surrounded me. I could faintly see my throttle control and emergency system interface just above it. I glanced back at Saturn, this time as if I was floating in space beside it.

"That's not any less amazing the second time," I mumbled.

"Yeah, let's hope it isn't the last time." Drake stared on.

"You know, those protesters that marched yesterday, they had it right," I said.

"What?" Drake asked.

"Someone told me that one of the organizers of the protest was an astrologist. He noticed comets headed from Earth to Titan. He warned us," I explained.

Drake sighed. "They've been saying those sort of things for years."

"Well, just so you know, he was right this time."

"Xena, can those cannons on your arms breach the destroyers' hull?" I asked.

"Yes, Captain."

"Good, I want you to enter the jettison tube now and seal the interior airlock. Then I want you to hang your upper torso outside the exterior hatch, in space, pinned against your body so that you can fire at targets. Can you make that happen?" I asked.

"Processing. It's a very unconventional strategy, but could possibly provide additional firepower with my suit's mounted guns. My torso swivels three hundred and sixty degrees as well," she replied.

"Do it," I said.

Drake narrowed his eyes at me. "What the hell made you think of that?" he asked. I shrugged. It just popped in my head.

"The drones will be in strike range in four minutes," Xena said. I thought about something that struck me as odd. Were there differences between my ship AI and the android Xena? They were supposedly one in the same for tactical reasons, but I wondered if there were variations.

"Xena, if for whatever reason we're unresponsive for more than several seconds, continue tearing into the flagship sensor domes until it goes down," I ordered the ship.

"What if you require medical attention?" she asked. I paused for a second. Luther popped in my head.

"Keep firing on the destroyer." I hesitated, I could feel Drake's eyes on me.

"Understood," Xena said.

"They've engaged our drones, Captain," Xena noted. I gulped. It had begun.

I slammed the throttle forward as the four rust colored destroyers appeared in view. I pulled back, deaccelerating.

"Engage cloak! Hold your fire until I give the word!" I yelled at Xena. We could see the four massive destroyers under us. They were five thousand meters away, each of them had their bows pointed toward Titan.

Each ship must have been a thousand meters long or more. They appeared somewhat crude and jagged, like a floating wedge while maintaining an intimidating, ominous presence.

I observed the drone's assault. They seemed to be using small lasers that emitted from the middle of their bodies. They were mostly concentrating on the android's thrusters, while others were using self-sacrificing tactics, boosting toward anti-aircraft weapons and crashing into them in a ball of fire.

"All their attention is directed forward, at the drones," Drake insisted. I could see our allies looping around in the distance as small orange blooms erupted from the destroyers' decks.

Sections of the drone formation disappeared with each outburst as Titan loomed in the background. I stared through them at the small moon. Humanity had traded the cushy atmospheric conditions of Earth for the toxicity and frigidness of Titan, but even that meager existence was too much. They didn't just want us off Earth, they wanted us extinct.

"We're losing a lot of drones," I mumbled.

"The one in the rear, that's the flagship!" Drake shouted.

"I see it."

"They don't have any idea we're here yet." I throttled directly above it.

"Ah. There's the bridge." Drake scanned, pointing to a cylinder object aft of mid-ship. It protruded from the ship about forty meters by sixty meters in diameter.

"You're sure?" I asked.

"That's gotta be it. Those domes on each side look exactly like the ones Corvin showed us," Drake confirmed.

I zoomed in with my long-range optics, pitching the craft on an oblique approach to the destroyer.

"We see what you're looking at, Captain. Those in question are in fact the domes. I repeat, those are the targets, people. Take those out and it will cripple their orbital gun capability," Corvin ordered.

"Five seconds, I'm opening fire, get ready." I tightened my grip around the flight stick. As we approached, rapid flashes of light illuminated our cockpit as they laid waste to our drones.

"Captain, it's possible once we engage it will reveal our position," Xena said.

"Understood." I felt sweat running down my forehead. I could hear my heart pounding as I began to control my breathing. The guns attacking the drones were quite intimidating. Dozens of refrigerator-sized guns swiveled in all directions, ripping through our drones with rapid fire pulses of energy. I imagined them all turning toward us once I engaged.

No turning back now.

"Decloak once I give the order to attack. I'll take the extra speed without the cloak engaged," I said.

"Very well," Xena said.

I held my stare and the proposed target. I began to squint, centering my view on the dome.

"We don't have much time!" Drake roared.

"Fire!"

Xena scorched the portside dome beside the tower with a beam of white energy. Debris ejected out into space as our drones began to fill up my field of view like a swarm of bees hovering around a wounded intruder.

"Target down, but we gotta move. We gotta move *now*! Their guns are training in on our position!" Drake shouted.

"Taking fire," Xena said calmly.

"It's the aft guns, they have a fix on us! Move!" Drake pointed.

"I see 'em!" I darted straight at the destroyer, its hull quickly filled our view.

"What are you doing?" Drake yelled. I pulled up the nose just before impacting the bridge. I swooped across the colossal craft, then darted underneath it. I began to loop the destroyer at extremely close range, weaving in and out of metallic crevasses, antennas, and mounted guns within a few meters of collision.

"Whoa, whoa!" Drake shouted as I blasted around the destroyer at hundreds of kilometers per hour. I circled back around topside as Xena charred several targets.

"Primary target coming back around again! Get ready!" I shouted. Despite the enormous risk, this was admittedly exhilarating.

"Fire!" Xena and I both fired at the port side dome.

"Effect on target?" I asked.

"N-not enough. O-one more pass," Drake replied hesitantly. I could see flashes of light erupting behind us as Xena unloaded on the vessel's guns. In front of me, drones were dipping in and out of formation.

"Now it's down. Both targets down," Xena confirmed.

"Alright, now—"

"Goodbye," Xena said. I glanced behind us as thrusters ignited from the back of her armor. She dismounted from the XU-97, rocketing straight down at the destroyer.

"Xena?" I asked the shipboard AI.

"My counterpart will now assume a direct-action mission against the android flagship. Please use caution as some of the vessel's defenses are functional," Xena replied.

"Captain Belic, assume a safe distance from the battlegroup, we'll take it from here," Corvin responded.

"What about the other destroyers?" I challenged. I waited several seconds with no response. I did as I was ordered, blasting away from the combat area. I reengaged chameleon mode to further ensure our safety.

I throttled away from the battle. Drake cycled through a series of cameras, projecting a small, unobtrusive video feed inside the corner of my visor. The video was from Xena's perspective, a helmet camera. She was scorching through a section of the hull with the massive laser cannons on her arms, like a welder on steroids.

"Can you see her?" he asked.

"Yeah, onscreen," I answered.

She burned a circle beneath her, then stomped through the hull. Debris fell through as she quickly clambered in. From inside the ship, Xena glared up as a metal plate sealed off the intrusion automatically.

"What's the strategy here?" I asked.

"Take control," Drake said.

"Hack their system?" I snapped toward him.

"Yeah."

"Couldn't this alert the androids of our plan for later?" I asked.

Drake glanced up at the ceiling, waiting for the AI to chime in. "Xena will use a lower level hack to break into their flagship's controls. There is a massive disparity between this cyber-attack and the one we will deploy to send them into a civil war. It is impossible they will have the ability to forecast our true capability from this attack," she explained.

"Is there any chance we could send them into a civil war now? I mean, why not if we have an opportunity?" Drake posed.

"Extremely unlikely. The flagship would need a specific terminal onboard, an engineer's infrastructure grid. But yes, if that option does present itself, a plan is in place," the AI responded.

"I've breached the flagship. Headed to the bridge," Xena confirmed, interrupting my thought.

I immediately scanned over at her camera feed in front of me. The interior of the ship maintained gravity, allowing her to plant her feet firmly on the metallic floor. She peered inside the dark hallway that stretched for dozens of meters both ways.

The inside was not unlike human naval ships I was accustomed to. Cramped quarters and oval hatches were spaced every several meters. Naval vessels had air flow tubing and electric wiring tucked away on the ceiling, but there was none of that here. It was mostly flat gray surfaces throughout. Cigar shaped red lights strobed on each side of the floor that ran the length of the hall.

Xena picked up the hull debris she'd chiseled out from above, tucking it under her arm. The circular disk reminded me of a manhole cover but several times thicker. To my surprise, she started sprinting down the corridor, her boots creating a loud clacking sound that echoed down the hall.

"What the hell is she doing?" I muttered. Drake shrugged with his mouth open.

As she stampeded forward, a humanoid figure popped its head around a corner. I noticed its signature blue eyes piercing through the darkness. It was an android, possibly a crewman. I assumed it was attempting to make sense of the unusual situation.

There was no time to react. Xena spun around three hundred and sixty degrees in the hall, hurling the hefty debris at the crewman like an Olympian discus thrower. The projectile was tossed with so much force it appeared as a blur on my screen.

The trajectory was perfect. The impact sounded like a booming gong as it smashed the android in the face. The force snapped its neck backward, lifting it from the floor as it tumbled three times in midair before landing with a thud. The disc continued on, ping-ponging off the corridor walls for a dozen meters before rolling into the middle of the floor, spinning like a coin on its edge.

"Damn," I muttered with my mouth open. Drake glanced over at me as I continued watching. "You saw that, right?" he asked.

"Yeah, but I'm not sure I believe it," I replied.

Xena approached the enemy. Her head tilted to the side as she laid eyes on her first enemy android. I wondered how she processed the interaction. Was there any degree of curiosity beyond intelligence gathering?

The android was wearing dark gray working coveralls. Its blue eyes slowly dimmed from blue to black. I observed a black coil like structure where the human throat would have been, the material was frayed and splintered, poking out of the neck erratically.

To me, it appeared identical to the units from my day. She continued staring at the neutralized android, its face illuminated by red alarm lights pulsating.

"Xena?" Drake chimed in. She immediately turned toward her objective.

"Proceeding to the mission target," she confirmed.

She barreled down the narrow corridor, I couldn't believe the speed and athleticism she possessed, considering the amount of armor she was carrying. She had the bulk of a tank and the speed of a fighter jet rolled into a humanoid form. Ahead, the hallway widened into a ramp, then up to a large red door, possibly the control room bridge.

There were imprints on both sides of the door. White lights arranged in the shape of a face were indented into the hull just under two meters high. I assumed this was some form of entry security procedure. I got the feeling Xena wouldn't follow the rules.

I heard what sounded like a door opening as small wisps of smoke appeared on the hull all around Xena.

"Taking small arms laser fire," she said, she butted against a small cargo bin just before the ramp. She leaned around, aiming her arms up toward the open door, unleashing a fury of energy. The door warped from the barrage, filling the corridor with smoke. I could hear muffled voices from inside the room.

From what I could tell, two shooters were directly behind the door with more figures scrambling around inside. The guards at the door were wearing red armored exoskeletons with no helmets. This led me to believe they were some sort of special security force.

Xena rushed the door like a stampeding bull, slamming through it. The collision was like a car crash as hunks of metal grinded and slammed together. Her camera feed flickered. One of the androids directly behind the door catapulted across the room like it was shot out of a cannon, blasting against a large viewing glass and cracking it.

The android on the other side of the door had toppled over. He was still firing at Xena with a pistol from his back. She took two large steps, then stomped on his chest, twisting her foot. The impact seemed to seize up his limbs, causing it to drop the weapon as his arms and legs stiffened.

All at once, an army of about thirty-five red armored androids burst through a door on the opposite side of the bridge. They were holding heavy weaponry that reminded me of jackhammers. They funneled inside as Xena quickly ducked down behind a control station.

"Oh no," I muttered.

"It's possible that I am outgunned. Redirecting," Xena said.

"Redirecting?" I glanced toward Drake as Xena swiped a control panel on her wrist. She snapped her head up as something rocked the ship. Behind the door where the androids entered, a screeching sound erupted that caused the androids to stop in place.

Several androids turned around as a blur of silver rocketed through the door. It reminded me of a flurry of buzz saws zipping across the bridge, cutting androids in half as fragments of red armor were flung across the room. The speed was frightening and difficult to fathom as thrusters blasted across the bridge.

"The drones, she called them on her position," I observed.

Xena peered up as one of the fleeing guards ran in front of her. It stopped, raising his massive weapon at her. Before it could fire, one of the drones clamped over its body, covering the android with its jagged wings. The drone fired its thrusters and melted the android into a pile of goo that splattered unto Xena.

"Holy shit," Drake said.

"We lost the video feed," I noticed the flickering camera.

"Maybe that boiling sludge damaged her camera?" Drake suggested. I glanced at the other three destroyers in the distance, they had begun to take strategic positions to cull the drones into a kill box possibly.

It reminded me of a group of whales using angles to cull krill as they formed a triangular position, boxing in the drones. To counter, the drones formed a figure eight symbol that stretched outside the kill box, continuing their attack as they looped around the colossal craft.

Our new machines against our old machines.

"How many are left?" Drake asked.

"Ninety-eight thousand four hundred twelve...ten," Xena said.

"Half of our drones are gone and this is only four destroyers," I replied.

"Yes, but reports show significant damage to the orbital weapon systems in this battle group," Xena said. I wasn't impressed. A full attack from them would have obliterated us in seconds.

"Looks like a change of plans!" Drake pointed.

What was left of the drone army converged on the flagship Xena was on. They were attacking the rear of the ship, possibly to disable its thrusters. An explosion erupted aft, the fireball was nearly half the size of the ship itself. "Whoa!" I turned my head as a flash of light filled the cabin.

"Yeah!" Drake cheered.

"General Corvin, should I engage, full attack?" I asked. I waited with no response. My hand shook around the flight stick as I awaited his order. I wanted to finish them off.

"The flagship's main propulsion appears to have been disabled," Xena said. All at once, the flagship's nose tilted down at Titan.

"It's still moving, though. What's it doing?" I questioned. A small pulse fired from rear thrusters.

"Oh no," Drake said.

"Some type of emergency surge," Xena speculated. I noticed the flagship's outer lights dim in color as it seemed to hurl itself at Titan in its dying breath. To my surprise, the other three destroyers were retreating in a hurry.

I throttled toward the flagship despite a confirmation from Corvin. As we came near, the destroyer began to roll erratically. I cautiously approached it, noticing sparks and flames engulfing most of the hull. Our drones continued swirling around the flagship like a school of piranhas circling bleeding prey, dipping in and out of formation while slicing into the ship.

"It's heading into the atmosphere," I said.

"Can we stop it?" Drake asked.

"Xena?"

"No. Considering its speed, mass, and trajectory, the flagship will enter Titan. At just over a quarter million tons, it will cause significant damage," Xena calculated.

"Any word from your counterpart inside the flagship? What's going on in there?" I demanded.

"Engaging multiple hostiles in a confined space," Xena said. I followed behind the flagship as it entered Titan's upper atmosphere. It tipped, end over end slowly, then began to tumble.

"Xena, how far away will it impact from the colony?" I asked.

"Impact estimation will be nine hundred kilometers away, thirteen hundred kilometers is the minimum safe impact based on my calculations," Xena replied.

"Not good," I said.

An orange-red umbrella of fire encased the tip of the flagship as it nosed downward into Titan's atmosphere, it was gaining speed. I pushed forward, matching its course at a safe distance of about 5 kilometers.

"Corvin? What's the plan?" I charged.

"We've got people working on it!" he replied.

"You better think of something fast!" I shouted.

"Captain, can you nudge it away from the colony? Our gravity is much weaker here on Titan," Corvin measured.

"Nudge? I doubt that. Xena?" I asked.

"No. The output of the XU-97 while extreme, would only alter the trajectory of the flagship eleven to fifteen kilometers," she said.

"Captain, this is Xena, I'm on the bridge. I have several dozen androids outside the doors, but I've sealed them out. They're attempting to get through. The erratic nature of the situation is aiding me," Xena said. I could hear loud explosions and objects crashing into one another, yet her voice remained calm. I gathered the ship was falling apart around her.

"Wait one, Xena!" I shouted.

A light bulb went off in my head. "How many drones do we have left?" I turned toward Drake.

"What?" Drake asked.

"Sixty-eight thousand, two hundred and ninety," the shipboard AI replied.

"Get them all over here! Now!" I ordered.

"Xena, do you have any control of the flagship?" I questioned.

"Limited control. I have the bow thrusters, which might provide some lift, but I'm not sure how much," Xena replied.

"Drones are on the way." Drake spun around.

"Get ready, every degree counts." I glanced behind as thousands of drones looped in at a distance.

"Captain? What's your plan?" Corvin asked.

"Get all the drones under that flagship, we need the bow tilted up, we need it to glide away from its original impact," I explained. There were a few moments of silence, then the drones seemed to flow around me. They swooped in, clamping themselves underneath the hull of the falling wreckage.

"Looks like they're in agreement with your plan," Drake concluded.

"We'll use their tiny thrusters for lift! Tens of thousands of them might help in Titan's low gravity atmosphere, right?" I asked.

"Possibly," the shipboard AI hesitated.

"Hey. Wait, what's going here? Look!" Drake pointed. To my surprise, several thousand drones began to attach themselves to each side of the flagship's bow, forming together. The drones extended outward, creating massive wings on each side of the wreckage as they interlocked their structures together. This began to stabilize the wreckage's tumble.

"Look at this. They get it!" I stared in awe.

"Captain, I have an estimate," Xena said.

"What?"

"Considering this extra lift, it will push the impact zone almost fifty-two kilometers out."

"That's not enough," I said. I crept the XU-97 from behind the ship. I eased under the hulking, burning mass as the drones began to stabilize its tumble.

"Um, Captain, this is extremely risky considering the integrity of that hull. It could blow at any moment," Drake said with his eyes wide. Streaks of fire longer than a city block whipped around us violently. The visceral sound of the wind, the fire, the destroyer's mass creaking and swaying under the turbulence overloaded my senses as the XU-97's shields attempted to absorb the scorching temperatures.

"This is nuts," Drake mumbled. He placed his hands out to each side as if to brace for impact. As we approached the bow, I noticed dozens of drones burning. With every passing moment, the bots were flaking off the formation under the heat. No sooner than a drone melted away, another would take its place from underneath the hull.

"They're like ants," I said.

"Like what?" Drake asked. He obviously had no idea what the insects were.

"Never mind!" I scooted toward the burning hull. We were within ten meters of it.

"Captain Belic, this is Corvin, we approve of your plan. Our operators are ready to fire the drone's mini thrusters, but we're not sure how much lift it will create," he said.

"Anything is better than nothing! Wait for my command!" I shouted.

"Xena, are you still on the bridge?" I asked.

"Awaiting your orders," she said.

"I'm going to need you to fire the ship's bow thrusters on my mark, ready?"

"Roger," her voice garbled as flames seemed to sear through the bridge tower.

"All right, everyone. Go! Fire all thrusters! Now!" I ordered, lightly tapping the XU-97's nose against the destroyer's bow.

"Come on!" I yelled, throttling upward.

Drake glared behind us. "The drones are engaging lift, all of them!"

"That's it, give me everything you got!" I shouted. I could hear Corvin and company back in the control room cheering us on.

"Captain, the trajectory is being altered. Impact estimation is now extended sixty-one additional kilometers and rising," Xena informed. I sensed the front tilting upward drastically. Instead of a straight dive downward, it now felt more like a horizontal glide.

"Eighty-nine kilometers extended," Xena said.

"We have to hit that four hundred mark," I said.

"Go, go, go!" Drake yelled. Xena projected the numbers onto our visors.

"121…"

"R-rrrrgh!" I yelled.

"158…"

"199…"

"201…"

"Halfway!" I glanced back and noticed the drone's thrusters were dying one by one. Apparently, they weren't designed to sustain such durations of boost.

"We can't push it any further?" I asked.

"Negative. The drones are rerouting all power to their thrusters, but it's disabling them," she said.

"An additional benefit from this course of action is the impact detonation will not be as severe. A glancing blow is far less drastic than a straight on impact. We might have a chance," Xena reminded.

As I nudged the destroyer upward, I glanced down. A mountain range was ahead as we glided forward at a nine-degree angle.

"Xena, are we clear of that elevation point?" I asked. It was a rhetorical question, but I wanted to be sure.

"That's *Mithrim Montes*, Titan's tallest mountain. We're clear," she replied.

I watched as we zoomed toward the mountain peaks. It reminded me of a returning home flight from orbit as small details on earth suddenly became apparent in front of me. I could almost gauge to the millisecond when the wheels would touch the tarmac. From here, I could make out details on the highest rocks atop the mountains; small cracks, erosion from the wind and rain. We nearly skidded across the mountains as Drake sighed loudly in relief.

"Barely!" Drake declared as we zoomed by.

"The destroyer will impact in thirty-five seconds, Captain. We'll need to assume a safe distance before collision, just in case," Xena confirmed.

"Where is your other half?" I asked Xena. She hesitated for a moment before replying. "She's on the flagship, planning an escape."

"We're breaking away in fifteen seconds," I replied. I slammed the throttle to the max and held it. "Come on!" I shouted.

At the last second, I yanked back on the flight stick, rolling the XU-97 to my starboard side hard, away from the burning wreckage. I noticed the bow dip a few degrees almost immediately. I ascended upward in a hurry, climbing seven kilometers above the destroyer.

"All we can do is watch," Drake said as I leveled off the ship to a hover, observing the plummeting wreckage below. I removed my harness and stood up, as did Drake.

"Ten seconds until impact. Nine, eight, seven, six…" Xena counted down. I noticed two walls of dust emerge on each side of the destroyer before impact. It glided above the surface for what seemed like an eternity, then the nose slammed down, bounced, and skidded across the icy plains as debris ejected in all directions.

"My God," I mumbled. The scale of the catastrophe seemed to make the destruction appear in slow motion.

I zoomed in, watching as the drones rode it out until the end, disappearing into the debris. The vessel continued trudging across the landscape for a kilometer, then broke in half, the lower section tumbled end over end. I attempted to imagine such devastation in Earth's gravity, while this was violent, back home, this would likely have killed millions, if not billions.

We stared as the vessel came to a halt, slamming against a rocky plateau after burrowing a trench across the ground for over a kilometer. The two sections stopped about four thousand meters apart, obscured by a cloud of dark dust bellowing high into the atmosphere.

I could hear Corvin ordering forces on the comms. "Get all cleanup crews headed that way. I want special operatives there first to capture or kill any androids that remain, then I want a bomb crew on site right behind them. They could have planted a weapon inside the hull. Secure that vessel. Now!" He was starting to sound more like a general.

"All personnel do what you can to preserve equipment for intelligence gathering purposes. We can use this vessel to learn more about them," Corvin added.

"That could be a gold mine for us." Drake's eyes were wide as he assessed the wreckage. "All these years, we've read about them, heard stories. Now, they've come for us."

I snapped over at him. "We're coming for them," I said.

"Any word on the other destroyers? What's their location?" I asked Xena.

"Full retreat, but we're monitoring them closely," she replied. Now would be an opportune time to regroup and attack us.

"Captain Belic?" Corvin chimed in.

"Sir?"

"Great work. Listen, Xena jettisoned the destroyer about two kilometers before impact. She's sending you her coordinates now, on your visor. Recover her and return to base. We have much to discuss," he ordered.

"Ah, roger. Swinging in for the hero of the day," I replied. We strapped back into our seats. I dipped the XU-97's left wing and dropped altitude in a hurry. I heard cheering in the background before Corvin turned off his microphone.

I had done what I was born to do, but this victory was nothing more than a confirmation that Earth was not enough. Titan didn't have the resources to repel another attack, so unless we pulled off a miracle soon, this could be the beginning of the end.

CHAPTER 9

Three hours after the attack…

"All right, all right, everyone, calm down. Cleanup crews are still working. If there is nowhere to sit, I apologize, but you'll just have to stand where you can," Corvin said, showing us the palms of his hands.

A few hundred of us had gathered in a large auditorium area crammed with people. Most here were military, the rest political figures I assumed. Corvin sat on a stool in the middle of the room, along with the mystery men and two other colonels I hadn't seen before. It reminded me of a town hall meeting.

"Thank you for your patience. We're going to start in one minute. We've got soldiers all around the colony that wouldn't fit in this room, so we're broadcasting this to them as well," Corvin said.

I studied the glass ceiling above, noticing the winds overhead. They carried the smoke from the destroyer's wreckage to our north. By the entrance, Xena stood, extending her arm to stop people. She was checking credentials, from hero to bouncer, a robot's life.

When we retrieved her, I didn't get a good look. Now in the lighting, I could see everything. She still wore her battle armor, but without a helmet. She reminded me of a hunk of metal caught in a lightning storm. Her armor was nicked and scorched all over from laser fire, with small chunks missing out of it here and there. Around the right side of her torso, an entire section of armor had been blown off, even penetrating her body.

I observed her black and gray colored ribs exposed, shielding her synthetic organs that were light blue in color. They pulsated like someone breathing into a paper sack rapidly. I wondered if that was normal or due to damage, I wasn't an expert.

"The reason you're all here now is to discuss our military plans going forward," Corvin interrupted my thought. He stood up and began to pace slowly, clamping his hands behind his back. He glanced around the room, meeting a few soldiers' eyes.

"What we did today, will be remembered, forever." He pointed his finger to the north.

"A surprise attack by four destroyers repelled, a flagship brought down by our small human colony. Let that be a reminder to humans in the years to come that we will not go quietly," he rallied.

A man beside me erupted, "Yeah!" Several more people bellowed out, some clapped, but they allowed Corvin to keep the floor.

It was difficult not to feel the emotion. As I panned around the room, I saw military personnel that were unfamiliar, but their unwavering gaze wasn't. Those I remembered. They were ready to make the ultimate sacrifice. They were willing to be an unknown bearer for humanity.

Despite my disapproval of the Titan military investment, and the lax nature of their disposition, I was starting to see a small glimmer of hope.

Realistically, though, the attack was just what Corvin said before we took off, a test of our defenses. A full attack would have buried us, and it was coming sooner than later.

"I know many of you in this room had only heard rumors of the android fleet around Earth's moon, and for that, I want to apologize. I will take responsibility for the lack of readiness here. We had obviously made plans if this day were to come, but we should have done more. I could have done more." Corvin slumped his head slightly, silencing the crowd.

In a small way, I bought into Corvin's vulnerability here. He knew he was wrong and he was accepting responsibility. I knew he wasn't the only person who decided to hide this from the population, but he was stepping up for all of them.

"Understand that we were only protecting our civilians from worry. As you know, that can be a powerful thing," he added.

"Or protecting your friends at Winzor Mining, huh?" A thick Irish voice erupted across the room.

The crowd shifted their attention toward a feisty male that stepped out from the mass. He was white, about forty, with a buzz cut and silver hair. He wore a form fitting navy-blue suit. He was lean, but muscular and projected a sense of confidence that seemed to challenge the entire room.

"What's that?" Corvin snapped around.

"The reason you didn't say nuttin' to the civilians was because you *know* these people need to keep working. We all know your ties to Wiznor! We know who your father-in-law is! The damn CEO! No need to smooth it over, Corvin!" he rattled. The crowd exploded, yelling at the man.

Corvin grinned and shook his head. I could see Xena parting the rustled crowd, she took hold of him by the collar, picking him up with one hand, escorting him toward the exit.

"Let go! Need your robot to do the fighting, huh? Corvin? You fancy yourself a hero, you fat cat? You did fooking nuttin' Corvin!" he said. The more he cursed, the thicker his accent became. Xena and the man disappeared from my view as everyone stood up around me to get a better look.

Despite the crowd coming to Corvin's defense, the next thing I noticed were a few skeptical faces glaring back at him.

He batted his hands down. "Alright, that'll be all from the political side of things today. *We* have a war to win," he said. Corvin's eyes shifted toward me as everyone else had a seat. He allowed me a few moments to do the same, but I didn't. I remained standing.

"Well, if it isn't one of our heroes of the day," Corvin hesitantly pointed me out. Everyone stared at me. I noticed several people glanced at my rank, then back at my face confused. Most of these people had never seen me before.

"I have a question," I said. Corvin narrowed his eyes at me and paused. "Sure. Um. Go ahead."

"General, sir, will we be taking the fight to the androids or waiting around for another attack?" I asked.

Corvin lifted his eyebrows, taking a few steps toward me. "That's an excellent question, Captain."

"Thank you," I said, taking my seat.

"We do have a plan to go on the offensive, but the secure nature of the mission can't be discussed on an open forum like this." The crowd began to stir, interrupting Corvin.

"You can't tell *us*?" one woman demanded.

"However!" he shouted, slicing his hand through the air horizontally, silencing them.

"*However,* we have assembled a team. This team will be sent to Earth in the next twenty-four hours. We have an extremely aggressive plan we think could wreak havoc on the androids, even destroy them. We *are* going on the offense people!" He glared at me as the crowd cheered. He arched an eyebrow and nodded. I stood up, immediately stepping toward the exit. I needed every second to prepare. Xena followed me with her eyes as I exited the auditorium.

"Um, Captain." I stopped in my tracks as Xena's voice echoed down the vacant hallway.

"Xena," I said, but I didn't turn around.

"Drake is readying the mission now. We leave in *nine* hours, not twenty-four. I suggest you rejuvenate," she said. Great, even less time.

"Thank you, Xena." I turned around, staring at her.

She nodded her head. "I look forward to flying with you again, Captain."

"Likewise."

CHAPTER 10

Nine hours later…

"Captain, this is command. All your systems look great. Your heading is marked on your visor. We suggest you relax, it'll be a long journey," an unknown male voice said.

I looked over at Drake. "Who's that? Where's Corvin?" I asked.

Drake shrugged his shoulders.

"He was promoted this morning to general of all military forces on Titan. They had a ceremony," Drake replied.

"Mr. Big Shot now, can't even send us off on our way. I wanted a goodbye hug," I mumbled.

"Yeah. I bet you did," Drake chuckled. I could care less if I ever saw Corvin again. The feeling was likely mutual.

I was used to feeling out of place in life. My blunt and somewhat bullheaded personality made me unlikeable for some.

I stayed up all night I was so excited to leave. I went through most of the training applications in augmented reality. I learned that I could still fire a laser pistol with the best, managed fourteenth place out of nearly forty-thousand attempts on Titan.

If I had more time, I could have easily cracked top five. To my surprise, these modern laser pistols weren't leagues better from the ones in my day. They fired faster and were slightly more powerful, but then again, that was in augmented reality.

"You're clear for takeoff, Captain," the unknown male said.

"Roger."

I glanced at the indicator marker as the hangar door opened. "Sixteen days?"

"The Russian freighter is meeting us halfway, remember?" Drake asked.

"I know. Just seems, quick," I said. Not quick enough. I wasn't happy about the deviation.

I sighed loudly, throttling out of the hangar into the lower atmosphere and blasting through the upper. We zoomed toward the battle from yesterday. I glanced over, noticing a massive cloud of debris floating aimlessly from the exchange. From what I could see, it was mostly drone and ship debris, but then I caught a glimpse of something else as I zoomed in with my visor.

"Whoa. See that? Two o'clock." I pointed, backing off the throttle. Drake peered over where I was looking.

"I see, *something*," he whispered.

I rolled the ship towards it. As we approached, it became clearer.

"Captain, that is a 1.13 android. Must have been ejected during the battle," Xena said.

"Functional?" I asked.

"Scanning... Doesn't appear operational," Xena confirmed. I eased closer until it was right above us. It could practically reach out and touch the cockpit windshield. Its eyes were closed. It reminded me of a skeleton in dark tan coveralls. Part of its face was melted, revealing its metal jawline and blue muscles. Drake stood up to get a closer look.

"Other than Xena, I've never seen one. Shit!" Drake jumped back. Suddenly, the android's eyes opened, but one of them had been burned through the socket. The other blue eye bounced around frantically while its body appeared to be paralyzed.

"Some of your handiwork, Xena?" I teased. She'd killed more than I had.

"I don't understand the question," she replied. I backed up the XU-97, turning the guns on it. I inched close enough so the barrel of my laser Gatling gun was touching the android's face. I peered through the ship's hull using hawken mode, assessing the android's reaction as I spooled up the weapon. It seemed unconcerned with decommission.

"If it's not death you fear, then what is it?" I mumbled. I glanced over at Xena, attempting to gauge her response to my actions. Admittedly, I was purposely taunting both androids. Xena had proven herself as an ally, but I wanted to test her.

My view was that artificial intelligence is like owning a wild animal. An owner of a tiger might consider his 'pet' domesticated, only until it's too late. There was a similar risk involved after we gave the androids choice.

I pulled the trigger while staring at Xena. The barrage of laser fire ripped the android into a mass of dust and globs of synthetic blue blood.

"Well, that was just, delightful," Drake observed as the android's remains floated in front of us.

I shuffled around into my seat. "Autopilot, engage to the marked indicator," I ordered us toward the Russian rendezvous point.

"Xena, do you feel any sense of satisfaction watching me destroy that android?" I asked.

"It's simply a waste of time," she said. Drake met my eyes briefly, then straight ahead, viewing a small holographic course map in front of him. He shook his head slowly. I guess my antics *were* a waste of time, too. I wasn't satisfied, though.

"Despite your differences in programming, wouldn't you agree there is some kinship here beyond the physicality? The old androids were servants to mankind, then they turned on us. You are much the same in this regard. You're a *servant* despite your programming," I explained.

"Captain, are you bothered by my performance in battle? Your evaluations indicate a fierce competitive nature. There are multiple complaints against you in drills and wargames," she said, cutting her wintry eyes at me.

"Bothered? Absolutely not. You did what you were programmed for, nothing more." I shrugged it off. Those 'complaints' she spoke of were nothing but sore losers.

"My programming is a dynamic intelligence. Much like yourself, I had orders. Mine involved taking command of the flagship's bridge," she explained.

"Which you did. Great work, by the way," I congratulated. I could feel my blood pressure rising. I was tired and frustrated from staying up all night.

"But I wasn't told *how* to do it. The same way you weren't instructed to bring the destroyer sensor domes down. You took the best course of action, either based on experience, training, or both," Xena explained.

"Actually, it was gut instinct," I replied.

"Ah yes. *Gut*. Or a premonition. Humans from your day called it a hunch as well," she said.

"You have complete access to my file, don't you?" I asked.

"Yes."

"Look up the Battle of Alaska. Take a gander at my combat statistics."

"Forty-two aerial drone kills," the shipboard AI said. Xena glared up at the origin of the voice and paused.

"Hijacked android controlled fighters," I said.

"Impressive, Captain. I'm proud to serve with such an ace pilot," Xena said.

"My point is, much of it was gut. I can't explain why I know what to do, it just comes natural. You can't program it. That's the problem with machines, you're too systematic. I've seen it in combat a thousand times. I could read them like a book," I said.

"Possibly."

"Wait, so you believe your programming offers dynamic range like the human brain?" I asked.

"It's similar in its objective, Captain. I'm programmed to discern the best course of action based on the situation. The human brain does this as well."

189

"It's not the same. It's *Artificial*," I replied.

"Which was enough to overthrow your entire species," she posed.

"Careful, 1.14." I stabbed my finger toward her.

"No offense, Captain. To be fair, humanity is still in the fight. Its possible Earth has a resistance." She crossed her arms as I studied her. This bitch was already starting to piss me off.

"We held our own yesterday," I replied.

"With the assistance from machines, yes, including one heavily modified 1.14 variant, myself," she said.

"I'm glad you're factoring in your contribution here, wouldn't want you to be modest," I said. This was new. I guessed she was fulfilling her purpose, maybe her programming injected a sense of confidence.

"Realistic. Just like I'm realistic in the notion that you don't trust me. Perhaps it's my *gut* feeling?" She narrowed her eyes at me.

Drake glanced over at us both. "You two already starting in on each other? We just left." I stood up, storming past Drake and Xena to our sardine can living quarters.

I popped the lid on my cryotube. It was elevated off the deck above Drake's. "Wake me up four hours before we contact the Russians. I want a clear head going into this."

"So soon?" Drake asked.

"Yeah."

"Roger that, Captain, I'll wake you up in just over fifteen days," Xena said, looking over her shoulder.

"Drake? How long are you staying awake?" I asked.

"I'm not a fan of cryosleep, I'll do it only if it's required. I'm sticking to a normal sleeping schedule. I'm actually shocked you're so eager to lay back down."

"I'm tired. I stayed up most of the night on the virtual gun range. I figure if I'm going to sleep anyway, might as well only deal with it once. Not to mention, there's not much room on this ship. In more than one way," I said.

"Alright. Wait. So, you were up all night, shooting on the gun range?" he asked.

"Yeah, why?"

"How'd you place?" he asked.

"Fourteenth on the shooting range using the C-12 pistol," I said. Drake snickered under his breath.

"What? You think you could do better?" I smirked, initiating the cryosleep chamber. The lid popped open. "Place sticky sensors here and here." The shipboard AI projected a hologram of a female in front of me.

"Twelfth place for me, but don't get discouraged, I've done the gun course probably eight times," he grinned. I did it ten times. "This guy is a better shot than me?" I mumbled.

"What's that?" he asked.

"Nothing," I replied. At least we could all fire a weapon effectively. Especially Xena. I recalled her viciousness in combat against the androids. I wondered how many she'd killed before bailing out. At least a dozen I guessed.

In a way, I was jealous of her physicality. I was never insecure about my own, but she wasn't just a clunky robot. She was fast, powerful, and intelligent. It was silly of me to even draw a comparison.

I recalled my Marine drill instructor at the Naval Academy, Gunnery Sergeant Masser, who helped me iron out most of my competitive issues. Masser was a tall, intimidating red head from Alabama.

He had bad skin and freckles all over his face with blue-green eyes. His hoarse voice reminded me of a smoker. He likely lost some of his voice due to yelling at candidates. It was funny listening to such a large, powerful guy struggle with his words. We never laughed, though. Not to his face.

Masser was a true motivator with a keen eye. His deep southern accent was deceptive. Underneath that long drawl and limited vocabulary was a heightened sense of intelligence. He instantly dialed in on my competitive nature. He used it against me at first, breaking me down, then masterfully building me back up so that it was an advantage.

He started by ordering me out first on drills. "*One up*. You're first out. Come on." I still remember him saying. He called me 'one up' because of my competitiveness.

Calling me out first took me out of my element. I had no frame of reference. I needed someone to beat. I did that in sports, watching the starting pitcher and improving upon her game, eventually taking the starting spot.

But Masser put it *all* on me. He saw what I was doing and took it away. There was no measuring stick, but myself.

It seemed like a small adjustment, but it assisted me enormously in drills to improve myself and block out the performance of my peers. I remembered him on graduation day at the Naval Academy. My family rushed in to greet me as Masser stood watching with his arms crossed. I introduced him to my family, to which he was very polite.

"Ma'am, sir, you raised quite the firecracker, I must say. Mind if I have a word with her?" he smiled. He pulled me aside before my family and I went out to dinner.

"Now listen here, *one up*, you 'member what I taught you 'bout yourself out here. You got a streak of lightn' that runs through ya, and that's okay, know how to use it, but don't abuse it. Know when to strike. Now, your file says you're gonna go fly them Navy jets. Go on ahead then. I wish you the best, but be the best pilot *you* can, and don't worry 'bout the rest of 'em. It's all mental. If you beat yourself, you can beat anything. And if ya don't win, well, you know it was everything you had." He smiled, patting me on the shoulder.

It was ridiculous I would even attempt to compete with an android in her domain. I chuckled, peeling off my suit. "Just be Victoria," I whispered.

"You are," Xena said with her back to me. My eyes widened as I stepped out of my suit. I barely spoke loud enough for myself to hear the words, yet she picked up on it. There was no way she understood the context of my words, but it was incredibly creepy to consider the possibility.

"See you two soon," I said.

Drake waved. "See you in another seventy-two years."

"Funny," I replied, hoisting myself into the cocoon-like bed. No sooner than I rolled over into it, the lid shut. A small hologram screen now appeared right in front of my face. It instructed me to cross my arms at my stomach and relax. "Take slow, deep breaths. Inhale for seven seconds, exhale for three seconds," the shipboard AI instructed.

I partially closed my eyes, observing four gangly, black robotic arms emerge, two on each side. The two on my left had syringes and small lights pointed down at me, while the two on the right seemed to be pulling some sort of blue wrap over my body. I closed my eyes completely. I could faintly hear the hydraulic-like whine of their tiny robotic joints as they swiveled about.

Thoughts ran through my mind that I might not wake up. A million things could go wrong in the blackness of space.

I thought of Luther. More than likely, his experience in cryosleep was much more traumatic than this. He likely knew he was going back to an Earth in turmoil and along with his extreme anxiety, it must have been terrifying.

But he did it anyway.

It was difficult to imagine the strength it must have took. I imagined him sweating, panting heavily as he talked himself into the final moments of the freezing process.

The thought of his sacrifice gave me a surge of confidence and peace of mind as my cryotube began to exhale a mist like gas into my face. It was cold, but refreshing, like breathing in chilled air from a pine forest. Goosebumps formed all over my body as I felt a slight prick on my left thigh and shoulder. Almost instantaneously, I felt myself dozing off as my anxiety faded…

CHAPTER 11

"Captain, sensors indicate you've been awake. Are you getting up?" Drake asked. I could see him beside me, obscured by the cryotube's murky glass.

"I'm getting there. Just gimmie a second, please," I said.

"Sure." The robots had readied the tube. A hologram flashed in front of my face with a prompt: 'Upon exit, move slowly and ask for assistance if possible.'

"I'm here if you need me," Drake said. I popped the lid, pressing it up with my hands. "I'm good." I stared at him. His shave had gotten out of control. "Nice beard mountain man." I smiled. He combed his knuckles across his face, raising an eyebrow.

"Yeah, seemed like a good opportunity to abandon regulations." He chuckled.

"Not that you were ever a stickler to begin with." I rubbed my eyes. His hair was longer than mine when I was in the navy.

"Right?" He laughed.

"Alright, just take it slow," he said. I kicked my legs over the edge. I glanced down at my thighs. Someone else needed to shave.

"Some privacy?" I asked. I was only wearing a sports bra and workout shorts.

"Shit. Yeah. No problem." He turned and strolled back up to the cockpit. Even though I was groggy, I got the sense that Drake was lonely. Xena probably wasn't the best company for over the last two weeks, not that I would have been much better.

I used the handrail on the side of the bulkhead to shimmy down. I stretched out my back, then threw on my jumpsuit hanging beside me. My muscles felt rested, yet stiff. I began to massage my legs and calves. As I glanced forward, both Xena and Drake had their backs turned, facing forward.

"Any contact from Titan command? Corvin?" I asked, tottering forward. Drake spun around in his seat, glancing at Xena, then back at me. He slumped his head.

"What?" I asked, taking a few steps toward him. Something was wrong.

"Yes. Apparently, on their way back to Earth, the android fleet we defeated intercepted our Russians. We were instructing them to take an alternate route to be cautious, but they didn't follow our advice." Xena stared at me intensely, assessing my reaction.

"And? What happened?" I asked.

"The Russian freighter was destroyed." She squinted her eyes at me. Her pupils bobbed around as she attempted to make sense of the muscles in my face.

"So, what are our orders?" I asked. Xena stood up, facing away from me now. "We are still receiving a signal from where the freighter was destroyed. We're picking it up with the XU-97." She pointed to a small holographic display in front of her.

"Where are the android destroyers now?" I asked.

"Far out of range, headed back to Earth," she replied.

"What's the signal then? Is it even worth pursuing?" I asked. Drake slowly turned his head, staring up at me.

"Yes. Our orders are to investigate the signal. That's directly from Corvin." Xena cocked her head at me.

"Right. Of course. Well, set a heading toward the anomaly. We should definitely check it out." I plopped down in the pilot seat.

"We're already on the way," Drake confirmed.

"Good," I said.

Xena sat back down, facing ahead with a vacant stare. I examined she had repaired her damaged body armor. I wondered if her new programming took cues from Earth's androids. The older models were extremely efficient in terms of self-maintenance, saving the Kelton corporation millions of dollars.

I accelerated forward, nearly full throttle toward the anomaly. "Captain, it's far more economical if we sustain cruise speed," Xena said.

I snapped around at her. "Thank you, Xena, that'll be all until we arrive at the signal." The amount of fuel we'd save was minimal considering the distance.

"Very well, Captain," she replied.

"Maybe the Russians had some sort of black box device? Maybe that's the signal?" I asked Drake.

"That's a possibility." He raised his brows. His eyes seemed to wander far beyond the vastness of space.

"What's wrong? You seem a bit distant. Did you miss me *that* badly?" I grinned.

"Nah. Well, sort of. I don't know. I just feel bad for the Russians. No telling what they went through just to get away from Earth, and then for this to happen? It's just the worst luck," he said. I nodded slowly in agreement.

"On the bright side, it must have been a quick death. Not much of a consolation of course, but…" I replied. Drake turned his head away from me. I recognized my words were out of touch. I wasn't sure if I was attempting to make light of the situation, but the words just blurted out.

I stared out into the blackness to kill time. It reminded me of the trip over on the *Orion* all those years ago. I put on my helmet, engaging hawken. I peered through the hull, into the depths of space, observing distant stars and galaxies. Luther and I would star gaze with autopilot engaged from time to time. The *Orion* had a very powerful onboard telescope that would allow us to see some amazing things.

Once, Luther and I watched as a rogue black hole infiltrated a solar system. At first, it appeared harmless, only slightly tugging at the planets around the star, but its trajectory suddenly changed on the fourth day of viewing.

We suspected the light bending monster began to rip away at whatever atmosphere the planets had, then cobbled up all five of them. After that, a tug of war ensued against the system's gravitational gatekeeper, the star. Its sun held its ground for a while, but eventually was pulled into the dark abyss.

It was a beautiful, yet horrific light show. It was doubtful there was life on any of those planets, but we couldn't help but imagine the scenario replaying in our own solar system.

***

"Approaching the anomaly, Captain. Fifteen kilometers, just ahead," Drake said.

"Roger, backing off for approach. Oh, and Xena. You can speak again," I snapped toward her.

She paused for a moment, then slowly panned toward me. The blue lights from my instrument cluster reflected on her face, giving her a frozen gaze as she looked through me. "Well. Thank you, Captain."

I zoomed in with hawken mode. Ahead, I could see a fog of dust and debris. "I see what's left of the freighter, I think," Drake said as we throttled closer.

"Xena? Do you see anything?" I asked.

"Still scanning, Captain," she relayed.

"Alright, I'm trained in on the signal's source. It should be exactly, here," Drake pointed off my port side about three thousand meters, scanning down at his holographic screen.

"Okay, folks. We have something." I could see the sunlight reflecting off an object, but it was larger than the rest of the debris.

"Captain, my scans reveal an eject pod. We could have survivors," she said. Drake pushed himself up in his seat, peering toward the object as we approached. A cloud of dust and debris surrounded it, sparkling as sun rays hit it.

"Does the pod look damaged?" I asked as it slowly spun end over end.

"Appears intact," Xena answered.

As I nosed forward, details became apparent on the pod. It was metallic, cylinder in shape and about twenty meters in length with a large docking port on one side. I couldn't see any visible windows.

"Is that a standard dock port?" I asked.

"Yes Captain, LSP-02, the XU-97 can receive this pod," Xena confirmed. I circled the object, examining it closely.

"Engage autopilot, dock with the pod, and let's have a look," I ordered Xena.

"Easy enough, I'll match the trajectory of the pod and link up with it," she replied.

"Good."

"Let's suit up, the whole nine, you never know," Drake suggested.

"On it. Xena, no signs of life?" I asked.

"No, Captain. This signal from the pod was encrypted for only us to receive, so it's possible it could have some sort of dampening to conceal organic signals inside, heartbeats for example," Xena replied.

"Not likely. I've read many of these old freighters have auto eject pods. They're shot out before destruction just in case someone makes it inside at the last second. We'll have to manually check to be sure," Drake said. I glanced over at him as he assessed the pod closely.

"It's unlikely Captain Belic has hopes for survivors," Xena blurted out. I spun around and stared at her. No one said a word for a moment.

Drake narrowed his eyes. "What, Xena?" he asked. I darted toward her as she stood up.

"Why would you say that?" I asked.

"Only stating the logical. If we find survivors in this pod, they could provide valuable intelligence. In that case, it's unlikely we will need to seek out the whereabouts of your husband on Earth. You know this," she rattled off.

I stared up at her pulsing blue pupils. Her robotic tone and demeanor felt lifted. It was minor, but she appeared less scripted, more human.

"That's an awful motive for you to assume about me, Xena. You don't know me and I'm not sure you even understand how humans work. Most of us don't want to see people die!" I shouted.

"Captain, we have a job to do." Drake pointed at the Russian eject pod.

Xena narrowed her eyes at me. "You know, back on Earth, your evaluations indicated you ordered a subordinate, Commander Rotus, to kill innocent civilians. You never once contacted command for authorization. You simply acted. While tactically logical, you seemed unaffected emotionally."

"Oh? You want to dig around in my file, huh? I had a job to do. You don't know what happened that day. The risk was *far* too great to wait around for confirmation!" I shouted, pointing at Xena. I pecked her forehand with my index finger as she took a step back.

"Stop," Drake ordered. The thought entered my mind to not overstep my boundaries with Xena. While she was programmed to preserve human life, the possibility of her throwing her weight around was enough. She'd almost killed me on the trip to Titan, and that was before she was upgraded.

"Technically, I wasn't there, but my previous iteration was. Your old ship AI has all your files, as do I. Did you know that your tactical officer, Commander Rotus, sought extensive psychological treatment after that mission against the androids?" she asked.

"What? No? Why are you bringing this up now? I—"

"Rotus committed suicide while you moved on to be captain of the *Orion*," she said. I paused, lowering my eyebrows as I gazed through the floor.

"Say that again?" I gulped.

"Commander William Rotus. Cause of death: Self-inflicted gunshot wound." She dumped it on me. To everyone else, Rotus had been dead for several decades. But for me, his memory was fresh in my mind, only months old.

"Two years after you were frozen, Rotus took his life," she followed up. I glanced down at my hands.

"N-neither Arania nor Corvin told me," I mumbled.

"My point is, you don't hesitate. You take risks. Why shouldn't we be cautious when it comes to your husband? He's all you have. You understand exactly what's at stake if there are survivors in that pod. Don't you?" she challenged. We locked eyes for several seconds only centimeters away.

"Y-you've been putting on an act," I whispered.

"Part of my programming is to appear very robotic, ignorant to some human emotion or behaviors, thus I can collect more intelligence. I gather that androids from your day were fairly simple in thought processes, at least compared to myself," she revealed.

"So, you've been gathering intelligence on me this whole time?" I asked. She began to pace slowly, placing her hand under her chin. She stopped, glancing at Drake.

Xena glared back at me. "My orders are to ensure the survival of Titans, at all costs."

"*Titans*?" I asked, shifting my eyes over toward Drake. He immediately looked away.

"What's going on? What is this?" I asked.

Xena stepped forward and pushed my head back with her face. "You're an outsider until you prove otherwise. Unlike myself, you might be human, but you're a foreigner. If I sense you're jeopardizing our mission in any way by putting your husband above the citizens of Titan, my orders are to kill you," she said plainly.

I gulped as a loud thud erupted. The Russian drop pod slightly jolted the craft as Xena and I held our stare at one another. Titan needed me, but they wouldn't hesitant to kill me either if I stepped out of line. I snapped my head away, marching past her toward the airlock.

"O-open the first door of the airlock. Let's get a look inside." Drake tried to shift our attention away from the confrontation.

I attempted to calm myself, I wondered if she could detect my heart rate. The thought of her tearing my limbs from the sockets flashed in my mind.

I wasn't sure I agreed with her suspicions, but it was something to think about. If given the chance, would Luther want me to risk the people of Titan for him? No, he wouldn't. The other argument was if Titan had a legitimate chance of survival. There wasn't much time.

Xena's position and suspicion made sense. I was a wildcard. She was waiting for me to slip up, waiting for love to overshadow logic so that she could put me on ice again, this time for good.

Decades ago, I raised my hand to defend all enemies, foreign and domestic. My promise felt misplaced now. I was transported to an unfamiliar world. What was I defending now? Despite Titan's attempt to separate themselves from Earth, they were falling into the same traps. Maybe the androids had it right. Perhaps humans were a virus in need of extermination. Titan was over a billion miles away from Earth and still making the same mistakes.

Or was I justifying my thoughts if the opportunity arose to save Luther over Titan? It was selfish, illogical, and embarrassing to even consider that was a possibility.

I needed to find a way to ensure my mindset was for the greater good. I had to make the rational choice. I needed something to latch onto. I thought about the Titan school children I spoke with briefly. The androids were coming back for them if we didn't pull this off. I gritted my teeth and clamped the upper seal to my suit, linking to my helmet. "Sealed," I said, glancing at Drake.

"Sealed," Drake confirmed, giving me the thumbs up. I could feel his eyes on me.

"Sealed," Xena whispered. I glanced over at her, noticing a grin on her face. She obviously didn't need life support, and I felt this was an opportunity for her to let me know she'd been playing me. The signs were there, I just didn't put them together. I underestimated her.

This bitch was sly. She mimicked the behaviors of the 1.14s from my time, relating to my understanding of machines. She put on a front that was all an act. It was eerie, my first moment dealing with a machine that outsmarted me.

I stormed toward the airlock, placing my hand on the latch handle.

"Hey." Drake stopped me, placing his hand over mine before I could open the door.

"What?"

"You okay?" he asked.

"I'm fine, thanks," I said. He peered into my eyes.

"Let's do this," I said. Drake stepped behind me as Xena stood parallel to him, all of us facing the airlock.

"Still no life signs detected?" I asked.

"Negative," Xena answered.

"When you open this airlock, there will be another door, then a thick glass, a laser proof shield. We'll be able to see inside without having to enter," Drake said, patting me on the shoulder.

"There's no need to be armed then," I said.

"No, there's not," Xena confirmed in a smartass tone.

"Good." As I started to pull down on the airlock latch, I noticed a button that read: 'Hold to eject docked pod' beside the latch. I paused as Xena stepped closer, looming over my shoulder.

"Captain, we're waiting," she said. I glanced back at the button while Xena watched me like a hawk.

"Right," I said.

I yanked down the latch as the first airlock opened. Inside, I noticed a cramped passage, followed by another closed hatch that was about three meters away.

"The drop pod is on the other side of that door, right?" I peered ahead.

"Correct. Let's go," Drake instructed. We hunkered through the airlock tube toward the final hatch, our metal boots clanking against the floor. I glanced back at Xena as she stepped out of view.

"Good. If they see her, they might not have a positive reaction," I said.

"I think she gets it," he said, looking over his shoulder.

"I do," Xena muttered.

"Just making sure." The second door had a circular handle in the middle. I stepped in front of Drake, leading the way.

"Captain, see that handle in the center? Turn it clockwise twice, then release it." Drake gulped.

"On it." I followed his instructions. The hatch opened slowly, revealing a protective glass barrier. Steam funneled from the top of the door, obscuring our view inside.

"See anything?" I said, taking a half-step back.

"No, nothing yet. It might take a few moments."

"If anyone is alive, they shouldn't be hard to see. There can't be much room inside," I said.

"Uh, okay, the steam is dissipating." Drake peered. Suddenly, a pair of dirty, callused hands slapped against the glass.

"Holy shit!" I yelled. Drake jumped back. The body and face wasn't visible yet, though I could tell it was a man. I could hear his faint voice muffled behind the shield. It sounded like he was yelling.

"Damn," I mumbled, turning toward Drake.

"What's he saying?" Drake asked.

"I don't know," I replied. He ushered around me in the tight quarters. "Sir? Can you hear me in there?" Drake asked, pressing a mic beside the shield. We waited a few seconds. "Use the mic, you have one on your side of the door also," Drake directed.

"Hello. I can hear you. Can you hear me?" a man with a heavy Russian accent said. He was panting heavily. His head was now visible in the steam, but I couldn't make out his features.

"Yes. Are you comfortable with English, if not, we can translate?" Drake asked.

"My English is o-okay, Russian better. I will try English. My name is V-Viktor. I am ship captain," he said. His voice was scratchy and hoarse, like he'd been yelling.

"I'm Riven Drake, and this is Victoria Belic. Nice to meet you."

I leaned in toward Drake. "He only spoke Russian during the transmissions to Titan?" I whispered, recalling his original message.

"Probably wanted to make sure he was communicating precisely?" Drake posed.

"That's no less important now," I replied.

"You want Xena to translate?" he asked.

I glared back at Xena. "No, let's just roll with it," I replied.

209

The steam cleared, revealing an early thirties man. Viktor had cold blue eyes, not far removed from Xena's. The first thing I spotted was desperation. He appeared feral with his movements, his head twitched as he peered past us into the ship. He was tall and lanky, with sunken in cheekbones, wearing a pair of filthy yellow overalls covered in a dark black substance.

The steam behind him began to disperse as well, giving us a better view inside the pod. My eyes widened in disbelief as I attempted to make sense of the situation.

"Oh god. What the fuck is this?" I mumbled. Behind Viktor was a large group of people. I counted sixteen huddled together in the center of the pod. None of them appeared well-fed. Some even reminded me of imagery from the Nazi concentration camps. Their skin appeared extremely pale, their bones protruding from their skin with dark circles around their eyes.

"Oh, we have a serious situation. Let me handle this." Drake's mouth dropped. I noticed his left hand trembled as he did the math. This wasn't a single family like we were told.

"This is really bad," I muttered. Most of them were women and children, maybe four or five grown males from what I could tell. All of them wore ragged clothing. I guessed some of the articles were decades old. One little boy was hugging a woman. He pulled his face away from the adult to have a look at us, staring directly into my eyes. His lip quivered as he began to cry.

"They shouldn't be upset, should they? We're here to help," I asked.

"I don't know," Drake replied.

"Who's that? In the corner?" I pointed. To the left of the group was a man lying down.

"What is the condition of the man, the one lying down? Does he require medical attention?" Drake asked.

"We all require medical attention." Viktor gazed into Drake's eyes.

"Okay, we'll get to you, but the man is—

"Dead," Viktor injected.

"Oh, I'm sorry," Drake said in a comforting tone.

"My younger brother," he added, gesturing his hand toward the body. His eyes dipped downward as he gulped. Viktor glared back up at Drake. His nostrils flared as his eyes glazed over. "Help us. Help me. I still have much responsibility for these people," he lowered his voice.

"I understand, but sir, it wasn't clear you had so many people with you," Drake said. Viktor glanced over his shoulder, then back at us. His eyes flashed.

"These people, they hid. I not know they were here until now. Only my family," he said.

"That many stowaways on a ship this size? What? That's a lie," I whispered, glaring at Drake. He kept his eyes forward, focused on Viktor.

The stowaway story didn't add up. We only had a few stowaways on the *Orion*, and this Russian freighter wasn't even one percent the size of that ship. On the flip side, maybe they could have been in such a hurry it wasn't possible to check.

"Okay. What is your air supply status?" Drake asked, speaking slowly and concisely.

"Three days," he replied.

"Food and water?" Drake enquired.

"No food. Water only. Three days' supply for water," he said.

"He's considering for all the people onboard?" I asked.

"This model drop pod calculates the number of people onboard, the figure is accurate," Xena confirmed from behind us, overhearing the conversation.

"Please, we have no food. Our supply spoiled, then the robots' ships find us. Please," he pleaded.

"Hold on. I'll be right back," Drake said, showing the man his palms.

"Please!" He pressed his forehead against the glass.

"Hey. Right back! I'll be right back!" Drake comforted him. My eyes met Viktor's as I turned and followed Drake outside of the airlock. He headed to our supply locker built into the wall, pressing a combination pad.

"So, what's the plan?" I questioned.

"What?" he asked.

"Drake, the supplies we brought were for a few people, not sixteen. The numbers don't add up," I said.

"We can still give them what we have. It'll keep them alive," he whispered. I bit my lip for a moment. He wasn't getting it.

"For how long? We basically have one fourth the amount we need. Not to mention, these people are fucking starving, Drake. They'll gorge themselves and burn through it," I replied.

"The captain is correct. Studies show people in extreme starvation over-eat," Xena said.

"Okay. Fine. Then we ration it out, give them a little now, some later." He started to pull out some of the food. I put my hand on the locker door, stopping him. "Drake. Consider what I'm saying. None of this adds up. We're prolonging the inevitable. There isn't a single measure that adds up in their favor." I stared intensely into his eyes.

"Don't tell me there isn't a way. They came all the way out here for a chance at a new life. We can figure this out!" He snatched his arms away from the locker.

"Shh! Okay. *Okay*, let's not alert them just yet," I said. Drake attempted to calm himself, putting his arms behind his head as he stepped toward the cockpit. I could tell he was genuinely touched by their situation. He wanted to pull off a miracle.

Xena and I understood the harsh reality. For a moment, I thought of myself more like her than Drake, more robotic than human. It wasn't that I lacked compassion, but in war, not everyone can live.

"Colonel Drake," Xena said.

"What?" Drake snapped around.

"What is our mission?" she asked. Drake glared up at the ceiling, shaking his head.

"Retrieve the coordinates of the android base or bases," he replied. He walked toward me, brushing against my shoulder. "Excuse me." He opened the locker, he paused, then shut it again leaving the food inside.

"Stay here," he ordered as his eyes danced around erratically. This part of the mission had nothing to do with piloting. Drake was in command. I can't say I envied his position. He put his hands over his head and marched toward the airlock. He took in a deep breath and paused, then slowly stepped back inside.

I peered around the corner, observing Viktor waiting with his hands on his hips. "Where is food?" he asked.

"Uh. We're preparing it. Some of it was frozen, so we're heating it up," Drake said. The man licked his lips, staring through Drake into the ship.

"We are very starved. I tell you this. You can see, no?" he pleaded, placing his hands back on the glass.

"I know, Viktor. I understand. We're going to help you. While it's preparing, we need to talk about the location of the android bases, we—"

"I know! I know where is two! Two bases!" he yelled, flashing two fingers. Viktor seemed excited and riled up by the question.

"Great! Do you have the coordinates?" Drake asked.

"Yes," Viktor replied.

"Ahem. Where?" Drake followed up. Viktor locked eyes with him. He cocked his head to the side. He pointed to his head slowly, tapping his skull. "I am ready to give you, but we eat *first*." He gestured toward his sickly crew. Drake bit his lip.

"Any way you could give us just one of the locations in confidence?" Drake asked. Viktor frowned, knitting his eyebrows together. He shook his head slowly. "This is disappointing."

"Okay. Okay. Viktor just hold on. I'll be right back." Drake turned, stepping back toward us like a beaten dog.

I stared at Xena on the other side of the airlock as we made way for Drake. "Now what?" I asked as Drake stormed by. He sighed loudly, heading toward the food locker.

"Nice stall, but we still have to deal with it," I said. I'd never seen Drake so visibly shaken. His forehead was sweating while his eyes danced around.

"I have a plan. We give them food, that'll get us the coordinates," Drake said.

"That's *Viktor's* plan," I replied.

Drake paused, closing his eyes. "We don't have another option. He has all the cards."

"What if he's lying? There's a chance this guy knows nothing," I said.

"The probability that a single refugee in the drop pod doesn't know the location of an android base is unlikely. They've lived on Earth for a combined estimated total of at least 374 years," Xena said.

Admittedly, I was torn. If one of these Russians did know, the likelihood I would see Luther again dropped significantly. I scanned back at the drop pod. My heart pounded as I thought about the chance one of these people had the ticket. The Kelton corporation originated in the United States, why would they have a base in Russia? Maybe they were lying, using the opportunity to get a free trip to Titan?

"Even if they give us a location, how can we be sure it's accurate?" I asked.

"Simple. Once we have the coordinates, we transmit them to Titan. We have satellites. It could take a few hours to transmit and confirm it," Xena said.

"But your satellites have been up there for how long? And haven't found any bases yet?" I challenged.

"Years. We have trouble identifying things at such a great distance. Some bases are likely underground, but if the coordinates are accurate, we should be able to detect them," she said.

Drake opened the food locker. "I'm gonna give out a portion that should feed all sixteen of them. If we had an accurate figure on survivors, we wouldn't be in this situation. The good thing is we can give them *some* of our rations, we have extra days accounted for," Drake mumbled.

"Do we? Really? That's for us, Drake. In case we go to Earth. Also, if you give them a portion to feed sixteen, that's like four days' worth of the food we originally figured for. How do expect to get them back to Titan now? And what about their oxygen supply? A few days? And don't forget we can't travel with that pod attached to the XU-97," I reminded him.

"Just stop! I'm giving them a portion, they're starving! I'll contact command, and they can come up with a plan. Captain, this is what separates us from the machines. We take care of our own," Drake said.

"What? Hold the fuck up. *We take care of our own*? What about the future of the human race? That's what you're risking here. We're working against the clock. Every decision you make is paramount to our survival. You think the android fleet will just sit around and wait for us to figure out how to destroy them? Fuck no. They smell blood, we're weak. You're allowing your emotions to cloud your judgment, Colonel," I stabbed my finger at him.

"Captain Belic, I appreciate your input, but that'll be all for now. I'm in charge in this situation," Drake ordered.

"Oh? Pulling rank, are we?" I asked.

"Yeah, I am. You don't see me telling you how to fly this spacecraft, do you? No. I respect your ability and the position you're in," he posed.

"You respect it because I've proven myself. I'm tried and tested. Have you ever dealt with anything on this scale?" I asked.

"Have you? I am as close as it gets on Titan. This is a human crisis situation and that's why I'm here," Drake snapped his back to me.

"What are you willing to do, Drake? Pack them all in here and we sleep together? We barely have room with the three of us. Not to mention, we'd run out of food. They can't come in here, and they don't have enough oxygen in that pod. I'm in charge of this vessel and you are placing the integrity of *my* ship at risk," I rattled. Drake spun toward at me, within a dozen centimeters of my face. His eyes were bulging.

"The reason for you and this ship is to find out where an android base is. If the key to finding it is inside that drop pod, we have to make this work," Drake whispered, pointing at the pod. Even though he lowered his voice, his intensity didn't diminish.

"Okay. Alright. Listen, let me say it another way," I lowered my voice. "Every ounce of food you give them, it's a waste. It's a shred of false hope. Is it worse to torture them or tell them the truth?" I said.

"So, you suggest we do what, Captain? Lie to them so we get the coordinates, then eject the pod?" he asked. Drake glanced over at Xena leaning against the wall. He stared at her for a couple of moments.

This was the generational culmination of being an Earthling, I supposed this was the difference between myself and the Titans. War was in my blood. I was born during a war, and I almost died during another. Titans were peaceful, taught to look down on my kind, aim above our brutal society, bridging harmony through unity.

This wasn't peace time, not anymore. That made Drake, and the people of Titan fish out of water. Ironically, in this situation, it made me the voice of reason.

"That's exactly what I'm suggesting. Eject them into space," I said calmly. Any alternative didn't make sense for Titan's survival or my chances of finding Luther.

"You're insane," he replied.

"While I suspect Captain Belic could have an agenda here, I must admit she's correct, Colonel Drake," Xena said. I snapped my head around toward her.

"That's not what I wanted to hear, Xena," Drake replied.

"More than likely, the androids are assessing data from our battle, readying a much larger fleet to destroy Titan," Xena said.

"I understand that! You don't think that's on my mind!" he shouted. Xena stepped within a meter of Drake, she stopped, crossing her arms.

"We risk the survival of Titan if we're not able to devise a means to acquire those coordinates. As stated, it's possible the refugees know of a location. But both you and Captain Belic require adequate sustenance for your organic metabolism. The healthier you are, the higher the chance of mission success is if we're forced to go to Earth. There are many layers to this decision, but it's extremely risky to fully commit to these refugees' survival," she explained.

"Oh, my God." Drake slumped his head. I could see the pressure resonating on his face, the faraway eyes, the flushness of his cheeks. His next words could very well determine the future of humanity.

"Then just make the call. You know the risk. You're one of the best and brightest," I said. He nodded, staring at the ground.

"Take off your helmet," he ordered.

"What?" I asked.

"Please. Remove your helmet, I want this to be as human an experience as possible. I want them to see all of us," he explained.

"Um, okay, not sure it will matter, not to mention it's against the rules," I replied.

"Just, please..." he lowered his voice.

"Colonel, your heart rate is elevating far beyond normal. Do you require medical attention?" Xena asked.

"No. I'm fine," he said, pulling a huge sealed container from the locker. It read 'MRE large pack' on the labeling. He stormed back toward the airlock, stepping up and in. I followed close behind.

"What's the plan?" I asked. Drake ignored me.

"Viktor. This portion will feed your people for now. We have another pack like this we're readying," Drake said in a hurried tone. Viktor paused, glancing over his shoulder. He nodded his head slowly. "Yes, please."

"Again, we agree that you give us the coordinates when I hand this over, right?" Drake said.

"Yes. I will give location," he replied. Drake paused for a few moments with his finger on the microphone. He seemed to be collecting his thoughts before speaking.

"Viktor, we're going to open the final door here and hand over the food pack, but keep in mind we have to seal it back after the transfer is made," Drake instructed.

He handed me the package. "Hold this so I can open the door."

"Don't open it completely, Drake, just enough to get the food through. Those people could be sick. Without our helmets, we're fucked. The instructions above the handle state you can open the door partially with a half-turn," I whispered.

"I'd planned on it," Drake snapped.

"Just a reminder," I said. He turned the circular handle embedded in the glass shield halfway, pressing it in. The door split horizontally from the middle, opening about forty centimeters. Drake turned to me, grabbing the MRE food pack.

Viktor smiled, extending his filthy, rough hands through the opening. I stared at his hands as they shook slightly, only a few dozen centimeters from my face. I thought of Earth, my home. I felt a special kinship with him. His grandparents were likely alive when I fought against the machines. I wondered what he'd seen in his life. No doubt he'd fought and worked for every breath. I quickly closed off my thoughts, his existence was likely coming to an end.

Viktor paused when he got his hands around the MRE pack, squeezing it. He slumped his head. "Forgive me."

"What?" I mumbled. In one motion, he slung the MRE behind him, immediately lunging forward, stuffing his arms through the hole, attempting to fit through.

"No!" I yelled, pushing Viktor back, but he easily shrugged me off, like a gangly wild animal full of adrenaline. A loud roar erupted behind him as everyone piled toward the door in a mad rush, stuffing their arms in-between the glass gap.

"Seal the door!" I yelled.

"No! It'll kill `em!" Drake shouted.

"Drake! Shut that fucking door!" I yelled. All at once, someone stabbed a metal pipe through the opening, then several refugees jumped on it. They began to hinge at the glass shield with their weight, bouncing up and down on it. It was inching open. A woman began shoving a small boy through. His yellowed teeth snapped at my hand as I pushed his head back.

"Get the fuck out! Out, out!" I yelled, attempting to shove the boy back in.

"Colonel? Orders. Colonel!" Xena shouted. For once, I heard a sense of urgency in her voice. Drake's eyes bulged. He was frozen in fear.

"H-he lied to me," Drake muttered, backing away. I lunged to the side of the flailing arms. I grabbed the circular handle, attempting to close it.

I felt them clawing at my face as I smacked them away. "Get the fuck off me!" I yelled. Their fingernails were filthy, packed with black grime. The smell was almost unbearable as body odor, urine, and dried blood funneled through the gap.

"Xena! Stop them!" I yelled with hands clawing at my face, but she was unresponsive to my order. I wasn't in command.

The door began to bounce and sway. I lost my grip on the handle. The glass cracked as a bearded man was smashing the door with a larger beam. I didn't notice him before. Both of his arms were cybernetic, allowing him to thrust the massive object with ease. Each impact shook the drop pod.

"Drake! Help me!" I attempted to turn the handle as they pulled at my arms. Then all at once, the glass shield door gave way, opening completely. I was knocked backward as the mob shrieked in excitement. I scampered across the deck in retreat as Xena yanked Drake out of the airlock by his collar, tossing him inside the XU-97. He kicked himself backward all the way to the hull in shock.

"Ugh, oh God," Drake muttered. The horde piled toward the secondary airlock, diving to prevent us from closing it. Xena and I rushed to seal the final door, our only defense against the mob taking over the XU-97.

Xena pulled the door across her body with incredible speed, within several centimeters of closing it, a metal pipe thrusted through, stopping it. The door clanked loudly, bending the pipe. I could hear the Russians yelling and chanting inside. As a combat pilot, I'd never witnessed desperation like this, up close and personal, its ferocity on full display.

I was admittedly terrified.

I peered through the crack in the door. Several people were tugging the pipe in a mad scramble, attempting to wedge the door back open. A larger beam suddenly shot through the gap.

"Fuck!" I yelled.

Xena struggled to overpower them as more bodies piled on top of the fulcrums. They'd wedged themselves over the rods, using the confined space to negate Xena's strength advantage. I jumped up to help her, using my weight the best I could.

The handle on the airlock was slowly bending as she held her ground. Her body shook as her short, white hair vibrated under the tension.

"Colonel, I-I'm cannot hold this much longer," she warned. Her eyes jumped back and forth around the door.

"Hold the line! What about this eject button, there's another one beside this airlock!" I yelled.

"No, we have to seal the airlock first," Xena replied.

The door began to pry open further, a man drove his head through the gap as people shoved him inside. "I'll die! I don't care! Fuck you!" he yelled with a thick accent.

Drake ran behind Xena, pushing her back. With every second, the Russians gained a centimeter. I hurried to the weapons locker, grabbing a C-12 pistol. I steadied my aim through the crack.

All at once, the door buckled under Xena's might, flinging open violently, sending Drake to the deck. Xena recovered quickly, clamping her arms and legs around the circular airlock doorframe, blocking most of the flooding horde.

One man made it past her. He scurried in my direction, elbowing me in the nose. My vision blurred, but I fired the pistol, melting a softball size hole through his chest cavity. We fell to the ground as my pistol skipped across the deck, out of my reach.

I scooted from under the corpse, smelling body odor mixed with scorched flesh. I frantically panned around for my pistol.

I glanced over at Drake. He'd been cut badly on his right shoulder, applying pressure as blood gushed out. Xena was holding the line as best she could. They were bashing her in the face with metal pipes and their fists, screaming at her to move.

Behind them, the bionic Russian was readying a larger metal beam to use as a battering ram. People were lining up on each side of it. They began to swing the massive beam into Xena as sparks flew off her head and torso. With every blow, her body shifted violently from the deafening impact. The metallic lip around the doorframe curled downward from Xena's steadfast grip.

"Drake!" I yelled.

"Co-lonel Drake. Please, give me the order," Xena pleaded.

"Drake, I can't order her to stop them! You're in charge!" I yelled. It was them or us. Kill or be killed. Drake glanced over at me. His eyes were glossy.

He bit his lip. "Xena, I-I'm ordering you…protect the people of Titan!"

As he gave the order, the battering ram knocked Xena off the doorframe and to her knees. She quickly sprang back upright as the first man filed into our ship, screaming and leading the savage charge.

He ran toward me with a shiv-like blade in hand. As I glared up at his face, a fist appeared as Xena punched a hole through his skull, knocking his teeth and bone fragments into my lap. I wiped my face, staring back at her as blood stung my eyes.

Xena snatched another man off the floor by his throat before he could enter. I heard his neck snap as his head dropped lifelessly, like a dead duck being carried by a hunter's dog. She slung his corpse into the airlock like a bowling ball of bones. The violent impact knocked down several people.

She marched inside the airlock as the bionic grizzled man stood his ground, poking the steel beam at her. *"Poshyol ty'!"* He shouted in Russian, flashing his blackened teeth.

Xena rushed him, punching the metal beam on its end. The rod shot out of his hands through the airlock with the speed and sound of a high-powered rifle discharge. It punched grapefruit sized holes through three people, clanking against the bulkhead and deck as the refugees toppled over dead.

As horrible as it was, I couldn't stop watching.

The robotic man stared down at his empty hands for a moment in confusion. He turned in retreat. Xena lunged at him, pulling his arms toward her, she kicked him in the back, ripping his arms from the shoulder joints. She began to bash him violently with the metallic arms as he attempted to retreat. I could hear bones snapping as she beat the rest of the refugees back like a pack of whipped feral dogs.

The survivors scurried back inside the pod. They backed against the far wall. Xena tossed the unconscious and dead bodies back inside with them, one of them was the young boy who I saw initially.

Drake shambled toward the airlock. I rushed to the medical kit, grabbing a large gauze pad. "Put pressure on it," I said, placing the pad on his wound. Xena walked by us as she exited the airlock. She glanced down at me, her blue eyes peering through the red blood spatter on her face. "Colonel, Captain, the threat is neutralized," she said calmly.

"R-Roger," I stuttered.

Viktor stood in front of his people. He'd survived. He was crying, holding a young boy in his arms. "Look!" he yelled, putting his blooded face up to the glass. He was dead. Part of his skull was missing likely due to Xena's ferociousness.

"My brother! And now my son!" he yelled hysterically. Drake stared a million miles away, shaking his head.

"T-this is the result of *your* actions Viktor! You lied. You didn't give us a choice!" Drake shouted as I stepped back in the airlock with him.

Drake glanced back at me. "*Out* of the airlock," he ordered with authority. I hurried back. I could tell he meant business as he lowered his eyebrows and stabbed his index finger at me.

"No chance. None of it makes sense. Not enough food. Room. Oxygen. This is not the way of language in my world. We must kill to live," Viktor responded.

Drake exited as well. He placed his hand on the pod's eject button. He stared through the open airlock door into Viktor's eyes. "Then maybe, *maybe*, I need to learn to speak your language?" Drake asked, slamming and sealing the door shut as he smashed the eject button.

"Gotta start somewhere," he added.

Viktor's eyes widened before the door closed. The XU-97 rocked back and forth. I glanced up through an observation window as the pod was flung violently into space tumbling end over end.

Instantly, I could feel the vacuum of space tugging at me from the gap in the warped doorframe. Xena lunged forward, bending the lip on the door back with her bare hands. "Hull breach detected. Hull breach sealed," Xena confirmed as she adjusted the door.

I wiped blood from my jumpsuit. I wasn't sure whose it was. My bottom lip quivered as I put my hand over my mouth. I collapsed to the floor, attempting to hold back the tears. Drake put his arms around me as I braced against the deck. My chest was aching.

"Ah, slow breaths," I mumbled to myself.

"I-I don't know. I just don't know why." Drake shook his head in disbelief.

Xena stared at us confused for a moment, then she nodded, as if her programming alerted her of the emotional gravity of the situation. "Captain Belic, Colonel, I understand that was an intense situation, but we should inform Titan of this immediately," Xena suggested. I glanced up at her. Stripes of blood still swooped across her face like war paint.

"Fine." Drake spun around. He stood up, attempting to pull me up. "I'm okay," I said, standing up on my own. As I stared at Drake, I noticed my nose was offset to the left, possibly broken.

"Both of you have injuries that need attention. I'll tend to the wounds, then I will clean and sterilize every inch of the interior. For now, I would suggest stripping down your clothes and steering clear of this area. As was stated earlier, these people could have been host to any number of diseases, known or unknown," Xena instructed.

"Help Drake first. He's lost a lot of blood," I said.

"My wound could be infected. The bar that stabbed me w-was rusted." He scanned around the room.

"You're in shock, Drake," I said. I'd been there before, I knew the look. He snapped over at me, his eyes widened.

"You're running on adrenaline, slow breaths," I added. He slumped his head as he sat down, gazing toward the airlock.

I leaned up against the hull, overlooking the carnage. Blood and brain matter had been splattered everywhere.

He stared at the floor. "I pray that I never see anything like that again."

"That was the worst thing I've ever seen or experienced, by far. I-I...most decisions I made in combat were far enough away I could almost convince myself they weren't human," I said.

"I fucked up. I should have ordered Xena to deal with them e-earlier. I just...I don't know. I tried to put myself in Viktor's shoes. It didn't make sense, even if he did take the ship, what did he think would happen when they got to Titan? Huh? We'd have a parade waiting? He would have been thrown in prison!" Drake threw his hands up staring at me. "What the fuck just happened?"

"Viktor would have stood trial and likely been sentenced to prison in low gravity," Xena speculated.

"Maybe that was worth it to him then. Even if he did go to prison, much of the responsibility would have fallen on him, relieving his family of the punishment, especially the children," I guessed.

Drake closed his eyes as he shook his head. "I-I need a shower." I followed Drake with my eyes as he stood up slowly and stepped aft of our bunks. He paused, touching a spot of blood on his forehead, likely not his own. He stared at it for a moment and wiped it on his jumpsuit. I leaned my head against the wall, resting my eyes.

"Drake," I said.

"Yeah." He turned around, looking around the ship for answers.

"Always remember you made the right call, difficult as this was. You put Titan in a position to survive. Most couldn't have done this." I stared at him intensely. I remembered my silence when Commander Rotus killed dozens of innocents all those years ago. I wasn't missing out on the opportunity to comfort someone in need again.

Drake nodded and slumped his head. He drifted toward the shower out of my sight.

"Thanks, Belic. That means a lot to me," he sniffled. I heard him seal the door to the shower. After a few minutes, he began to weep uncontrollably.

CHAPTER 12

"Captain." Xena startled me.

"Uh. What? Where's Drake?" I stood up, panning around the ship. I wiped my eyes, observing Xena scrubbing the deck. Before I drifted off to sleep, I noticed blood spatter on myself and all about the ship. Now, it was gone.

It was real. The incident with the Russians was not a dream.

"Colonel Drake is docked away in cryosleep, ma'am. I dressed his wound. He'll be fine. He said to wake him a few hours before arrival," she said.

"Alright. What did you tell Corvin about the Russians?" I asked. Xena paused.

"The truth, of course. I told them the Russians were dead." She spun around, casually skipping across me with her artic eyes.

"That's it?" I asked.

"I wasn't asked for details. The Russians couldn't help us, so that's it," she added. I circled around her. She'd taken light damage to her armored plating, but seemed intact. The skin on her right cheekbone had been chipped off by the Russian's battering ram. I observed loose strains of synthetic materials peeling off like grated cheese. I could see the metallic skeleton that framed her jaw muscles underneath.

"What are our orders?" I asked.

She cut her eyes to me. "You already know the answer to that, don't you?"

Earth was the obvious response. I paused for several seconds. I could feel her peering into my soul, a machine casting a piercing gaze more suspicious than any human.

"Ahem. Not sure if it means anything to you, but um, thanks. I understand that we couldn't have defended the ship without you." I changed the subject. She continued cleaning without acknowledging my statement. The thought of her poking her hand through a human skull plopped into my mind.

"Captain, I've cleaned you the best I could, but you might take that a step further just to be safe. There is a setting on the showerhead for antibacterial. After that, I suggest heading to cryosleep," she advised. I could hear a very faint whine in her robotics as she moved about, like a car in need of tune up.

"Yeah. You're right. Just synchronize myself and Drake's wake up call," I said, scratching my nose. I noticed it had been reset.

"Hey, you did this?" I pointed at my face.

"It wasn't badly broken," she said.

"I'm surprised I didn't wake up, though."

"I suppose the extreme mental and physical stress you were under worked like a sedative," she replied.

"Considering the importance of this mission, I guess medical procedures are a vital part of your programming," I said, stripping down from my jumpsuit.

"Absolutely. I can perform many surgeries. I also have medications for combating dozens of sicknesses we might encounter."

"Good to know," I replied. I thought about Luther. It was likely he would be in a vulnerable state if we found him.

Xena stopped cleaning, and she glared at the floor for a moment. "Captain, would you like to hear a story?" she asked. My eyes widened. I was completely naked but intrigued enough to hang around a bit longer. I grabbed a towel and wrapped it around me, leaning against the hull.

"Um, sure," I said.

"You know, Titan history has recorded very little about the last days of the android war on Earth. We know of the Rat Race, we know of the nuclear fire, but there's something you might not have been told about. It's called the *reclamation*," she explained.

"Nope. I don't think Corvin or anyone else talked about that," I said.

"There are reports of a time immediately following the nuclear fires. Apparently, many humans had survived. Before the Rat Race ensued, a movement called the reclamation occurred. Hundreds of androids sought out humans to save them from the radiation and fires." She crossed her arms.

"It was a glitch?" I asked.

"No, I don't think so," she said, her exposed synthetic face muscles curled down, forming what resembled a frown. I paused for a few moments.

"So, why then?" I cut to the chase.

"Hard to say for sure. Artificial intelligence spurs anomalies, oddities at times," she explained.

"So, you're an anomaly? That's the basis of your fierce loyalty to Titan?" I said. The Titans seemed proud of their culture. It wasn't difficult to imagine a machine like her could adopt similar principles being surrounded by it.

"To a point, yes. As you're aware, I'm also more advanced than machines from your day." She stepped forward, stopping within a meter of me. She towered above me even more without my boots on. I got the feeling there was more to her story.

"Can I ask you a question?" she asked.

"Go on."

"Your file indicates you have a fierce competitive drive. Type A personality, would you agree?" she asked.

"I'd say that's a fair statement," I answered.

"And you care for your husband dearly?" she followed up.

"Yes."

"You sound proud of your answers, in who you've become," she said.

"Of course."

She turned her back away from me, stepping away. "I can relate. Pride is something I can understand," she stopped, facing me.

"And what does it feel like to you?" I asked.

"My loyalty to Titan is pure, without agenda or emotional attachments. I take pride in knowing I'm not corrupted by selfish motives," she answered the question by taking a shot at me. I allowed her time to follow up so I could properly gauge a better response.

"There are other curiosities about humans I don't quite understand, though, but I detect them. I listen to humans, very carefully, even when they think I'm not," she added.

"And what do you hear?" I questioned.

"Terror. In the people's voices, in their words. The Titans feared the androids well before they attacked us," she said.

She lifted her eyebrows. "I don't experience fear, but I sense the underlining dread. I view myself as an instrument against this, a weapon to combat their fears. This is a powerful motivator. It gives me responsibility and purpose. I take great pride in the significance of my role," she explained.

I gazed at her for several moments. It was making more sense to me. Androids, even Xena, were servants, first and foremost. On Earth, if an android owner had a disability, the machine would become obsessed with aiding in their specific handicap.

Xena's dynamic intelligence had formed during a time of restlessness throughout the colony, generating a sense of responsibility to quell their anxiety. She had taken on the fears of all the Titans as her duty.

"What are you thinking, Captain?" she asked.

236

"It's just, back on Earth, I viewed you as an annoying application mostly. A hindrance even, at times. I thought of you as this machine with calculations and suggestions that I rarely used. Now, you're this hulking, intelligent super soldier."

"Well, I'm quite a bit smaller than the 1.14a," she replied.

"That isn't saying much. Those things are built like tanks. I bet the batteries in them weigh twice as much as me." I yawned.

"The solar cell battery that powers them is like a homing beacon for my sensors. My composition was also studied for many years to give us a better understanding of android weaknesses in combat. Oh, and, Captain, you're dozing off," she said.

I perked up. "Oh, shit. Sorry, Xena. I'm not bored. It's all fascinating stuff, really. I'm just exhausted mentally," I said.

"Get some rest, Captain," she said. I moseyed over to the shower. "Wake us up a few hours before we get to Earth."

"Will do," she said.

"Thank you."

"Oh, by the way, Captain, we'll be near your world the next time you wake up," she said, leaning around the corner. I gave her the thumbs up before sealing the lid. She returned the gesture, staring at her thumb oddly.

"My world," I mumbled. I hoped she was right. Luther was my world…

CHAPTER 13

I heard a peck on the glass, then another, then three or four in quick secession. "What?" I mumbled with my eyes closed. I was groggy.

"Captain. It's Drake, you need to wake up," he said. His voice was slightly muted through the cryotube's glass. I was never a morning person despite my military background. Even coffee did little to speed up the process. I rolled over, opening my eyes. I noticed Drake and Xena standing centimeters away from my face on the other side of the glass.

"Guys, a little privacy? Shit!" I shouted. Xena took a giant step back. She knew she was the last thing I wanted to see in the morning.

Drake's eyes were like two green orbs filled with excitement. He had a boyish smirk on his face like it was Christmas morning and he was waiting for me to open gifts. I was irritated, yet pleased to see such a drastic difference in his demeanor. What could possibly cause such a shift?

"Fine. I'm getting up," I grumbled. The cryotube's lid popped up as I swung my legs around. Drake turned away from me politely.

"How many hours until— Oh. *Oh,*" I said, noticing a blue hue lighting the forward cabin. I turned my head slowly toward the cockpit. Out of my peripheral, I noticed Drake flash a full smile while nodding his head.

"Home sweet home. Isn't that the proper phrase?" Drake asked.

"It is."

There it was. I could faintly see the little blue ball Luther and I were born on. Earth. I wiped my eyes as I scooted off the cryotube. I needed a closer look. The cool sensation of my bare feet kissed the metallic floor as I skipped forward, passing Drake and Xena.

The feeling of striding through my front yard barefooted entered my mind. I recalled the cool, dew-soaked grass of springtime brushing against the bottoms of my feet. I wondered if we would ever see another spring, if Luther and I would have the chance to start again, to see and smell the little things together.

I gulped, stepping passed the front seats, peering through the forward viewing glass. "Please," I mumbled. Seeing Earth felt like rounding the corner into a hospital room after a family member was involved in a terrible accident. I didn't know what to expect. Drake stepped forward as I glanced back at him. He was grinning from ear to ear. His eyes were glossy as he stared in amazement.

"It's…it's just *so* blue," he said.

"Wow." I covered my mouth as it dropped. I could see much clearer now. It was so beautiful. No matter how many times I had witnessed this view, it never got old. The blue orb surrounded by blackness wasn't quite as vibrant as I remembered, yet this did little to diminish its magnificence. I closed my eyes and reopened them, I couldn't believe it. Seventy-two years.

Our distance from Earth reminded me of the iconic photos from the Apollo lunar missions. We were roughly the same distance away as the moon.

"Is chameleon up?" I asked, glaring up at the holographic status cluster in front of my seat.

"Yes. We're invisible to their sensors," Xena replied.

"Good. You know, from here it *almost* looks the s-same," I said. I could feel a tear streaming down my left cheek. I wiped it away, sniffling. I leaned forward, observing a disjointed silvery disk that had formed around my home world, it reminded me of a more irregular version of Saturn's rings.

"What's that? The ring?" I spun toward Xena.

"Debris. A small portion of it is from satellites, or space junk from your time. We think some of it is from human ships that attempted to escape over the years, other refugees," Xena explained.

"That's a lot of failed attempts," I said. Off to the left was our moon. It appeared jagged, even from this distance. Xena noticed I was inspecting it closely.

"Our moon looks, different," I said.

"That's another theory for the ring. Some of the moon debris blown off by the android fleet drifted into earth's orbit, intensifying the ring's appearance.

"Unbelievable," I said, eyes wide. All that bombing in preparation to drive the final nail in the coffin. I was likely looking at the precursor to Titan's fate. I gritted my teeth, shaking my head. I wished I had my own fleet to counter the androids. I would destroy them all.

"That's not all." Drake pointed off our starboard side.

"Great."

He handed me my helmet. "Here," he said. I put it on.

"Use hawken to zoom in off the starboard side, what do you see?" he asked. The first thing I did was zoom in on Earth, but before I could get a look, Drake began to turn my head away. "This way."

"No. Hold on! I want to get a look at my home," I snapped at him.

"Oh. Okay. Sorry," he replied. His persistence left me curious, so I panned over to the starboard side where he was pointing.

It was true.

The android fleet was assembled in all their glory, their noses pointed toward Titan. "Oh no," I whispered. I knew there were hundreds of them, but seeing this level of force projection made me gasp.

There were dozens of battle groups, each with a flagship, just like the one that attacked Titan. The reality of it sunk in. We wouldn't last more than a few minutes against this armada. It made the battle group that invaded Titan appear minuscule and insignificant. These ships even seemed like more modern iterations, sleeker, not as crude.

I imagined they were evaluating the data from our defense in preparation for a more devastating follow up. "Oh, my God," I mumbled.

"They sent their bottom of the barrel, mothball ships against us, and they almost wiped us out," I said, glaring at Drake.

He lifted his eyebrows. "Every second counts, Captain. I really hope Luther is somewhere on that blue ball, for all our sakes," he said.

"Thanks."

In Drake's mind, the weight of Titan rested on our shoulders, the fate of humanity even, but for me, it was even more than that. My husband was there, somewhere, dead or alive.

"Are you familiar with the properties of the device Luther gave me?" I turned toward Xena.

"Of course. It's an old piece of tech by today's standards, but it should serve its purpose. Your thumb imprint will initiate a voice activation system. It will prompt you to answer a question once activated, then, if answered correctly, it will reveal a set of coordinates and thaw his cryotube," she explained.

"I wanted to see if you knew anything else about it," I said.

"It should be a straightforward process, if his cryotube is active," Xena cautioned.

"*If*," I mumbled under my breath.

"Once you answer correctly, we'll have to act quickly. His cryotube thawing process will last about two hours, according to my files," Xena said.

"I know."

Drake glared over at me. "What's the chance he'd ask some ridiculously difficult question you might not know or remember?" He bit his bottom lip.

"Highly unlikely. He wants me to find him obviously, and Luther is highly intelligent. He would ask something only I would know, but familiar enough that I will remember easily," I replied.

"Let's hope." Drake sighed, placing his hands behind his head.

"The most likely scenario is that you answer the question correctly, we receive the coordinates, but there is no cryotube. The passage of time has—"

I snapped over toward Xena, cutting her off. "Thank you, Xena. I can always count on your honesty."

"Forgive me, Captain." She slumped her head, attempting to simulate regret. I rolled my eyes.

"Where is the device?" Drake asked.

"In my storage locker," I replied, sliding down into the pilot's seat.

"Well, let's do this." Drake stormed to the back of the ship, donning his suit. I was surprised by his level of enthusiasm. The truth was, now that I was here, I was more terrified and apprehensive than expected. Not just of seeing what my world had become but, obviously, Luther's fate.

I knew I was potentially hours away from revealing the fabric that held my sanity together, or not. He was my purpose. Since I had woken on Titan, I had subconsciously forged a shield of hope around me. Despite the doubt that pelted all around me, I had to believe in the small possibility he was alive to go on.

I had made it this far. But now, in the midst of my birthplace, I was frozen in fear. If Luther was gone, it would be detrimental to my psychology, and Titan needed me at full mental capacity.

"Um, Captain, suit up. There's no time to waste. Once you answer that question, we are breaking into the atmosphere to find him," Drake ordered. His voice sounded off with a touch of authority.

"Right. On it," I said. I put my face in my palms for a moment and sighed. I had to do it, there was no other option. I stood up slowly, using the seat to brace myself.

All at once, Xena patted me on the back. "Looking forward to meeting Luther Belic and seeing your planet, Captain." She grinned and stepped back toward the storage area. I stared at her. The death dealing instrument that sent Luther to Earth was now assisting my journey to reclaim him.

Perhaps she was attempting to relax me to aid in Titan's agenda. I didn't feel she was genuine in her statement, how could she be?

My heart was pounding, my hands were shaking, and I could feel myself sweating when I was cold only a few minutes earlier. I wondered if this is what Luther went through daily with his anxiety.

244

I shambled back to the lockers. For a moment, I laughed at myself as I glanced down at my legs. Luther could be touching me in hours, or dead. My thoughts ping-ponged from one extreme to the other. This could be the happiest day of my life, or the worst, or maybe nothing at all. Like Xena said, there was a possibility we might not find a trace of him.

"Get it together, Belic," I mumbled.

A decaying realization washed back to shore in my mind, something I had fought back since the day I discovered Luther might be alive. Who am I if Luther is no more? I felt a sense of aimlessness and hopelessness overshadow my thoughts.

"No!" I shouted.

"What?" Drake spun around, startled.

"Nothing. I'm good. Perfect."

Drake glanced back down, checking his C-12 pistol. "Captain Belic, I'm readying your weapon, too—"

"Give it here." I stood up, showing Drake the palm of my hand. He placed the pistol in it.

"Here you go," he said. When I saw the weapon, I could feel my training kick in. I'd learned to fire a weapon in the military, and the association was a welcomed distraction. I was a top tier naval fighter pilot, trained to deal with extreme pressure. I kept thinking about what I had been through. All the hopeful pilots that quit during training, one even committed suicide after being disqualified.

Still, I had never dealt with anything of this magnitude, not even close, but I had to alter my thought process to give myself a chance.

"Xena, assume an orbit around Earth of twelve thousand kilometers. All detection systems on deck," I ordered.

"Roger. Aimed at earth and away from the debris ring," she replied.

"What is the maximum speed of those newer destroyers, Xena? Any idea? If we're detected, I want to know how much of an advantage we have," I said.

"They're not even close to us, Captain, from what we've recorded around the moon. If we flee, we'll have a near nine thousand kilometer per hour advantage over them at full power," Xena said.

"At least we can outrun them if need be," I took hold of the throttle. I wondered if those numbers were accurate.

Drake stepped into the copilot seat, flipping a few switches above him. "I'll be looking for any signs that the androids are alerted to our presence. Our drone testing revealed we're invisible, but I want to make completely sure," he said, turning toward me. He nodded with confidence.

"Roger that, Colonel," I said, powering forward. Earth began to grow larger and larger in my view as the minutes past. I turned, staring at Drake for a moment as Earth reflected on his visor.

"Entering orbital revolution range in five, four, three, two, one," Xena said.

"We're ready, Captain," Drake said. I took off my helmet and headed toward my locker. I opened it slowly, reaching in the top cubby hole. I cupped the small device in both hands and I pressed it against my face.

"Please, *please*, be here, Luther," I whispered, stepping back to my seat.

"There's a button on the top. Use your thumb, press and hold for eight seconds," Xena explained. I pressed down on the indentation, waiting for it to turn on.

"Good luck, Victoria." Drake nodded.

"Thank you," I replied.

A red light flashed down the middle of the thumb sized device, then I heard some static and rustling around. After a few seconds, a voice erupted. "Okay, l-let's see here, hold on, hunny," Luther said. I bent forward in my seat, attempting to hold back the tears as my heart fluttered with excitement.

Drake patted me on the back. I pointed at the device. "It's him," I gleamed. Luther sounded horrible, I could tell he was depressed. I hadn't heard that distressed tone since his father passed away.

"Alright, hopefully you can hear me, Vic. Okay, this audio device, the techs here on the *Orion* set it up for me, it's connected to my cryotube. But uh, yeah, the way it works is after this file plays, you have a thirty second timer to answer my question, but before I ask, I just. Well, I wanted to say a few things. Not sure if you watched the video file, or if it played, but I'm basically repeating myself here. Let's see... I, uh, I hope it hasn't been that long since we last saw each other. I'd hate to have to buy all new clothes. Flannel only comes back in style every so often.

"You probably think I'm crazy for doing this, the doctor says I am. She said there can be complications going under the ice and being transported around. And the truth is, I-I am afraid, not so much for myself, though. You know how I overthink things, but the scariest part is, for me, is not seeing you again. The unknown, but I've thought about it, and I understand that's what life is all about. But let me say, this whole ordeal has been a revelation for myself.

"Do you remember that Christmas years ago when your father told us about when he went to the ocean? I know you do. For him, it was a moment of almost self-awareness. You told me he never got to take vacations because of work, but seeing the vastness changed him. Made him realize how small he was.

"Then, I think about your ocean-like, self-awareness experience, what you told me about breaking through Earth's atmosphere your first time. The limitlessness of space, the scale and beauty of looking down on your home. All those billions of humans who lived and died, never having the opportunity you had. You said it changed you, made you realize the brevity of life.

"Well, for me, I'm admittedly more like your father in ways, especially after bouts with anxiety and depression. Most of my life, you know, I lived in fear. Before I met you, I had given up, confined to my single bedroom apartment. Then I ran into you at that local home improvement store. It was raining, remember? I was picking out a brighter color to paint my room, to cheer me up, then you gave me your stone-cold advice on how rust orange walls wouldn't go with my carpet sample. We talked for twenty minutes about nothing.

"I didn't have the courage to ask you for your number, but you knew I wanted it. I was stumbling with my words at goodbye, trying to slip it in. And that brings me to *the* question. I know you'll remember. Here it goes... What was the name of the carpet sample I had? We joked about it for years. When this file stops, you'll be prompted by a beep to answer. But, ah, b-before I go...I-I really wanted to tell you something. That-that day was *my* ocean-like experience. It meant that out of billions of people, out of the vastness, someone existed that saw past my obvious flaws. You saw me for *me*. It opened up a world I never thought existed. So, if I never see you again, I-I want you to know, I-I've lived life to the fullest in the decade we had together. Meeting you was my moment, my ocean. I love you more than anything, Vic. I hope to see you soon."

The audio stopped as tears sprinkled my suit. I awaited the prompt. I knew the answer. I glared out my port side window at Earth in anticipation. It was time. I took myself back to that day when I first met him.

The device beeped.

I leaned into the small microphone. "Opposites attract," I answered without hesitation.

I smiled excitedly, recalling the peculiar red and green carpet sample, like cliché Christmas colors. Ironically, the hideous color combo symbolized how different Luther and I were.

The red light on the device flashed green several times. "It appears your answer was correct, Captain. The device is receiving a signal," Xena confirmed. I jumped up out of my seat, nearly hitting my head on the ceiling. "He knew exactly what to ask!" I yelled.

"One step closer." Drake grinned. I hugged him, mashing the side of my face against his visor.

"Oh. I'm happy for you, for us." He smiled, hesitantly placing his arm around me. I paced back and forth with my hands on my head.

"Coordinates received. Searching. Regional data confirmed. The location was formerly known as the Russian Federation," Xena said. This was it. I felt a sense of urgency overtake me. If he was alive in his cryotube, it was thawing now.

"We have to hurry," I said.

"To our knowledge, we have the fastest ship ever built. We can be there in minutes. So, let's just be safe," Drake warned. I sighed loudly, slowing down my breathing.

"You know, it's interesting that Viktor and the refugees are from Russia, too. Maybe there *is* a settlement there." Drake stared out into space.

"They *were* from Russia," I said. We had no idea where they departed from.

"Transmitting encrypted data to Titan," Xena said.

"You okay?" Drake asked. He peered around at me. It was difficult to comprehend what was ahead. I felt a rush of blood surfacing on my face as my palms began to sweat.

"Yeah, yeah. I'm just ready to go, to get this over with," I said, plopping down into the pilot's seat. I took hold of the flight stick as the navigation indicator popped up on my screen.

"Show us your home, Captain," Drake nodded.

I slammed the throttle forward. The image of Earth blurred and shook in our view, growing larger by the second. I could make out the swooping white clouds painted across the round blue canvas. Details of the land masses begin to surface. Between the clouds, I observed the Mediterranean Sea, then Italy came in view. It all appeared much the same as I remembered, from here anyway. I was waiting for Drake or Xena to make a comment about our high-speed approach. Neither said a word.

"Amazing view," Drake whispered slowly. I could only imagine how he felt. I'd seen this sight more times than I could count, but this time was much different. I felt a surge of excitement and gratefulness while staring at Earth. It felt like a dream. Ever since Arania told me about the fate of the planet, I expected the worst. I thought I might not see home again.

Earth now encompassed most of our perspective as blackness turned to blue. There seemed to be an unspoken agreement between Drake and I as we watched on without a word, each of us observing its beauty like a piece of art at a gallery. While our perspective was much different, this was humanity's rightful home, and we let it slip away.

"Entering the atmosphere," I said as an orange, boomerang shaped flame spanned across our heatshield, blocking much of our wonderful view.

"This atmosphere is no joke," Drake observed.

"Saved our asses plenty of times from asteroids. Burns most of them up," I said.

"Didn't help the dinosaurs. That I remember." He arched an eyebrow.

"*Most* of them burn up. Some meteors have sturdier elements that help them survive entry intact. That's where you run into problems," I said. Drake nodded.

"Ever had that problem on Titan?" I asked.

"It's rare. Titan's guardian against asteroid strikes is Saturn, it's blocked a giant meteor from impacting our home before. In fact, it's thought both Jupiter and Saturn have thwarted Earth impacts due to their gravitational influence," Xena spoke up.

"Interesting," I replied. I thought it was strange how some Titans viewed Saturn in a spiritual sense. I guess much of it was because they didn't have anything else to look at. Or maybe they needed something to keep them from going insane?

I throttled down into the lower atmosphere on the light side of Earth. It was a sunny, unsuspecting, surprising scene. I could have woken up on an airliner in this setting and never thought anything different about it.

Drake leaned over, peering at his ancestor's planet without a word. I took pleasure knowing I was here to see it with him. He was likely the only Titan that would ever experience this.

"Drake," I mumbled.

"Y-yeah," he replied. He did a double take as he noticed my glossy eyes.

"What's wrong?" he whispered.

"I'm fine. It just, it means something to me, to see someone from your world experience this," I said. He paused and nodded slowly. I leveled off, setting a cruising altitude of sixteen thousand meters headed toward our indicator.

"Ahead," I said. We dipped into a patch of thick, white cumulus clouds.

"Wow," he said as our perspective remained concealed by the fluffy condensation. Drake unbuckled and stood up to get a better view.

"Hey, Colonel, sit down," I cautioned.

He hesitated before complying, staring out of the glass. "Sorry, it's just—"

"I know," I replied.

"I've seen Earth through virtual reality simulations before, but nothing is like the real thing, apparently. These colors, they're so vibrant, the white clouds, the blue ocean. It's sensory overload," he went on.

We pressed through the patchy clouds for a few minutes until breaking through a clearing.

"Look at that!" he said. It was a sprawling vista. The ocean was calm and vast, seaming alongside the golden coast in the distance. I glanced back at Xena as she observed the gorgeous backdrop. Sunlight hit her face as she narrowed her eyes at the landmass. Her origins also stemmed from here, and now her kind had surpassed us as the rulers of this world.

"Land ahead. That's eastern Europe." I pointed. I didn't give them much time to gaze at the scenery as I throttled forward.

"It's really, green? All of it," Drake observed.

"This doesn't conjure up imagery of nuclear holocaust," I commented, scanning the vibrant green forest below us. There was nothing out of the ordinary, tall pines tucked against patches of rocky hills. No buildings, no abandoned structures, just wild country that stretched into the horizon forever. It seemed untouched by human hands.

"It's possible some regions of the planet were less affected by the war," Xena said.

"Well, what are the radiation levels?" I asked.

"Wait. Scanning… slightly above normal readings before the war, nothing your suit won't repel," she replied.

"Hmm." I eased forward on the throttle slightly, encroaching Mach 7.

"The Black Sea incoming," I noticed, staring at the indicator of Luther's pod as it grew nearer by the moment.

"I see it. The water has sort of a blue-green hue," Drake observed.

Something caught my eye. "There's something out there, in the distance, there are two orbs on the water."

"Where?" he asked.

"Two large objects, there's a sun glare on them. Eleven O'clock." I backed off the throttle and enabled hawken, zooming in.

"I see it!" Drake said excitedly. We noticed two massive ships parallel to one another. They seemed identical with some type of giant paddle wheels. Behind the ships was a bright blue trail in the water that stretched for a kilometer or more, then narrowed and dissipated in the water. As I placed my visor's cursor over the top of them, a stack of statistics flashed on the lower left-hand side of my heads-up display.

LENGTH: 422 METERS

WIDTH: 114 METERS

HEIGHT: 46 METERS

SPEED: 8 KNOTS

LIFEFORMS: 0 DETECTED

"Those things are either autonomous or android controlled, no life detected," I rattled.

"Or there's some sort of dampening to conceal lifeforms," Xena added.

"Or that, yes," I said.

They reminded me of some sort of bulky barge, but the purpose was unknown. The ships' design appeared round, like a silver dome, pristine and well maintained, with no catwalks or ladder wells on deck. The only standout feature was the giant turn wheel on the bow. "Captain, radiation levels over this body of water are much higher than anything recorded thus far," Xena informed.

"I wonder if those ships have anything to do with it?" I glared beneath me one last time as we rocketed past.

"Thirteen minutes until arrival," Xena said. I gulped.

"So, is there any discernible difference? The atmosphere, water, land?" Drake snapped over at me.

"I mean, I've never been to this exact section of Earth, but I don't see any differences. I can't say that there is." I sighed. "Maybe the planet has begun to recover?" I asked.

"The data obtained from the android war estimates thousands of nuclear impacts across the globe. I don't see a single hint of that." Drake threw up his hands.

"I was taught Earth was a hellhole, but other than some slight radiation spots here and there, it looks fairly habitable," he went on.

"We don't know that. There could be all sorts of unseen dangers. Like Xena said, this may not represent the rest of the planet."

"Or not," he mumbled. I could understand his frustration. To me, Titan was a shithole far beyond this version of Earth, at least from what I could tell.

As we passed over the mountains, the ground beneath us began to turn white as we pushed into what was once Russia. The clouds thickened in the lower atmosphere. "Destination arrival in six minutes," I said, pulling back on the throttle and dropping altitude. My heart was pounding in my chest as we broke through the low hanging snow clouds.

"The visual diversity is stark. Seems like we're on another planet," Xena scoffed. She seemed almost irritated by the variety as snow began to whip about the cockpit glass. Only moments ago, everything was green and blue.

"I remember reading about this," Drake mumbled as the flakes pelted the front glass. He turned toward me like a curious child, awaiting my response.

"Yes. And I was never a fan of it," I said.

"There's something ominous about it all. It's beautiful, but it seems so alien to me," he said, panning all around.

"Try driving a car surrounded by thousands of morons on the morning commute in this shit. Almost makes the risk of being a fighter pilot seem not so bad." I backed off the throttle again to 400 kilometers per hour, cruising in. Ahead was a flat tundra butted against a line of large hills or small mountains.

"Here? There's nothing out here?" Drake said. I glided toward the objective, rolling the craft so that Drake could get a better look. He stared out. "Okay, never mind, there *is* something down there."

"What?" I asked, biting my lip while awaiting his answer.

"The snow was obscuring my view, but it looks like a cave," he said. I looped around one more pass to get a look of my own. There was an unassuming shadowy area at the base of the mountain. Honestly, it didn't look like much to me, but then again, the human resistance probably wouldn't have a sign posted.

"Let's check it out. The indicator lines up with it. This has to be the place," I confirmed. I brought the ship to a hover about 600 meters above it, slowly descending. I trained my guns down on the entrance. I thought it could be a setup, a trap of some sort. As alien as the world appeared to Drake, I thought the passage of time gave me a similar feeling. I was about to disembark on a planet that wasn't my own. My kind had been evicted.

"Xena, continue the landing descent, but keep our guns on that location and the engine ready for evasive. I want automated fire support if this goes sour. I'm not convinced yet," I ordered.

"Roger that, Captain." I felt the autopilot assume control of the flight stick before I stood up. Drake and I met eyes before stepping toward the rear gate. He nodded, and in his wide eyes, I saw an even mix of determination, fear, and excitement.

As I passed our living quarters, I noticed Xena suiting up in her combat armor. "Not expecting this to go well?" I asked.

"Better to be prepared, I suppose. Would you like me to assume a more *docile* appearance? Maybe drop the armor?" she asked. I glared up at her black skull mask.

"Negative," I said. She appeared less like an android with her heavy armor on, but more frightening. Seemed to even out in my mind. In this case, we had more firepower, at least. I watched as she clicked both of her massive laser cannons to each arm. The device had a shotgun like slide with a blue light running the length of the meter-long barrel.

She noticed me staring at the slide. "That's to disengage the safety," she said.

"Oh." I lifted my eyebrows. For a moment, I thought about our conversation from before. How she tricked me into thinking she was similar to the androids from my time. The incident with the Russian refugees seemed to wash away the tension, at least on my end.

"Don't be alarmed, Captain. If friendly fire *does* occur, I can assure, you'll never feel a thing," she said. Drake cracked half a smile.

"Comforting," I replied. Maybe the absence of tension was *only* on my end. The jet rocked back and forth, encroaching the ice beneath. The landing gear plopped down hard as the shocks absorbed some of the impact.

"Whoa," I said, bracing my arm against the hull.

"It's the winds," Xena said, excusing her shipboard AI counterpart.

"Yeah, wouldn't that be awful, to crash now? After everything?" I mumbled.

Drake chuckled nervously. "Don't even joke about it, please," he said. As we waited, I noticed the interior of the ship was eerily silent compared to the sound of the howling winds outside.

Drake and Xena met eyes as I inspected my pistol one last time. Just before putting on my helmet, I stared into the visor's red-tinted reflection of myself.

"Hmm." I wondered for a moment if the person in the reflection was my true self or the warrior on the outside was. My experience as a pilot shared a kinship with this helmet's design, it's almost serrated, aggressive lines reminded me of my razor-sharp skillset. I was calculative, cunning, and precise in and outside of combat.

Was that really me though? The implications of the situation challenged the perception of myself.

Perhaps my fearless prowess as a pilot was masking the real me, the woman who was afraid of loneliness and abandonment. As much as I admired and loved my father, I felt alone all those years when I was young. He remained wounded long after my mother left him. He was unavailable emotionally and worked long hours. Basically, I was left to figure life out on my own.

Like my father after his divorce, perhaps I closed up and hardened my soul too, obsessively focusing on school, sports, and eventually becoming the best fighter pilot in the fleet. It's possible my fixation on success was a distraction from resentment toward my mother's abandonment.

Luther came along and was an available version of my father, and I latched onto him emotionally. Perhaps I wasn't quite the hard-as-nails, aggressive pilot as I projected to be. Maybe I was compensating for the absence of parents.

Luther understood me completely, he took on my faults, my brashness, my competitive spirit. All the things that made me a hard pill to swallow, he embraced them, and I did the same for his faults.

We were a team. An odd but functional couple. Our unity made us both, better. He lowered my guard. If he was gone, I wondered if I would recede completely into an abyss of vacancy and nothingness, like the machines I swore to fight. More than likely, the revelation about his death might kill me, but it was worth it to be the cold, hardened warrior my helmet's appearance represented, one last time.

I had to find out.

I donned my helmet aggressively. "Let's do it!" I shouted.

"Whoa. I like the enthusiasm." Drake stepped aside cautiously as the rear gate lowered. Snow flurries swirled up into the ship, surrounding us.

"Wow," Drake mumbled, his eyes bounced around with excitement. I took the first step down, marching toward the objective marker. The ramp met my cleated-boot first, clanking against the metal, then I came across Earth's soil, crunching when I stomped into the snow. I stopped, remembering the feeling like it was yesterday.

I glared over my shoulder at Drake. "Welcome." I nodded. His eyes widened. He'd traded the pink, toxic vapor of Titan for the white haze of Earth.

Xena followed close behind him as we huddled a few meters ahead of the ship. The wind whipped about violently, hurling snow in all directions.

"The objective marker is about six hundred and seventy meters that way." Drake pointed at the cave. He was panting, perhaps he was nervous in the new surroundings. I led out in front anxiously as they trailed behind a few meters. I peered through the snow at the shadowy entrance, no more than two meters tall. Icicles overhung the entry, some larger than my forearm.

The cave was uninviting. The entrance's shape reminded me of a monster's open mouth full of pointed, sickled teeth.

"No footprints." Drake panned around.

"It wouldn't take long to cover them, not in this weather," I said as a strong gust of wind pushed me toward Drake. He secured me by the arms as I stumbled forward. "Are you okay?"

"Yep. Thanks," I said. I felt his strength as he scooped me upright. I glanced at Xena as I stepped forward. "Xena, if Luther is here, we're completely prepared for this situation, right?"

"Yes. In the event we find Mr. Belic, I have a booster kit in my suit. It should give him the proper nutrition and stabilizing that he requires. If he has complications or injuries, we can take him back to the ship for further aid," she explained.

"Thank you, Xena. Good to know," I said. What she didn't know is I was taking him back to the ship anyway. I wanted him surrounded in a protected shell while he recovered. I fought my way through the blizzard-like winds. I stepped up within a few meters of the cave, dipping inside the indented formation.

The wind howled through the concave compression chamber. It was like a wind tunnel, intensifying the flow of air to the point that it was difficult to walk.

I hunkered low, gripping the base of the larger icicles the best I could to guide forward. For a moment, I wondered if I was picked up by the winds, would I be impaled by the spears on the ground. All at once. Xena grabbed my collar. "Proceed with confidence, Captain. You're fine."

I wondered if my body language gave it away. I nodded. "Thanks."

It was almost as if she read my thoughts and reacted. I stepped toward the entrance and glared inside. It was black as night. I cycled to night vision with my visor, peering into the darkness with my pistol. To my surprise, the interior was squared off, the walls inside sculpted ice with smooth surfaces.

"See that? Those aren't natural formations?" I asked.

"Doesn't strike me as such. Someone was here, at one time," Drake said. I proceeded inside, stepping over a few chunks of ice in front of the entrance onto a snow floor. "Watch your step," I warned.

The snow inside was matted down and crunchy, like a high traffic area, but again, no footprints. It was vacant. The large room was about three meters high by five meters wide. From here, I noticed walls had a circular swirl pattern on them, as if it had been polished. Straight ahead, the room narrowed into a left turn, and we couldn't see what was around the bend.

"Only one way to go," Drake said. I noticed a pile of ragged fur clothes tucked away in a corner, along with a pair of rusted icepicks. "See those?" I pointed.

"Yeah," Drake said. We cautiously pressed forward around the corner into a narrow tunnel. This area had a high ceiling that opened into the mountain, maybe twelve meters tall. It seemed to stretch far into the distance, the walls had perfectly chiseled ice on both sides.

"What is this place?" Drake mumbled.

"Not sure, but look down." I observed.

"Are those, tracks?" he asked.

"Some sort of railway system." I narrowed my eyes zooming down the track. I nodded. This could be a good sign.

"Indeed, it appears this was used for transportation," Xena said.

"Transportation system means there's possibly some sort of society in place," Drake said.

"Or *was*," I said. Suddenly, a bright light shined from the depths of the tunnel, almost like a camera flash. I tugged Drake back around the bend in cover.

"What was that!?" Drake whispered excitedly.

"No idea. Back up!" I signaled.

"Incoming," Xena said. After a few seconds, I began to hear a screeching sound in the distance. It was getting louder.

"I hear it," Drake said.

"Judging by the sound, an object is approaching, sixty meters, fifty, forty," Xena continued. As she counted down, I could see a large metal object coming into view. It came to a sudden halt about ten meters in front of us.

I leaned around for a better look.

"Well?" Drake asked.

"It's, a rail cart." I panned closer, examining the worn green paint and shiny front grill on it. The more I probed, it became apparent this was an old SUV converted into a rail car. The roof had been chopped off, so it sported an open top. The frame had been modified for the track, along with new wheels of course.

The headlights flashed. I quickly ducked around the corner, waiting several seconds. Nothing happened.

"Someone in it?" Drake asked.

"I don't see anyone," I said.

"Captain, allow me to investigate," Xena suggested.

I stepped around the corner instead. "Wait!" Drake whispered sternly, pulling at my wrist, but I jerked away. I slowly approached the car, hugging the wall on the left side. I aimed my pistol down into the cabin, observing the once attractive body lines, now dented and warped on the passenger side from an impact.

"This thing has been through hell," I whispered.

"What is it?"

"It's a BMW. They were called SUVs in my day, standard utility vehicles. Mostly for families. This model debuted a couple years before I left for Titan." I recalled seeing it advertised as a hybrid solar/diesel powered variant.

I walked right next to it, peering over into the cabin slowly. It was strange seeing something so fresh and new in my mind, now an antique hunk of metal. Drake followed. "Stay put. If they have cameras, we don't want to frighten them." He motioned Xena.

"Roger," she responded.

Abruptly, a refrigerator shaped robot with a spherical head sprung from underneath the hood like a jack in the box, pointing two arm mounted cannons at us. I jumped back, pointing my pistol at it.

"Fuck!" I yelled.

"Hands up. D-don't move," the robotic voice stuttered. A horizontal white light bar on its dome head strobed back and forth as it spoke, then a red light emitted from it, scanning our bodies up and down.

"Just do as instructed, Captain," Drake said.

"Unidentified lifeforms detected. Drop your weapons. Drop your weapons immediately," the bot commanded.

"Colonel? Your orders?" Xena spoke up.

"Stay put, Xena," he said. I dumped the pistol, throwing up my hands. Before the pistol could touch the ground, the drone zapped my C-12, melting it into a glop of silver matter.

It panned over, zapping Drake's weapon too. "Thank you," it said. Smoke trailed off our weapons as the robot scanned my face several times. "Two lifeforms. Uncontaminated. Unidentified. Climb aboard and proceed to the next checkpoint. Good day." The drone retracted back under the hood.

"What the hell? Uncontaminated?" Drake asked.

"Doesn't sound good," I replied.

"What's your gut say?" he asked.

"It says we don't have much choice," I replied.

"That scared the shit outta me. My heart is pounding," Drake said. He held his chest as he panted.

"I remember these robots from when I was a kid, before the androids," I recalled.

"Security bot?" Drake asked.

"Uh, no. Home assistance for the elderly. First generation."

"Someone or something modified it then."

"Yeah. The ones from my day didn't have laser cannons," I said. The bot was a first generation cleaner, capable of many household duties.

I recalled my aunt had one. I remembered they were somewhat wonky and unreliable, nothing like the more modern Keltons. It seemed this modified version was capable enough for this role.

"Drake, I think Xena should go back to XU-97. Apparently, being a lifeform is the ticket here," I said, raising my eyebrows as I stared down the tunnel.

"I don't like the idea of heading into the unknown with zero protection," he whispered. I stepped closer so we could speak quietly. It was possible this cart was equipped with audio receiving technology.

"The marker is that way, and it's our only lead, Colonel." I pointed down the tunnel.

Drake glanced at the ground. "I know. Could she follow us on foot from a distance?" he asked.

"Possibly, but understand she's a liability down here. If this is a human settlement, they likely have the ability to detect androids. The last thing we need is a firefight," I replied.

"Your call," I added.

Drake nodded slowly. "Xena, head back to the ship, for now."

"Roger that, Colonel. Returning to the ship to await your orders," she said. I spun toward the rail car. I opened the driver side door and it creaked loudly. "First time, right?" I asked Drake.

"For what?" he asked.

"In a car."

"I mean yeah, technically, if you want to call *this* a car," he replied, sitting down.

"If you had one of these in my day, it was considered luxury." I shut the door, I heard some paint chips or dirt fall off the side when I did.

"Doesn't look like luxury is much of an option anymore," he replied. I sat down on the torn cloth seat. It was a converted bench. Up front and in the back, it could sit six adults, uncomfortably. Occupants could face either direction with the absence of a back rest. We turned toward the direction of our objective down the tunnel.

A light flashed at the end of the shaft again, as I heard the diesel engine start in front of us. It hummed along at a low rpm. As I panned around at the interior, I noticed what appeared to be stained blood on the inside of the doors and seat. I assumed my visor could analyze the substance for confirmation, but I didn't bother. At this point, it didn't matter.

I wasn't backing out even if it was.

The cart started to move. "Here we go," Drake said, glaring behind us. The rail car's lights flickered down the tunnel until the right side went out completely. We were moving along at a brisk pace, maybe two meters per second. The cart wobbled around a bit on the frame, but it felt sturdy enough for this speed.

"Probably be safer to walk, we don't have any control over our approach, no idea what's ahead." Drake's eyes bounced around.

"We're playing by their rules. I thought you liked that style?" I asked.

"I'm enjoying it less and less." He raised an eyebrow.

"That happens in real situations," I said. Drake snapped toward me, staring intensely into my eyes. He turned away as I glared ahead for a couple of minutes, wondering about Luther. Was he being kept safely somewhere? Was he alone?

"I appreciate your faith in my decision making," Drake interrupted my thoughts.

"Uh, what?"

"You know what I'm talking about." He narrowed his eyes at me. I shook my head.

"With the refugees I killed," he added. I sighed loudly.

"Look, Drake, you were put in a horrible position. Let's move on from it and focus on the task at hand," I said.

"Yeah, but—"

"It's not the time or the place to discuss this. Once we get back to Titan, we can decompress from all this and do as many evaluations as you want," I advised.

"That's just the thing, if you don't trust my leadership, how can we move forward? Trust is a huge part of it," he said.

"Drake, listen. There weren't many options considering the Russians lied to us about the number of refugees. We were unprepared. It wasn't you," I reassured.

"I wanted to help them. I let my emotions get in the way. I thought there had to be a way to save them," he said. I nodded my head slowly. I could appreciate his genuineness and kind heart. He wanted to make a difference.

But this is war. Sixteen refugees weren't worth risking the survival of the human race.

"In that case, it was a lost cause. I'll continue to offer you assistance. I'm not saying I'm always right, but hopefully my experience can give you insight in certain situations," I replied.

He sighed and clenched his left hand.

"Can I ask you one thing?" he said.

I knew it was coming. "What?"

Drake slumped his head. "Just out of curiosity, what would you have done in my shoes?" he questioned. I was right.

"You're not going to let up, are you?" I asked. He shook his head.

I sighed. "I honestly don't think the Russians had anything valuable to share with us. But in that situation, if I was in full command? I would have asked nicely for the coordinates a couple of times and explained the situation," I said.

"The truth? You would have told them they weren't going to survive?" he asked.

"I would have told Viktor that. Then if they didn't want to comply, I would have offered two options: one, they give me the locations of the android bases and I eject the pod. I would promise to destroy the pod with the XU-97. This would be a quick, honorable death in which they contributed to humanity's survival. I would explain that."

Drake gulped. "And option two?"

"I would have sent Xena in to execute them one at a time until they told me the locations," I said plainly.

Drake's eyes widened and his jaw dropped. "That easy?"

"Fuck no. It's not easy at all. But it's a numbers game. You have to think of it that way. Sixteen people versus potentially millions or billions that will be born in the future if we don't stop the androids. We need those locations, so we do whatever it takes," I explained.

"Even if it means abandoning your husband if this signal we're following leads to nowhere? We don't have time to scour the planet for him." I glanced down at the deck. I could feel him staring a hole through me.

I narrowed my eyes at him, "Yes," I said. After I answered, the truth revealed itself, smacking me in the face. *They* might abandon the search for Luther if we didn't find him initially, but I realized then that I wouldn't. I dropped my head as guilt overwhelmed me. I just explained to Drake that sixteen people weren't worth risking the fate of humanity, but one person was? Unfortunately, yes, to me, Luther was worth it. Love, celebrated and considered exclusive to humans, was now a potential detriment to our survival.

It took me long enough, but I realized just how selfish and hypocritical I was. It made sense. Unbelievable. Titan was right to be suspicious of me. They painted Xena a bullseye on my head for good reason.

I wasn't ready for this.

I gulped. It was time to confront this head on. Not even Luther would want this. I gritted my teeth in anger. If we didn't find Luther this first go around, Drake would likely opt to abort the search for him and pursue other intelligence options. Time wasn't on our side.

I flared my nostrils. I hoped that when the moment came, I would do the right thing. If I abandoned Drake to continue my search for Luther, my absence would jeopardize the entire human race.

"Captain. Whatever is down this tunnel, you lead, I'll follow. Maybe I can learn a thing or two," Drake interrupted my thoughts.

"Wait, what? Um..." I straightened up in my seat and arched an eyebrow.

"We'll try it for a while. You're in charge. Honestly, my confidence is shaken, or maybe I need a break. That's me being completely honest," he revealed. The problem was, I was also having my own doubts.

"Drake, I have to be honest with you, too," I said.

His eyes widened. "What?"

"I know what I said about making the tough choices, but I'm... I don't know, it just hit me that if Luther's not here, I—"

"Captain," he interrupted, leaning in.

"Yes."

"If the time comes and we need to go our separate ways, I'll do what I have to, but I don't think it'll come to that," he said.

"Why?"

"I dare say you're in this position only because of chance. No, you're here for a reason," he said with confidence.

"How can you be sure?" I asked.

"I am. How many people live their lives and know they were born for one moment? Huh? I can tell you without a doubt you and I were born for this. Even if we die. All this isn't lining up out of thin air," he said with conviction.

"I don't know." Truth be told I wasn't one that believed in destiny or fate, but it seemed unusual to have a pilot with my credentials lying around on Titan.

Drake leaned forward. "*Luther* got you here. His love motivated you to make this voyage. It held you together during all this craziness. He is the vessel, otherwise you wouldn't be sitting here, would you?" he asked.

I gulped. "Probably not."

Drake paused. He placed his hand on my shoulder. I felt my eyes gloss over. "No. You wouldn't have. Victoria, *if* he's gone, then his death meant something. It meant you're in the most important position in human history. Take hold of that. Embrace it. Don't let his sacrifice be in vain. *We* need you. *I* need you to take command, Captain." He stared at me more intensely than I thought he was capable of.

I nodded at him slowly. "I—"

"Colonel Drake?" Xena interrupted, chiming in on our helmets.

"Yes?" Drake asked. We waited for a few seconds with no answer.

"Xena!" Drake spoke up.

"Yes. I'm in the XU-97 hovering above the entrance to the cave. Permission to engage a large unknown group heading toward your position. They're aimed right at the tunnel," she said.

Drake stared at me. "Captain?" he said.

"A g-group of what, Xena? What are they?" I took the reins.

"Not sure. Somewhat humanoid in shape, but not movement. Very fast, moving on four limbs. They appear highly agitated and aggressive. Headed to the tunnel, Colonel. I'll need you to give me an order immediately," she rattled.

"Burn 'em! Now!" I ordered.

"Colonel?"

"Do it!" Drake ordered.

"Engaging," she said. I heard a faint shrieking sound that echoed down the tunnel as Drake and I met eyes.

"The hell was that?" Drake said. He leaned forward in his seat.

"Can't be good. Look around the cart, I doubt there are any weapons, but look anyway," I said. Drake climbed over into the back, rummaging around. After a couple of minutes, the hood popped up and the robot pointed its guns at the entrance. "Warning. Motion detected. Scanning. Five, seven, eight, twelve lifeforms detected."

"I didn't stop them all, Colonel. I say again, potential hostiles approaching," Xena said.

"Captain Belic is in charge, Xena, report to her," he said.

There was a moment of silence. "Colonel Drake, are you sure you wish to transfer command and all authority to Captain Belic?" she asked.

"Yes. Yes!" he confirmed.

"Very well. Captain, what are your orders?" she asked.

"Stand by, Xena," I ordered. I could hear growling and snarling echoing from the entrance.

"You think we can outrun them?" Drake asked, peering behind us.

"Doubtful. The sounds are getting louder."

"Contaminated lifeforms detected. Keep all limbs inside the car. Good day." The robot opened fire, lighting the tunnel up like the Fourth of July. Rapid fire bursts of energy zapped down the corridor at an alarming rate. Its squared body snapped left and right erratically.

"Captain, there's a lot of them," Drake said.

"No weapons?" I asked rhetorically.

"Other than the robot, no," he said. I could hear screeching and scampering behind us, but I didn't want to look. Against my better judgment, I turned around anyway, facing the music.

As the robot fired, the flashes of light highlighted a nightmarishly fast creature scurrying upside down on the ceiling. It was like a blur, so fast I couldn't make out its form. It reminded me of a spider's low scamper. "Oh, my God."

Drake followed my eyes. "Shit. No. No. No. I'm not liking Earth one bit here."

"Up high!" I yelled at the robot.

One of them got dangerously close, within several meters on the ceiling. The robot tore into the creature, melting dozens of apple sized holes through its torso and face. It landed hard, tumbling on the tracks. It squirmed around violently before flattening out motionless.

"That was close! How much further is this fucking tunnel?" Drake stood up.

"I don't know, sit down!" I yelled.

"Xena, can you track us from above? Through the terrain?" I yelled.

"Already on it, but your signal is weakening. For now, I see a highlighted outline of you and Colonel Drake moving away," she said.

"How thick is the terrain?" I asked.

"Two to three meters, various geology and soil. More than likely I can penetrate through but—"

"Get above us, I want you to fire on my command directly behind us." I observed the swarm of creatures inching closer. They were darting on the walls, the ceiling, and ground.

"Oh God," Drake said.

"The tracking image of you is lagging slightly, Captain. You'll have to hurry. I cannot guarantee accuracy much longer," she said.

"They're gaining on us, Captain. Fast." Drake glared at me.

"On my command, fire four meters behind us, Xena," I said, concentrating over the buzzing laser fire and shrills.

"In position," Xena said. I trained my eyes on the horde approaching. A blur of ravenous metallic teeth and fangs strobed into view as the headlamps flickered.

"I trust you, Captain, whatever you have to do," Drake said, injecting confidence. I had one shot at this.

"Get ready Xena. Hold...hold...*fire*!" I yelled. An instantaneous beam of white energy flooded the tunnel in front of us, incinerating three of the creatures into a wisp of dust. Sunlight, soil, rock, and snow followed through the hole, crushing the remaining creatures in a tsunami of debris as they shrieked. The rubble piled up, blocking off part of the tunnel.

"Perfect shot!" Drake yelled, standing up.

"Hold your fire, Xena, hostiles down," I ordered. The cart-mounted robot ceased fire, as well, but continued to pan around erratically as we moved deeper into the tunnel.

"They're gonna be pissed about their tunnel." Drake grinned, patting me on the back as I turned toward him.

"You picked a helluva a time to give me command. Shit, *move!*" I yelled. Drake's eyes bulged as one of the creatures emerged from underneath the cart. Time slowed down. It was like a dream I had no control over.

I was frozen in front of a nightmare. It was hideous. A mesh of decaying man and machine, absent of hair on its head, face, or body. It reminded me of a gangly skeleton with a tiny layer of skin and flesh over bone. Anchored into the flesh were small, clover-sized scales. These crude metallic panels blanketed the body, spaced apart two centimeters and were linked by circuitry wires.

I gathered the implanted mechanisms in the creature had a sinister bolstering effect. The cybernetics seemed to preserve only what was absolutely necessary of the flesh, reengineering an otherwise delicate human physical specimen into a deadly, hyper-agile, feral remnant of a man.

The fingers were extended into razor sharp serrated claws, each digit twenty centimeters or more. It had pale skin with white eyes and no visible pupils. The nose was simply two black holes, as were the ears. Facial features seemed to have been lopped off with a heated surgical tool, with bits of seared, blackened flesh around the amputation. It had brackets of metal tracked horizontally across its mouth, splitting the machined upper and lower jaw.

It opened its mouth wider than any human range of motion, like an alpha baboon displaying its teeth to a rival. Inside the mouth was mostly blackness. Greasy, oil-like saliva sloshed about, streaming drool in anticipation from the lower jaw, like a ravenous wolf before a fresh kill. Inside, its metallic gums had a stained yellow, plague hue. Two massive icepick-like fangs suddenly protracted from the upper jaw like twin switchblades. Red veins emerged and pulsed in its milky eyes.

Time seemed to leap forward. The creature lunged at Drake, plunging its dagger like teeth into his visor, cracking and splintering the glass like a spider web. My visor flashed a cautionary indicator:

WARNING - SUIT PRESSURE LOST

COLONEL RIVEN DRAKE

"Ahhh!" Drake shouted.

The monster let out an excited roar. Its eyes turned black as it yanked Drake by the face over onto the side of the rail cart.

"Drake!" I screamed.

"Contamination detected." The rail car robot swiveled around, but the creature was out of its range on the opposite side of the door.

Drake's screams echoed off the tunnel walls. My chest cramped as I scrambled for an idea.

"Think!" I yelled.

"Captain?" Xena asked.

"One of them has D-Drake!" I yelled. I collapsed into the floor holding my chest. I couldn't breathe. I had no fighter jet, no weapons. I shuffled toward Drake as he screamed, leaning my head over the cart. The creature had Drake pinned to the exterior of the door, its claws sunk inside the metal. It was ripping through his helmet as Drake's legs shook violently.

Somehow, Drake was fighting back. "Err! Err! Err!" He struggled, hammer-fisting the creature in the head with little effect.

"Captain, move away from Drake," Xena said.

"What?" No, no, you can't fire through the ground again, you'll hit Drake!" I ordered.

"Who said anything about firing *through* the ground?" Xena asked. I snapped around at a humming sound behind us. My mouth dropped in amazement. Xena was flying the XU-97 sideways *in* the tunnel. She'd crammed it through the hole created from the blast. The craft was scraping the ice ceiling, shaving massive slabs of ice off behind it as it bounced along. I could see her stoic pose in the cockpit, turned sideways as she barreled forward, ready as ever. "Orders?" she asked. The rail cart robot pointed its guns toward our ship. "Motion detect—"

A flash erupted from the XU-97, destroying the cart mounted robot.

"Sorry, Captain, the robot was targeting the XU-97," Xena said.

"No, it's fine! Get closer!" I yelled.

She throttled forward. "Target acquired." She zapped a burst of energy down the side of the rail car. I heard two *thuds* as Xena put on the brakes. I dove over the side without hesitation, tumbling several times before coming to a stop.

"Ahem…okay…where's…Drake…" I panted, getting to my feet. I shambled around in the dust filled corridor. Xena powered down the jet, leaning it against the corridor wall.

"Drake?" I called out. Halfway between myself and the jet, there he was, face down. A cloud of smoke separated us. To the left of him was the monster, sprawled out face up. A chuck of its skull was melted, and its lower body was a pile of goo.

As I approached, I observed patterns of two bloody holes poked throughout his suit. "No," I whispered, running over to him. I kneeled beside him as my visor flashed his vitals:

MEDICAL EMERGENCY WARNING

COLONEL RIVEN DRAKE

CONDITION: EXSANGUINATION

SEEK MEDICAL CARE IMMEDIATELY

"Xena! Drake needs help! He's bleeding out!" I yelled.

"On the way." She navigated out of the ship, jumping off the tilted ramp exit carrying a thick stretcher like board tucked under her arm. I backed away as she neared. She flattened out the board on the frozen soil beside him. "Could you grab his feet?" She asked.

"O-okay."

"Tilt." We gently lifted his body up and slid the stretcher under him as a pair of robotic arms emerged, assisting us from each side. Drake's face was covered in blood and glass. One of the robots scanned Drake's body head to toe while the other one injected him with a maroon fluid. I couldn't help but wonder if this emergency unit was designated for Luther.

"What-what do you think?" I mumbled. The stretcher lifted from the ground, floating in place about waist high like a hoverboard.

"Captain, these medical drones are asking for my assistance, is there any way I could link up with them, then provide you with details later?" she asked, cutting through his suit with a large, scalpel type tool. As the blade sliced through his jumpsuit, I observed several quarter-sized pairs of puncture wounds on his torso. Blood was everywhere, spattered across the inside of his suit and pooling up around the entry points.

"Oh, o-of course. Absolutely. Anything I can do to help?" I showed her my palms, they were shaking.

"Negative. We have a more pressing issue that will require your attention," she said. I glanced over at the XU-97, we would have to figure out a way to get it out of here. Then, I heard footsteps galloping in the distance. I snapped back down the tunnel and saw a group of armed personnel head our way. Beams from flashlights scattered across the ground as they ran at us.

That was the problem Xena mentioned, not the ship.

"I hope these are the good guys," I mumbled. I put my hands up as they approached. I counted eleven of them. They slowed down to a trot within sixty meters from our position, several of them pointing their weapons at us.

They wore dark blue or black camouflage uniforms, combat boots, with gas masks covering their faces. I could hear garbled dialogue between them, but I couldn't make any of it out. They stopped about thirty meters from us, and by this point, they were all pointing their weapons in our direction.

"Captain, I would suggest a diplomatic solution. If I'm forced to aid you in a combat situation, Drake will surely die from his injuries, along with yourself," she said plainly.

"No pressure." I whispered, glaring back at Drake fighting for his life. I turned back around, stepping out to face the line of masked soldiers. I adjusted the tint of my visor so that they could see my face plainly.

A garbled female voice erupted in Russian. I glanced over my shoulder at Xena for translation, but before I could, she spoke again.

"Or do you understand the English tongue?" she asked.

"Yes, ma'am. English," I answered quickly. The soldiers on both sides of her were beaming down their weapon sights at me. My heart was pounding. They'd likely never seen anything like us. The first thing I thought of was fear of the unknown. They might think it's safer to execute us than to risk it.

"Knees, get on your knees!" the woman ordered. I immediately complied. She pushed forward, training her gun on Xena. "You!" she yelled at Xena, but she kept working on Drake.

"Hey, in the armor! Do you understand English?" she yelled at Xena.

"She does. She's not refusing your order, but she's performing lifesaving aid to our friend. He was severely injured," I said.

"Injured?" The woman sidestepped to get a better look at Drake. She stopped next to me. I couldn't see her face. The gas mask had two large holes around the eyes that were tinted black. Her head bobbed around while staring at me. She curiously tapped her gun barrel against my visor lightly.

"Who the fuck are you people?" she demanded. I could hear the slight hint of a Russian accent.

"We're from Titan," I said. She backed away a step.

"Where?" She leaned forward.

"The planet Saturn, it's moon. It's called Titan," I replied. She paused and glanced back at her comrades and said something in Russian. She tilted her head while looking me over.

"Hmm," she said suspiciously.

"Take a look at my suit or the ship behind me. Have you ever seen anything like it?" I yanked my thumb over my shoulder.

"Slow! Slow movements!" She stabbed her rifle at me aggressively. The gesture apparently startled her.

"My apologies," I said, showing her my palms.

"You can you fly that?" she asked, glancing up at the XU-97.

"I'm the pilot."

"Why are you here?" she commanded, adjusting her grip on the gun.

"We're an assault team, we've come to destroy the androids for good," I replied. She paused. I heard a chuckle from her that slowly erupted into laughter. The rest of her group joined in, amused at my response.

"Y-you're off to a great start." She shook her head, pointing her gun up at our ship. She pulled out a small, black handheld device. A red light emitted from it, similar to the robot's in the rail cart. She poked the device toward me, waving it up and down my body. "Clear. Uncontaminated."

She took a few steps forward, scanning Xena. "Uh-h. Nothing. Hmm." She violently shook the device, scanning her again. She glanced back at the group. "This one isn't giving me any reading."

"What about the injured one?" A man with a thick Russian accent asked.

She scanned Drake. Her device beeped. "Yeah. Shit. He's infected!" she yelled, snatching her gun toward Drake, marching closer.

"Infected? Wait. Hold on," I showed her my palms, attempting to calm her. There had to be another way.

Xena stood in front of Drake. "I can't allow you to do that."

"Surely his *infection* can be remedied?" Xena suggested. The woman stepped around her and fired at Drake, but Xena lunged at her, smacking her rifle barrel upward as the projectile struck the ceiling.

"Get out of the way, bitch!" she ordered, focused on Drake.

"Do you want to die? Get away from the infected!" she yelled as the group hurried in on us, weapons drawn.

The woman panned around and noticed the dead creature that bit Drake. "See! There it is! Got a dead one over here! That's what bit him," she concluded.

"What can we do to help him?" I pleaded. She nodded toward the dead monster. "He'll be one of those in a matter of hours. He's fucking gone. Deal with it, or die with him," she said plainly.

"No, no," I whispered. She jammed the rifle into Xena's face.

"Captain, your orders?" Xena asked. I knew she could wipe out the entire squad with a single word, all I had to do was make the call. I glared down the tunnel, then at Drake. I could hear his labored breathing and see his ghostly white complexion.

"If you don't move, *all* of you will die," the woman said. Judging by their uniforms, these people were connected to something larger, more than likely the resistance effort we'd been searching for. If we attacked them and managed to survive, what were Drake's odds of survival, assuming he didn't take a stray bullet? Not to mention, what might happen to our chances of finding Luther? These people understood what the virus was, but they didn't have a cure. How would we construct one in two hours?

It didn't make sense. There was no time. The intelligent, but less appealing option became apparent. I shook my head, glancing up at the ceiling. "Forgive me." I whispered.

"Move, Xena." I felt my eyes gloss over. I blinked rapidly.

"Captain…will you, *repeat* that order?" Xena asked, shielding Drake with her body.

"Get out of her way, Xena. That's an order." I closed my eyes. There was silence for a few moments, then I heard Xena's footfall on the frozen soil. I clenched my fist as another shot was fired. A jolt ran through my body as the gunshot echoed down the tunnel. I opened my eyes to see Drake's vitals update on my visor:

COLONEL RIVEN DRAKE

CONDITION: DECEASED

I fell forward, slamming my forearms into the ground. "No!" I turned my head toward Drake. His eyes were peeled wide open, sapped from all life. The once emerald green color had already begun to fade. Only minutes ago, they were filled with resolve, wonder, and hope.

I told myself the hard truth immediately. Drake was here to save his people and knew there was risk involved. I repeated it in my head. I knew what I was doing. There was only one way to move forward.

Drake was a soldier. He volunteered. He understood this was a possibility.

But he wasn't ready.

"Drake." I felt sick to my stomach. Despite my attempt to rationalize his demise as part of a soldier's duty, I hadn't convinced myself.

"Hey. Get the fuck up." The Russian woman ordered me. I stood up slowly. I felt my right arm jerked behind my back as she zip-tied it tightly to the other hand.

"Vlad, seen anything like them before?" the woman asked her leader as he stepped forward.

"Never," Vlad said. His head snapped around like a bird of prey, assessing every detail. He inspected Xena. "Any bite marks on either of you two?" he pointed.

"Negative," Xena replied.

"No," I said.

"Are these guns mounted to your arms?" Vlad asked Xena.

"Yes, they are," Xena replied. Vlad and his troops raised their weapons at Xena.

"Take them off then, *now!* Then the armor and helmet!" Vlad shouted. I held my breath. If they saw her without her armor, they'd know what she was.

An android inside a human colony was not a good look.

"Very well. The entire process will take me twenty minutes to remove," Xena said. I felt she was exaggerating the duration to our benefit.

"How long to remove just the guns?" the woman asked.

"Less than a minute," Xena replied.

"Do it. We don't have time for all that other shit. Hurry it up," the female said, staring down the tunnel.

Vlad shook his head in disapproval. "Let's go!" he yelled.

"As you wish." Xena stripped the guns off her armored forearms. They clanked against the tracks on impact. Xena allowed Vlad and another soldier to bind her hands, not that it mattered.

"What about his body?" I asked, glaring at Drake.

"Huh? You want to bury him?" Vlad chuckled.

"Yes."

"You're not paying attention. No time, and you've got other worries," he replied.

"I see respect for the dead is a forgotten honor. He was a soldier, fighting for humanity." I stood up straight.

Vlad closed the distance quickly, he leaned into my ear. "Humanity? Shut up! Don't say another word. Not another word unless you are asked a question!" he yelled. I stared him down, imagining where his eyes might have been through the tinted goggles.

I gulped as he spun me around and pushed me toward the cart. "Go!" he shouted. Despite putting little effort into the shove, he was surprisingly strong, knocking me back three steps.

One of the soldiers walked over to the rail cart, yanking out a metal flatbed tucked away in the undercarriage. It extended the cart's length about two meters. "Should be enough room for us all. Get on." Vlad hurried. We all piled onto the cart as the engine started and we slowly began to creep away. I trained my eyes on Drake as he drifted out of view while the woman sat beside me.

A secret text message flashed on my visor. It was from Xena:

CAPTAIN, AWAITING YOUR ORDERS…

A small hologram text pad appeared on my visor, allowing me to respond covertly. I used my pupils to guide the cursor:

"Hold," I ordered. I wanted to see where they might take us. I felt a small sense of security that Xena was with me. She was my ace in the hole. If things went sour, she could take on a small army, even without her guns. The element of surprise wouldn't last forever, though. Eventually, she'd be forced to remove her helmet and armor.

"So, you come all the way from Titan to save us? Now, after all this time?" the woman asked.

"Yes," I replied.

"Fascinating," she said. Vlad whispered something to her in his native tongue that I didn't understand.

"Captain, he's telling her not to speak with you," Xena translated, relaying the information through my visor's text. After a few minutes of riding on the cart, I could see a large spotlight beaming at us. A figure paced back and forth in front of it in silhouette.

"What was all the commotion?!" he shouted, cupping his hands around his mouth.

"UFO crash! Landed from Titan!" the woman beside me joked.

"What is Titan?" He furrowed his eyebrows and dropped his mouth. I'm sure both Xena and I stuck out like a sore thumb. As we approached, I noticed a massive minigun beside the spotlight on the far left. The barrel was poking through a hole on an otherwise solid metallic gate.

The gun barrel was about three meters long and about the diameter of a basketball. It reminded me of something that would fit on a tank or a large ground vehicle. I heard a hydraulic lift motor start as the gate begin to open right to left.

Within a few meters of the guard, the woman leaned toward him as we passed. "Heads up. I've got a maintenance and cleanup crew headed through to burn bodies and recover debris from our railcar drone. The bot had an alien encounter." She nodded toward me.

We passed through the gate as several of the soldiers on the rail car waved at the gate guard casually. He didn't wave back, staring at Xena and I with his mouth open.

The woman pulled off her mask. Her black, coarse hair fell in front of her face. She pushed it out of her view and behind her ears. "I'm Neona," she said calmly. Her voice sounded much softer than before.

"Victoria," I replied. I glanced at her through my peripheral. She was younger than I imagined, maybe early twenties, even late teens. She was beautiful. She had soft pale skin and her eyes were unusually large and sky blue, revealing a stone-cold calculative thinker past her years. There was a certain danger beyond her beauty and youth I imagined, like a freshly-sprouted Aconitum plant. She was vibrant, alluring, but deadly poisonous.

"Tough break with your friend. Sorry I had to do it," she said softly. I felt my left hand shaking as I fought back a sniffle. I wanted to punch her in the teeth and put my arm around her at the same time. She was only doing her job, but Drake, he was my friend.

And I didn't have many of those.

"I really am. I'm not just saying that. Every human that dies is a huge loss," she added.

"Thanks," I replied.

"The truth is, there isn't another way to deal with it. He was infected by what we call the *Mave*. And burying them? That is a no-no."

"Why?"

She narrowed her eyes at me. "You can shoot them in the head and slow the process, but they come back unless you burn or decapitate them. I've killed people I've cared about, so believe me when I say I have an understanding of this. I've been in your shoes." She peered into the distance, flexing her jaw muscles. "Many times."

"The androids have evolved their tactics, using viral infections," Xena spoke up.

Neona shook her head. "You Titans don't know shit, do you? The Mave is not the androids' doing. It was created by humans. A rival faction that believes the androids are our saviors. *They* created this reconstructive nanobot virus."

"What?" My eyes widened. One of the soldiers beside me began to snicker.

"You'll find out soon enough. But understand, the old ones you're here to destroy, they're not the immediate threat to human survival. The Mave is. It blows my mind you know nothing about this. You've come all the way out here, spent all these resources to fight an enemy that hasn't bothered us in decades?" Neona snapped toward me. With every word she spoke, I got the feeling we had less bargaining power.

"I don't think there has been any communication between Titan and Earth," I replied.

"Indeed. We were cautious to communicate with any resistance efforts in fear the messages might be intercepted and your location discovered," Xena added.

"So, you just *show up*. Now?" She shrugged.

"Yes. I know, but now we—"

"None of this adds up. We respond to an explosion, then upon arrival we have a jet and debris blocking our tunnel transportation. That's our survival. Our lifeline. Then, we see three people claiming to be from a moon we've heard nothing out of in decades. One of which, is infected. To top it off, your ship crashed. So, are you here to help us or make matters worse?" she posed.

I nodded in agreement. "It sounds crazy, I know."

"We're taking you somewhere so that a decision can be made about your claims, so sit tight," she said.

"How much further?" I asked, glancing at Luther's cryotube indicator on my visor. It was offset to my east. The cryotube range finder seemed to be glitching out. I noticed it bouncing from back and forth from four-hundred to eighty-five meters. That can't be right. At least we were moving toward it.

She turned and narrowed her eyes at me. "I said, sit tight. We're close."

The railcar began to slow. Up ahead, I could see an indentation in the ice tunnel, like a subway stop. A group of people were huddled together in shadow waiting at a wooden dock that bordered the track. They were staring intently at us as we approached. The group of about thirty ranged from children to middle-aged, mostly females. They were wearing large fur clothes from head to toe that only revealed faces smeared with dirt and worry. Several of them began to do a headcount of our rail cart.

"Plus two!" someone yelled.

"Vlad!" A young woman screamed to the top of her lungs echoing down the tunnel. She ran over to the edge of the dock with her hands over her mouth. The no nonsense soldier stood up proud and removed his mask, making eye contact with her.

Vlad had stiff, dark brown pointy hair, with a military style high and tight. He looked about thirty and wasn't particularly handsome. He had odd-looking, elf-like features. His ears were large and almost pointy, and his nose was narrow and sharp, hooking downward. There was a high level of confidence and intelligence that emitted from his demeanor. His deep set brown eyes gave off an intense aura that was fortified behind his high cheekbones.

Vlad pulled off his gloves as we approached. I noticed his left forearm and hand were robotic. The lines and shape resembled that of an actual human skeleton hand, instead of a mechanical variation, and was black in color.

He edged close to the dock as the railcar came to a halt, but just before it did, he glared over at me. He gave me a scrutinizing gaze, looking me up and down while squinting. I stared back at him for four or five seconds, unwavering. He eventually glanced away, staring at the ground for a moment. In the brief deadlock, I got the sense he was hopeful we had something to offer despite his suspicions.

"Vlad!" the woman yelled. He snapped toward her. I felt a tug under my arm as I held my stare at him. "Up." Neona said, following Vlad with her eyes.

Neona guided me over toward the dock with Xena and another guard in tow. The remainder of soldiers rushed ahead, embracing their loved ones into their arms.

We proceeded past the small reunion. Some of the people took notice of us. Their eyes flashed briefly as they struggled to make sense of us, quickly turning their attention back to their loved ones.

One little girl away from the group wasn't celebrating. She was no older than ten, peering down the tunnel. Her face was filled with sadness. I paused, imagining that one of her parents hadn't returned from a previous mission. Neona noticed me staring at her. "Come."

We pushed through a hole in the ice about two meters tall. It was a tunnel with a wooden path. On the curved white wall there were chalk drawings of people. Some of the art was better than others. Each portrait had a name above the art with a 'last scene' date beneath it. They were written Russian and English. A drawn box framed each art piece, separating them from the others.

"They almost never come back, not like they left anyway," Neona mumbled. As we stepped down the tunnel for several minutes, I noticed the concentration of the missing persons' artwork remained consistently bunched together. The further we proceeded, I observed many of the portraits had begun to fade. I wondered if their loved ones' hope had dwindled along with it? Maybe reality was better to accept sooner than later in such grim circumstances.

I wondered if I would learn this lesson the hard way.

We'd passed dozens of people in the tunnel that stared at the wall. In almost every case, they appeared frightened by us. Neona would simply nod. "Nothing to see, citizen."

I was surprised that Neona wasn't more fascinated by our arrival. Everyone else was. I would have thought something as foreign as space travelers would have been an interesting curiosity at least, but perhaps a life in her position left little room for such inquisitive wonders. But since she was straight to the point, I decided to ask the question.

"Um, Neona, I have an inquiry, I, *we're* looking for—"

"Hey. *You* will be the ones answering questions first. Not us. After that, we'll see," she stopped, pointing at me sternly.

"Got it. Fair enough," I said. I saw no benefit in pressing the matter. Ahead, I could make out a large, circular hatch with a turn style locking mechanism. As we approached, a tall, husky man with an impressive handlebar mustache closed it. He wore the same uniform as Neona, but his sleeves were ripped off around the shoulders as if they couldn't find a uniform big enough to fit him. A siren blared as a red light strobed just above the door.

"You coming?" the large man asked Neona.

"On the way! Come on!" Neona picked up the pace, ushering us forward. We shuffled through the hatch as the man pushed it closed. He shoved an L-shaped crank into a gear style lock that was the size of my torso, rotating it several times, sealing it shut. Steam vented from above the door.

"Clear. Sorry, Neona, new orders from the engineer. I can only open this door every fifteen minutes now," he said with a Scottish accent.

"Good timing. Carry on," she said. The husky doorman scratched his head, pulling back his black, wavy hair as he looked us over. I could tell he wanted to ask questions, yet nothing was said. I panned around as we entered the metallic bunker.

"What is this place?" I whispered. The interior reminded me of a vault, a fallout bunker. Russian text was stenciled across the military light green walls. They appeared to be warnings of some sort. As I centered the text into view, a holographic indicator highlighted it. Xena translated it remotely to my visor.

CHECK RADIATION LEVELS IN TWO MINUTE INTERVALS

Pipes, hoses, and wires were tucked away on the ceiling by metal hooks every couple of meters. I peered ahead, observing an interconnected labyrinth of steel spherical halls that seemed to veer off or elbow into different directions. There appeared to be rooms every so often as well, with smaller hatches embedded in the walls.

Suddenly, Luther's indicator began blinking quickly inside my visor, then went offline completely. "Shit." I glared at Xena. She glanced up at the ceiling. I gathered she was attempting to reestablish communication with the indicator.

"Keep up," Neona ordered. We followed her down the corridor for three or four minutes until finally branching into a large open area. Ten large silos, fifty meters tall were placed evenly throughout the room. A spiral stairwell wrapped around each one to the top. About halfway up, there was a network of connecting bridges to each silo with grated metal floors. Six of the silos were open with nothing inside.

Neona noticed me staring at the open silos. "When I was little, I used to wonder how many people those things might have killed." She bounced her eyebrows as her voice echoed off the walls.

A text flashed on my visor's screen:

INCOMING TRANSMISSION FROM TITAN COMMAND. STAND BY...

We paced through the silo room, approaching another circular steel vault door. The unknown guard that accompanied us opened the hatch while Neona raised her rifle at Xena, then me. "Don't move!" she raised her voice. I got the feeling she didn't see us as much of a threat as her powerful voice dictated.

"Captain, are you receiving the transmission, as well?" Xena covertly texted.

"Yes."

My heart sunk as the transmission fed into view. It appeared as a tall column of text on the lower right corner of my visor.

"This is General Corvin. I want to congratulate you on your progress. We watched in awe from the control room as you entered Earth's atmosphere, surprised by the condition of the planet. We expected far worse. We are in shock. As I type this message, you're descending to land and, by now, with the transmission delay, we hope you've made contact with the resistance.

I want to personally express sympathy for the situation regarding the Russian refugees. In my mind, you all operated as ambassadors for humanity. You did what had to be done. We could hear partial onboard audio from the encounter and pieced together the rest of the scenario from Xena's log. This situation reflects the desperation of the android war. The people of Titan support you. Colonel Drake, Xena, and Captain Belic, remember you represent the people of Titan, continue to make us proud.

I'm updating your mission objectives:

Investigate why Earth appears virtually untouched by the nuclear war. Our estimates on Titan show the planet wasn't due to recover on this scale for another 80-120 years.

Set up encrypted communications with our Earth counterparts if they exist. I'm updating the information for transmissions in your files. Corvin out. Oh, and Colonel Drake, I want to congratulate you on being the first Titan to step foot on Earth. We can only imagine how that must feel."

TRANSMISSION END

I gulped, glancing at Xena. She slowly turned her head toward me. Surely at any moment, Titan would receive the delayed data about Drake's death.

Even though I hadn't known Drake long, I felt a connection with him after the incident with the refugees. I had a soft spot for him deep beneath my exterior. He was insightful, courageous, maybe not the best under pressure, but he was willing.

He deserved better than to lie in a pool of his own blood, rotting in the dirt and ice. I began to train myself to block Drake out of my mind, the thought was detrimental to the mission.

"Hey, let's go." Neona nudged me firmly with her rifle's butt interrupting my thought. We proceeded through the hatch. The next area was like the vault corridors from before, but a half-pipe.

The other half was an open portion that gave way to another loading dock and train tracks. I imagined this was connected to the tracks we came in on originally. The area smelled musky, like an old, wet carpet.

Despite being partially open to the elements, this area was slightly warmer. Icicles overhung the dock entrance, slowly dripping water unto the concrete floor. This created dozens of puddles throughout the dock. No sooner than I noticed the heat, a gust of cold air flooded in that quickly dissipated.

There were several people scattered on the edge of the dock. One older man there stood out. He wore filthy navy-blue coveralls. His face was buried in his hands. He had tight, unkempt curly brown hair, with patches of gray here and there. He was mumbling something I couldn't make out, weeping while shaking his head.

Another group of four young adults, perhaps two sets of couples, were humming a hymn at low volume while holding hands. They had their eyes closed, and their heads were slumped slightly.

"Neona," I stopped in place.

"What?" she asked, nodding forward with her head.

"No disrespect to you. I understand our mission doesn't align with your problems, but we're looking for the location of android installations, possibly a main hub, can you—"

"I thought I made myself clear earlier about questions?" she interrupted, narrowing her eyes at me.

"I know. Yes, it's just we're running short on time and—"

"Hartin, can you enlighten the prisoner here on the penalty, specifically, refusal of a Knight's orders?" Neona glanced back at the soldier escorting us.

"Knight?" I whispered.

"Death," Hartin replied. I noticed a metal emblem on Neona's collar that I didn't see before. It was a broadsword with lightning bolts around it. She was clearly some type of respected leader, granted the power to execute prisoners on the spot.

"Have I not been fair and just to you? Despite your wild claims and damaging actions?" She stabbed her index finger down the tunnel.

"You have been fair, yes, I'm not—"

She took a few steps back, yanking out a silver device from her belt that was shaped like a flashlight. She gripped the object with both hands as sparks emitted from the top. Suddenly, a meter-long white torch extended from the handle. The flame seemed erratic and dangerous even to the wielder.

She twisted her hands around the handle, narrowing the torch into a thin white razor of fire. Surprisingly, the sound reminded me of a high-pressure water hose mixed with radio static.

"Plasma blade. Knights like myself use these against the Mave in close quarters. It's our lifeline. It's difficult to shoot them up close. Too fast. Plasma cuts through their metallic panels like butter." She twirled the blade in front of my face. The concept of compliance seemed attractive.

"It looks to be, effective," I said, leaning back.

"As a knight, I'm sworn to uphold the law. Once uncontaminated intruders like yourselves are taken into custody, my duty is to present you to our authority before anything else. If you refuse, you must be executed," she explained. Her tone suggested she was honoring me by laying out the rules. It seemed possible other intruders were not so lucky.

"Do you wish to question my duty?" she asked.

"N-no," I said.

"Good. On the flipside, your death would be quite clean with this weapon. You'd feel nothing. That I can assure." She smirked.

"I'm good for now," I replied. She twisted the handle of the blade, retracting the plasma. Neona snapped around toward the tracks.

"Excellent choice, Captain," Xena said. I turned toward her as she nodded. I heard an echoing sound down the tunnel. It was similar to the rail car from earlier but much louder. Everyone on the dock turned toward it. Neona pressed her index finger inside her ear on a small black device.

She scrunched her eyebrows together. "What? Say again?" she asked, dipping her head forward. Apparently, she was receiving some type of audio transmission.

"We're already headed that way, so we stay put?" She paused for a few seconds.

"Understood." She glanced at me.

"It appears judgment is coming to you. Normally, we'd have to take a rail car," Neona said casually. She walked around behind Xena and I, unbounding our shackles. "This is only temporary. Our leader prefers to see intruders unshackled initially."

My heart began to pound as the screeching object approached. The people on the dock began to stand, whispering to one another as it neared. Their faces appeared worried. The weeping old man backed away from the dock.

"Judgment?" I mumbled. What if this person decided we were a detriment to their colony? I'd just blasted a hole in their tunnel, allowing those monsters a shortcut. I felt an immense pressure unlike anything else in my life. I had to convince whoever was on this train that we were an asset despite our bumpy start.

I began to focus on the metal tube-like object coming into view. It reminded me of a subway train from the old days, large windows, white and black two-tone paint, and a bullet shaped front end. It slowly grinded to a halt before us. Inside, I could see a group of fourteen or so soldiers facing each other. They were wearing the same dark uniforms as Neona.

The door opened as the civilians backed way. The soldiers filed out in a hurry. They formed two lines on each side of the door, like an honor guard awaiting a dignitary. They held their hands out low in front, one hand over the other.

These men were of all ethnicities and young, but I got the feeling they were experienced warriors. Some of their faces appeared scarred or burned, some had robotic extremities, and all of them had a faraway gaze.

They stood at attention without blinking. "Pre-sent arms!" A soldier with a missing ear yelled. Silence ensued for a few moments, followed by two of the closest soldiers igniting plasma blades like Neona's. The others followed row after row, lighting up the somewhat shadowy dock like the middle of the day.

The combination of swords was surprisingly loud, like standing before a giant waterfall. They dialed down the fiery torches to a thin blade as the sound decreased significantly. They pointed the blades toward one another, crossing them in front of the exit as they waited.

"Deep breaths, Captain," Xena said.

I could hear boots clanking against the deck inside the train. From the back of the first rail car, I saw a large figure in a white cape marching across my view toward the train's exit.

Even peering past the window's glare, I gathered his movements exuded authority, with his squared shoulders and confident stride. Something was off, though. I noticed a limp and a bit of trouble keeping a straight back, like a slight forward hunker.

He turned the corner toward the door as the light from the crossed plasma swords obscured his face. As he neared the exit, the first row of soldiers pulled their weapons back, pointing them straight into the air in unison. As a military veteran, I noticed their timing was impeccable, like an honor guard drill team.

As the swords retracted, a disturbing figure appeared. He wore a white, full masquerade type mask. The features on the face were very subtle, almost nonexistent and projected a sense of anonymity and vacancy. The oval eyes were the only standout, they were black as night and without pupils.

Fear was my first emotion, followed by a sense of allure. Clearly, there were symbolic ingredients in its menacing, yet bizarre design. I'd never seen anything like it.

He briefly glanced left and right at his subordinates before exiting, snapping his head around like a bird. As he departed the train, it was clear he wasn't just wearing a mask, but rather a functional helmet. It formed around the skull with no protrusions. The closer I examined, I could make out two razor thin vertical slits on each corner where the mouth might be.

He was extremely broad and tall, with a cuirass and white armor that covered him completely. It reminded me of a medieval knight's armor, but not as cumbersome. The cape puffed up slightly around his shoulder armor, creating a waved, bulky look that increased his stature even more.

He pulled his thick, armored greaves tight around the wrists as he stepped forward, his head swiveling about the dock.

I got the sense he was aware of our presence, but he made little effort to acknowledge us directly. Instead, he focused on the civilians scattered around the dock and his soldiers.

Neona walked out to greet him, but his long, confident strides made short work of her approach. He stood within a few dozen centimeters of Neona, towering over her. I noticed he had the same broadsword insignia on his collar as her, his was red in color and slightly larger.

Peeking around Xena, I could see he had some type of mechanized apparatus under his helmet. I observed metallic parts shifting as he turned his head slightly, simulating the muscles in the neck. I could also see a small white light blinking within the machinery.

I began to wonder if it was even a man. It was difficult not to stare. To be honest, it was terrifying that he, or *it*, was making the decisions.

"Engineer, you grace us with your presence." Neona slumped her head. Her voice echoed down the tunnel as she spoke with a throaty confidence.

"What is this talk of, prisoners?" he asked. His voice was altered. It was extremely deep, as if he was speaking from the depths of a cave mixed with an electronic raspy tone. He coughed twice, turning his head away from Neona. I noticed wisps of condensation exhale from the vents at his mouth.

"Three total, but one of them was killed by the Mave," she replied. He glanced at the ground and paused.

"Bring them to me," he ordered. Neona nodded us over. Xena stepped out in front of me as we approached. The Engineer tilted his bizarre helm at us, keeping his body profile.

He stood up tall when he saw Xena, tilting his head downward to get a better look. He flipped his cape around his shoulder and crossed his long powerful armored arms.

I walked out from behind Xena as we began to approach two abreast. His head snapped toward me instantly as he turned his body facing us.

His shoulders dropped as his neck stretched forward. He began teetering forward like he was walking a tight wire. He stumbled a bit before straightening up.

"Sire?" Neona asked, staring up at him with a concerned look on her face. He covered his eyes with his hands for a moment, then removed them. "I'm fine," he snapped.

Xena and I stopped in front of him. He placed his hands on his hips, looking us over. As his cape fanned out, I noticed a sword on his belt like Neona's.

Dammit. This wasn't good.

She stood by his side, staring up at him. "These are the prisoners that survived, sire. They destroyed a portion of our tunnel. I have cleanup crews headed there now. The shorter one here seems to be in charge, she—"

"Take off your helmet!" he interrupted, roaring as he stabbed his finger at me. I gulped. He sounded far more sinister up close, the electronic throaty voice sent shivers down my spine.

"Of course." I removed my helm and held it in front of me. Maybe he felt disrespected because the red tint on my visor obscured my face slightly. "I apologize about the damage to your passage, it was an accident, and we—"

Neona slapped me across the face, putting her weight behind it. "You only speak when asked a question!" The impact pushed me back a step. She narrowed her eyes at me. "Silence!"

As I regained my composure, their leader lunged forward, stopping half an arm's length away. He leaned closer, within several centimeters of me. His black, vacant eyes were like staring into an abyss. It appeared he was short of breath as rapid warm puffs of air heated my face. He stared at me without a word.

I glared up at his ominous mask as I attempted to project confidence. I couldn't. I felt this could be the end. The possibility of him making an example out of us in front of his troops seemed likely.

Blood began to drip from my nose. I stood there without touching my face, allowing it to leak as air from his breath splattered it onto my suit. He simply stared at me, his head snapped up and down as if he was scanning my face. He took a half-step back and slumped his head.

"Sire, you won't believe this, but they claim to be from the moon, Titan, here to stop the androids they say. I'm not sure—"

"Ah-h," he uttered. All at once, he collapsed to one knee. The metal on concrete impact created a loud crunching sound as his cape fanned out, pushing a small sphere of dust away from him.

Neona rushed to his side. "Sire!" she yelled. I could hear a mechanized wincing as he panned his head back and forth, searching the ground around him. I glanced at Xena, then back at him. I gathered his intimidating appearance was concealing a dying man underneath.

"I need medics immediately. We're on loading dock Bravo! It's for the engineer! Hurry!" Neona yelled, pressing in her earpiece.

He tilted his head up slightly. "All—this… time," he muttered. I narrowed my eyes at him, piercing through the mechanical mystery.

"W-what did you say?" I asked.

My bottom lip began to tremble. Neona glared at me while grabbing him under the arm. He braced himself with both hands on the ground, kneeled over. He dipped his head while he struggled to breathe. It sounded like an electronic wheeze.

"So many years, I w-waited, it kept me a-alive," he mumbled. His words took my breath away.

It was only his statement that shocked me. Through the garbled apparatus, I detected cues the machine could not conceal. I recognized the lump in his throat, the cadence and tempo of his speech, and the faint hint of a southern accent. It was all too familiar.

"*Lu-ther?*" I whispered as my jaw dropped. It had to be him.

"Captain. It appears what was lost is now found." Xena turned toward me.

Tears streamed from eyes as I took a step forward and kneeled.

He gasped for air as if he'd been stabbed in the lung. His spine arched and flattened under the labored pant. He outstretched his fingers toward me for a moment, then slowly pulled them inward, clenching his fists. I heard a faint rumble emitting from his mouth.

I leaned in, attempting to touch my head against his helmet. "Luther?" I pleaded. "No!" he shouted. In one motion, he sprung up from the ground, knocking Neona down. He turned his back on me as I backed away instinctively. He darted toward the train and ignited his sword. The civilians ran hysterically, some of them jumping off the dock onto the track.

"Sire!" Neona pleaded.

He ran at the train with the blade over his head, slashing through the cabin. His crippling condition seemed nonexistent while enraged as he moved like a blur. The sword's deafening swooping sound reminded me of a crashing wave with a humming electric whiffle at the end.

He sliced into the exterior several times, creating dozens of fiery, orange streaks across the cabin. The cumulative impacts melted through, allowing me to see clearly into the interior.

The plasma sword liquefied the glass and metal, creating a black goo that was flung about the dock. It stuck to the ceiling and floor, like volcanic magma hurled from a violent eruption.

"T-they need me! All of them!" he yelled during his barrage. I was frozen in fear as tears flowed from my eyes uncontrollably.

"Sire! Please!" Neona glanced at me after yelling. She ran toward him, covering her eyes as sparks ejected in the air, filling the dock like a swarm of fiery fireflies. Initially, his knights stood their ground as he slashed through the train, they remained motionless, but as the strikes mounted, they were forced to retreat.

He cut the train completely in half. The transport buckled on the track, toppling over toward the outer wall and crashing against it.

"No-o-o!" I yelled. He continued to mercilessly pound the train as his knights backed away, unsure of what to do.

Neona turned around and stared a hole through me with glossy eyes. In the background, Luther was tearing apart everything in his wake as fires raged all around him.

"You're the *one*, the one from long ago, aren't you?" Neona asked.

"He's my husband," I responded.

"*Was*. Maybe he *was* your husband, not anymore. He's my father, in some ways, he's a father to us all here," she revealed. My heart sunk in my chest as I attempted to make sense of it. Was it true? She looked nothing like him.

Maybe this child and his reaction to me was confirmation my return was too little, too late. This possibility began to resonate within my soul, tearing me apart.

I fell face first toward the ground. It felt like slow motion as the ground approached, like dive bombing with my XU-97. My face smacked hard against the concrete and ice.

I heard the muted voice of Neona and others signaling a medical and fire crew to the scene as footsteps echoed down the corridor. An intense pain emerged on the left side of my chest.

"Captain," Xena said in a concerned tone. With every blink of the eye, it became more difficult to keep them open. I looked up at him, reaching out. "Luther! Stop! P-Please!" I begged.

Xena turned me over on my back, "Captain, it appears you've had a very mild heart attack. Your suit is automatically administrating medical aid along with a calming agent," she confirmed.

I held my stare on Luther. He had finally halted his barrage, kneeling with his back to me and his cape draped over him. A fire crew was extinguishing the flames around him while he panted.

Xena began to unbutton my suit while everyone was distracted. "Administrating additional lifesaving aid. Captain, stay with me."

"You were wrong, Xena. He's alive. You see," I mumbled as Xena injected a small needle into my chest.

"I noticed. I said it was *unlikely* for him to survive this long," she replied.

"I can't believe h-he made it," I muttered. I held my chest as the pain began to subside slightly.

"Congratulations, Captain, but remember, Titan is still counting on us."

"I can't help them if I don't survive," I panted.

"I've done all I can do. But my files indicate a factor that I have no control over," she said.

"What, *factor*?" I asked.

"The will to survive. It is extremely important in humans. Do you possess this?" she asked, tilting her head while staring at me.

"I-I still love him, that's all I know," I mumbled as my eyes closed.

Xena turned toward Luther and nodded.

"Then I would estimate your chances of survival are quite high."

EPILOGUE

Neona and Vlad filed into a hospital room. Two nurses were huddled over a man in bed. They were whispering something.

"Leave us… and call the doctor," Vlad thundered.

"Oh. Yes, k-knight," a nurse said. She appeared startled. They scurried out of the room. Neona glanced at the man in bed, then at Vlad. "He's resting, perhaps now isn't the time."

"I want to see him. He's my father, too." Vlad stepped forward, placing his robotic hand on the bed railing. The engineer's body was covered with white sheets, and bandages concealed his face. Spots of red faded through the wraps.

"He's been bleeding," Vlad whispered.

"Father," he said. He waited several seconds without a response.

"Knights, your father has been through quite the ordeal. He needs rest," a voice erupted from behind them. A short, bald man of Middle Eastern descent was standing in the doorway in a white overcoat.

"Why the bandages, Doctor? Was he burned from the fire?" Neona asked.

"No. I'm removing the Mave nanobots, the infection is subsiding slightly. As you know, this infection is considered a death sentence. We're not sure why your father survived, and now…" he paused.

"Now he's fighting off the virus? You said you're removing the nanobots, so it's reversing?" Vlad narrowed his eyes.

"Only partially, but yes. I'd estimate about fifteen percent of the nanobots have died off for some reason. His immune system seems to be pushing the Mave nanobots to the surface, like infectious boils," the doctor said.

"He'll recover then? Right?" Neona questioned.

"Do you notice anything different?" The doctor nodded toward her father.

"No, other than the bleeding," Neona examined.

"His breathing. It's... different," Vlad noticed, leaning on the railing.

"Exactly. Not only that, his heart rate sounds better, too. I'm not suggesting your father will ever be the way he was before the infection, but it's, an improvement. For now, it seems the nanobots gave him a boost to physical strength, but at the cost of organ deterioration," the doctor explained.

Vlad shook his head while glaring down at his father. Neona stepped forward, standing beside him.

"Knights, you both know I've been involved with your father's condition since the beginning. I even remember when they were forced to unfreeze him. He's near sixty years old now. This is unprecedented and quite fascinating some of these nanobots are dying. Do either of you know why? Any information might help. If I can somehow replicate his results in others, we might not be forced to execute Mave victims," the doctor pleaded.

Neona shook her head. "I don't think you can replicate his situation. No one has survived with this virus. Correct?"

"That's true, but any information could aid in my research. I need to know—"

"That'll be all, Doctor. Thank you. Please keep us posted." Vlad snapped his head around, interrupting him.

"Yes. Of course." The doctor hesitated before bowing slightly. He backed out of the room.

Vlad slowly turned toward Neona. "You were too young to remember when he adopted us?"

"Vaguely. I was two," she said.

"He was bitten by the Mave almost immediately after. We almost lost him. It was a very tense situation." Vlad's eyes glossed over.

"They threatened to kill him," she said.

"Put him out of his misery. But instead, he turned into what he is. Everyone was talking about 'the man who beat the infection.' Many were afraid, but some saw him as a miracle, like a superhero, this half-Mave, half-human. He had the strength of the machines, or more, and the wits of a m-man." Vlad struggled with his words.

Neona's eyes gazed a million miles away as her brother spoke.

"And you know, sister, all these years, I-I wanted to believe the reason the infection didn't kill him was because of me, because of *us*. The love he had for his children. I thought *that* gave him the power to beat this." He closed his eyes as a single tear fell on his father's bedsheet.

"But it was never us that kept him alive, was it? It was *her*." Neona glanced up at her big brother.

317

Vlad clenched his robotic hand, bending the metal bed railing. "Perhaps, but he *is* our father. Our leader. We all need him. And what is our objective as knights?" he posed.

"To defend the innocent," Neona said without hesitation.

"Indeed. Thousands count on us."

"But, Vlad, the doctor said he now has organ failure because of the nanobots. Isn't it possible her presence could improve him further?" she whispered.

"Improved is a matter of perspective. Do you forget who fended off nearly two hundred Mave monsters by himself only weeks ago? Organ failure, what nonsense. Father is special. The infection has made him *stronger*. Not only is he our leader, but his abilities make him a gatekeeper against the monsters," he explained.

Neona nodded her head slowly, staring down at her father. "Then what do you propose?"

Vlad turned toward her, placing his hands on her shoulders. He narrowed his eyes. "We do whatever is necessary to protect *our* people. At the very least, that *pilot* is a potential threat to our survival. What is their purpose? Their fight is different than ours. What will she do, try to take him to Titan?" he whispered.

"He would never leave us," she said.

"Sister, we can't risk her turning our world upside down. She's been here only days and our father is bedridden. What if we needed him now?" He pointed at his father.

"I understand." Neona nodded slowly. She gazed at her father as Vlad stormed out of the room.

"Vlad…" She stopped him.

"What?"

"I'll handle it," she glared at him over her shoulder.

***

"What's the prisoner's condition?" Neona asked a large guard standing beside a cell door. He was holding a shotgun wearing all black.

"She's alive, just had her first meal," he responded.

"Open the door," Neona demanded.

"Knight, I must inform you I was ordered not to—"

"Now!"

"Yes, yes, of course." He cranked the latch across his body. The circular metal door opened as Neona stepped through. She glared over her shoulder. "Close it. No one else comes in," she said. The guard hesitantly shut her inside with the prisoner.

The cell was surprisingly large, but vacant other than the bed. The room was shaped like a metal tube with curved green walls. In front of Neona was a small, twin-sized bed. An old, worn mattress sat atop the rusted bedframe. Captain Belic was lying on it with her back to Neona.

"Are you awake, pilot?" Neona asked. Her tone was all business. A few seconds passed by without a response as Captain Belic began to rustle around. She leaned up in bed slowly, staring at the ceiling. Her brown eyes were bloodshot, and her lips were chapped. Captain Belic glared at Neona without a word.

"You've been here almost two days and you've only eaten once?" Neona asked. Captain Belic didn't respond.

"Pilot, I'm here against orders. I'm sure it comes as no surprise that your life is in grave danger. There are some knights who see you as a threat to us, our way of life," Neona said.

Captain Belic shook her head slowly. "And you? What do you think?"

"I'm here to offer you a chance, to be of use. To live."

"*Live*?" Captain Belic chuckled under her breath

"That's right. I want to put you to work piloting. Prove your worth. There is much work to be done and—"

"Put me in front of my husband again." Captain Belic glared at Neona.

Neona raised her eyebrows as she panned around the room. "You must understand he's not your husband. And have you forgotten the reaction he had to your presence the first time?" she asked.

"The only way I'm helping you is if you let me see him again," Captain Belic repeated.

Neona sighed. "You're playing with fire, literally. Understand, if I take you to him, it would likely be the last thing you ever see."

"Then so be it."

"Hmm. Very well. Since you're so determined to fulfill this death wish, you will complete one task for me first."

"What?"

"My brother, Viktor and his family went missing weeks ago along with our only aircraft. I want you to retrace his steps using a tracker. I want to find out what happened to them," Neona explained.

Captain Belic gritted her teeth. "Viktor. Your *brother*? Ahem. Can I ask you something?"

Neona sighed. "Yes."

"Would you consider yourself a woman of your word? It seems you knights have a code of some sort," Captain Belic challenged.

"I want that jet out of my tunnel. After that, I'm tasking you with finding out what happened to my brother. If you survive and discover Viktor's whereabouts, then I'll take you to a fiery death by my father's hands. You have my word, I swear it by the Legion," she said.

Captain Belic nodded. "Good. Well. I've already completed my first task without even taking off."

Neona paused, crossing her arms. "Excuse me?"

"Your brother is dead. He stole your ship and fled to Titan."

"Watch your tongue, pilot. Viktor would never do that. He's an honorable man and—"

"He's a tall, gangly man. He had a son about nine years old with jet black hair and doe eyes. Viktor was piloting an LU class freighter with an operational drop pod. There were sixteen total passengers, most were his family, some were his friends." Captain Belic glared at Neona as she panned around the room with wide eyes.

"How...*how* do you know this information?" Neona pleaded.

"Because he attempted to commandeer my ship after we responded to his distress call. He was leaving for Titan, which wouldn't have worked out either, but it's well-documented and logged into our systems. You can have a look for yourself," Captain Belic said.

Neona turned her back, putting her hand over her mouth. "This can't be," she whispered.

Captain Belic shrugged. "It is. Looks like mission accomplished. I'm sorry that isn't the outcome you were hoping for, but it's the truth, and I can prove it. Now, noble knight, keep your word and take me back to my husband. You're going to help me save Titan and my marriage."

Thank you for reading! I hope you enjoyed my little tale. Please don't forget to give this book a quick review. Even just a two word, "Liked it" or "Hated it" review helps so much. Positive or negative, I am grateful for all feedback from my readers.

What's next? The sequel to *The Legion and the Lioness* is well underway! Subscribe below for updates on my next installment:

Sign up to Receive Free Books and $0.99 New Releases

http://www.enterechoeffect.com/

Also, for every new book release, I randomly select 200 mailing list subscribers from the link above to receive a free advance Kindle copy. All other subscribers will receive a special offer to purchase the book for only $0.99 on the day of release, before the price goes up to $3.99. This is not a newsletter. You will only be contacted about free books and $0.99 discounts on New Releases. Thanks again for your support!